To deare[...]

Happy C[...]

and enjoy reading

over the holidays

with our love

& best wishes

for the New Year

from

Allan, Churchill

A[...] [...]

Christmas 1997

Secrets

Secrets

DRUSILLA MODJESKA

AMANDA LOHREY

ROBERT DESSAIX

MACMILLAN
Pan Macmillan Australia

Acknowledgement is due to Faber and Faber Ltd for permission to
reproduce 'At last the secret is out' from 'Twelve Songs',
Collected Poems by W.H. Auden.

First published 1997 in Macmillan by Pan Macmillan Australia Pty
Limited
St Martins Tower, 31 Market Street, Sydney

Reprinted 1997

National Library of Australia
Cataloguing-in-Publication data:

Modjeska, Drusilla.
Secrets.

ISBN 0 7329 0863 9

1. Australian prose literature – 20th century. I. Lohrey,
Amanda. II. Dessaix, Robert, 1944–. III. Title.

A828.30808

Designed by Mary Callahan
Typeset in 11/14pt New Baskerville by Post Pre-press Group
Printed in Australia by Griffin Press Pty Ltd

Contents

DRUSILLA MODJESKA

'Ripe to tell'

1

AMANDA LOHREY

'The clear voice suddenly singing'

173

ROBERT DESSAIX

'At last the secret'

275

At last the secret is out, as it always must come in the end,
The delicious story is ripe to tell to the intimate friend;
Over the tea-cups and in the square the tongue has its desire;
Still waters run deep, my dear, there's never smoke without fire.

Behind the corpse in the reservoir, behind the ghost on the links,
Behind the lady who dances and the man who madly drinks,
Under the look of fatigue, the attack of migraine and the sigh
There is always another story, there is more than meets the eye.

For the clear voice suddenly singing, high up in the convent wall,
The scent of elder bushes, the sporting prints in the hall,
The croquet matches in summer, the handshake, the cough, the kiss,
There is always a wicked secret, a private reason for this.

W.H. Auden

DRUSILLA MODJESKA

'Ripe to tell'

The story that is ripe for me to tell, begins early this century on the gravelly bed of a small lake in the dense, rather succulent country of north-west New Guinea. To find it you will need a large-scale map. Tucked into the hills between the coastal ranges and mountainous spine, the intricate waterway of Lake Sentani is hard to find, even on a map.

Not that this has protected its people from the scrutiny of the West. Rugged mountains and treacherous rivers did not deter the missionaries who found their way there a hundred years ago. They went in looking for souls, and instead found art – not that they used the word – which shocked them deeply: squat figures with huge penises and crested heads, powerful birds in flight, spirit figures that blended the human with the animal as if one was as sacred as the other, mythic mothers with round, protuberant breasts. Figures that are now prized by museums and galleries around the world were taken as evidence of malignant spirits, and the deranged workings of a heathen mind.

These prurient outriders of a protestant god stripped the villages of idolatory, and threw everything that offended them into the lake. Even the prows of canoes were wrenched off and consigned to the deep. Spears, gongs, masks, ornate serving bowls followed the carvings from the sacred spirit-houses into this watery grave. One of the finest collections of Oceanic art landed on the bottom of Lake Sentani where it stayed, waterlogged and silty, until the end of the twenties.

In 1929 it was hauled out by two adventurers who arrived from Paris on a mission of rescue in the name, this time, of Surrealism. Jacques Viot, whose idea it was, needed to pay his debts – many of them to the dealer Pierre Loeb – and he knew that a haul of Oceanic art would do more than that. His friend Claude Ferraris – if friend is the word – needed money to finance his extravagant hopes and bolster a meagre talent. So Pierre Loeb put up the money, and André Breton provided credibility for a venture that amounted to little better than plunder. There were good prices to be extracted from the masks and carvings of Oceanic spirit beings.

A couple of years earlier the Surrealists had seen an exhibition from the Dutch East Indies at the Musée des Art Décoratifs; there the tapa cloth from Lake Sentani had aroused, according to Breton, *an irresistible need to possess*. Skeletal spirit men danced across a landscape that made no distinction between the actual and the mythological; dark figures with huge eyes, octopus-like limbs and swirling tails kept company with recognisable creatures; ochred reptiles spiralled between strange plants and ghostly bug-eyed spirits; little fish swallowed huge fish; a swordfish speared a man; a turtle gave birth to a bird. You can see the echos of this mythic world in the work of artists like Joan Miró, Man Ray, and even Picasso.

Oceania, Breton wrote, *inspired our covetousness as nothing else.*

When Claude and Viot reached Lake Sentani, they found a place worthy of Surrealist as well as covetous imaginings. Lying behind the mythically named Cyclops Mountains in territory that is now controlled by Indonesia, and then belonged to the Dutch, the lake was given its shape by the roll and tumble of foothills, so that in whichever direction they looked they could see bays and promontories, narrow spits of land and secret inlets. Hills as round as breasts lay across the still water of the lake.

Tucked into the bays and inlets were villages built on stilts that leaned out over the water. Rising above the modest houses of pandanus and thatch were the peaked and decorated dwellings where the elders engaged in their mysteries of ritual, mythology and art. *An enchanted castle,* Viot called Lake Sentani, in deference to André Breton's enchanted garden – though from the photographs I'd say he'd have done better to stick to the original and call it a garden. On the round hillsides that dipped into the lake were more prosaic gardens, ripe with fruit, where the women bent to their daily tasks.

Claude and Viot were not interested in the gardens, or the fruit, or the villages, or even the drama of the spirit-houses. What they were after lay deep in the lake. When slender canoes were floated out across the surface, they looked down into the water and – rocking dangerously – made their bargain. They would restore the treasures from the bottom of the lake to sunlight and the elders, and in exchange would be free to buy from the haul. They showed the silver of their coins.

Neither Jacques Viot nor Claude Ferraris dived personally. Of course they did not; they were artists and did not wish to wet their hands. Instead they paid as boys and young men dived. They paid in small coinage, and counted their profit as the masks, the gongs, the canoe prows, the bowls, and carvings redolent of the spirits, were raised from the water. Still wet from the lake, the best and the greatest of these treasures – gongs and spears, prows and masks, the carved figures of the spirits

– were added to the crates packed for the journey back to France.

Once there, Loeb took his share, Viot sold enough to pay his debts, and Claude satisfied his immediate urges. In the division of the rest Claude, who might be described by that old-fashioned term *a ladies' man*, took the carving that is at the centre of the story I am to tell you.

A life-size double figure, it stands almost six foot high, a primordial couple, male and female, man and woman. Carved of wood the two beings grow from the same root, standing on a small block as if tethered at the foot; the two bodies flare upwards and out, their heads turn slightly from each other; their expressions, eroded by the water, are sombre, a resigned melancholy. A grimly magnificent coupling neither complete – there is no romance here – nor sundered: a union demanding struggle.

That the figure went to Claude was, perhaps, a fitting fate – for Claude, if not for the figure.

By the standard of Claude's times, though not of ours, the expedition would have to be credited as a success, bringing to its adventuring heroes not only money but considerable prestige. Viot wrote a book about Sentani which was published in 1932, before he gave up Surrealism and switched to writing detective novels. Claude was still trading on the heroism of their journey decades later.

When I heard the story from Isobel Cullen in Sydney during the seventies, Claude's name was attached to it as if engraved on a trophy. Isobel told it often, and she liked to quote Breton that *Oceania has always had the supreme ability to unlock our hearts,* as if mere acquaintance with the figure from Lake Sentani could turn the course of a life. I was young enough to believe her, and believing her aroused my own covetousness, though it took many years for me to see that this was so. My desire was for a ripe and juicy story, not the figure. That I left to others.

But the figure, as it transpired, had a life rather separate from the version, and the event, with which its story originated. There was one piece of information, one twist in the plot, that Claude kept well hidden. He kept the secret, and perhaps it was for that reason that he could not keep the figure.

Claude gave it to Isobel in 1948, not long after Merle was born.

Isobel gave it to Merle in 1976 when she married Simon.

Simon stole it from Merle in 1982 when they divorced.

It could be said that none of them should have had the figure, and – as you will see – it didn't make any of them happy, least of all Simon who of all of them prized it the most.

1 SIMON'S SECRET

Simon was once the sort of man women dream about. *Heavenly,* was a word used of him, or *divine,* not because these dreaming women thought of him as a god exactly – language has become debased – but because he evoked in them an unnameable longing. I know because I was one of the dreamers. The tense I use is past, and so are the dreams. It is a compensation of age that one no longer falls in love with men like Simon. These days something dramatic has to happen to remind me to think of him at all. Like Merle returning to Sydney.

That morning, as if we needed waking from forgetfulness, we'd opened our papers to the extraordinary photo of Merle with no hair. Rosie, my niece from New Zealand, was staying with me. We were still at the breakfast table. I'd pointed out the photo of Merle and said that she was a friend. That's all, just a friend.

Then I'd passed Rosie the paper with its half-page article about the quartet which was here from New York for a short concert series at the Opera House. There was nothing surprising in that, the tour had been widely publicised – I'd already bought tickets – and I read with a kind of weary familiarity the breathless description of Merle, the only woman and, to add spice to sensation, the only white in the Quatrain Quartet. Journalists can smell a story, as I know, and I laughed (a quiet chuckle) as I read their attempt to find it. All the questions they asked were wrong, they had smelt the wrong rat; they were obsessed with the blackness of black and the whiteness of white, as if that was in itself some kind of secret. And there was Merle, married to Charlie Quatrain, taking up her cello, the sexiest of instruments, beside this fabulously sexy husband. No wonder the press rushed to photograph her. That shapely head. That veiled gaze.

It was only as an afterthought that we were told that Merle still used the name she called her Australian name and the paper called her maiden name. Merle Cullen, the article told us, was the third child of Tom Cullen, who had established the prestigious *Cullen's* Gallery and *brought modern art to Australia* (as if he had personally lugged it here, which in a way I suppose he had). And here was his daughter returning to us with a quartet given entirely to modern and esoteric music. *Like her father,* the paper said in its nauseating – and actually misleading – rhetoric, *Miss Cullen's ambition is to bring this century's classical music to world notice.*

Roll over Beethoven, the article was headed, over the astonishing photo of Merle.

'How gross,' Rosie said, registering a weary shock, as only a twenty-year-old can, as if our newspapers were a personal slight. So when the phone rang I left her to answer it. 'It's bound to be for you,' I said. She gets a lot of calls and, besides, she was trying to find a job – or I was trying to find one for her – and every ring of the phone was received with a measure of hope.

The shock I was registering had nothing to do with the crudeness of the heading, or the silliness of the reporting. I was transfixed by the grainy newsprint photo. Gone was the halo of hair without which Merle had always been, until that moment, unimaginable. Long, crinkled, a darkly brilliant red, it had graced her with the power of a pre-Raphaelite beauty. It was all gone. Not softened into a bob, or fashionably short at the side with plenty on top. I mean gone. Cropped to the skull, there was nothing to deflect attention from the lines around her eyes, the slight drop in her cheeks. She was no less beautiful, but her stance had changed. It was a stance entirely uncompromising.

The phone wasn't for Rosie.

'It's someone from some clinic,' she said, and I leaned across to take the receiver from her.

A polite male voice – urbane and slightly gritty – introduced himself as the director of a clinic up at Pittwater, on the other side of Sydney, and said he was telling me *in the utmost confidence* that he had Simon in his charge. Simon had asked him to ring as he wanted to see me, he seemed to have some kind of confession to make. Would I be able to visit, and if I did, which he very much hoped I would, would I call first at his office.

'Well,' I said cautiously, 'I might be able to come on Friday.'

'I think,' he said, 'that he needs you now. Look, I'll put you onto him, and hope to see you soon.'

The line went dead, there were a number of clicks, a female voice said *I'll transfer you now.* I knew at once – of course I knew – that whatever it was he had to say, whatever it was that had brought him there, would have to do with Merle and the Sentani figure that still divided them. That he was in a clinic startled but didn't surprise me. He'd skated too far and too long on the wrong sort of success. The fate of men like Simon, especially when they are successful, is to be emptied out by the dreams of women. Merle's dreams, as I well knew, were ferocious.

In the thirty seconds of waiting and listening to the phone click, I ran through my stock of excuses. Trekking across Sydney was not what I'd had in mind when I woke that morning to a rare day at home, away from the magazine.

'You're not to tell anyone I'm here,' Simon's voice said suddenly.

'Why not?' I asked.

'I just don't want it advertised.'

'Okay,' I said. 'But tell me what this is about.'

'I need to see you,' he said. 'There's something I have to tell you.'

'Can't you tell the doctor? He sounded okay, the one who rang.'

'I can't,' he said. 'It has to be you.'

'Why?'

'Because you know why I took the figure,' he said. 'And because you know Merle.'

'That doesn't necessarily make me sympathetic.'

'That's the point,' he said, and I thought I heard something on the line, I can't be sure, that sounded like a breath drawn in, a sob. 'Don't you see?'

'No,' I said. 'I don't think I do.' But because, despite it all, despite all that had passed, despite my capacity for forgetting him, I couldn't quite turn my back; and because the curl of history – if that's not too grand a term for it – had brought me to this moment, leaving something to be discharged, I said, *Well, yes, I suppose so, all right* – and promised to drive straight up.

'I suppose you've seen the paper,' he said in a more normal tone of voice.

'Yes,' I said. 'I was just reading it.'

'What's she done to her hair?' he said. 'It looks bloody awful.'

'I was thinking it looked rather good,' I said.

'What a cock-up,' he said.

'Who's Simon?' Rosie said, her face sharp with inquiry.

'Simon was married to Merle,' I said. 'Ages ago.'

'It's weird him ringing the day she's in the paper.'

'Not really,' I said. 'Not when you know the story.'

'Well, tell me,' she said, filling our cups.

'It's no good settling in,' I said. 'If I'm going to tell you, and I'm not sure that I am, it'll have to be in the car.'

'I'll come if you promise to tell.'

'I might.'

'Fuck *might*,' Rosie said.

I knew that I would tell her – *the delicious story is*

ripe – but still I hesitated. It was not reluctance – on the contrary I knew there would be pleasures in the telling, there always are – but nevertheless a hesitation. It was a strange, intense moment. What I was confronted with wasn't just the aftershock of a long story that I had entered many years ago when I was her age, but whether or not to speak of it, which parts to tell, which to conceal.

If we are to speak of secrets this question of revelation is at the heart of it. There are those dark, shameful secrets that we never want to tell anyone, which weigh on our conscience until we have to let them out – if only to a stranger, a priest, a psychiatrist. But in my experience it is more common for secrets to hover in a murky realm between being hidden and being revealed. We tell some people, not others; we tell part of the story, not all of it, letting the versions change shape like sea creatures weaving through the rocks and weeds of our lives.

I thought of this image, the rocks and weeds, the depths of our lives as we set off on the long drive across Sydney. It's obvious, I suppose, living in a city like this.

It was early spring. One of those days when great towers of cloud bear down on the city, their edges catching the sun, and underneath we are caught in a hectic wind. The harbour was choppy with yachts scudding about drunkenly. It was the sort of day when one expects to see fights outside pubs, children chasing dogs, shoppers tugged by their parcels into the wind. As we drove up onto the bridge, past the Opera House where Merle would play that night, I thought about what it means to live in a city with so much water, beside a harbour that is counterpoint to the glitter of stylish surfaces, a reminder, as the waves catch the sun, of both the transience of reflection, and the truth, the challenge and the danger of deep water.

So when Rosie said again, *Who's Simon*, this time I took her back to the beginning, not right back to Lake Sentani, but eastwards along the north coast of New Guinea to the Sepik. And I am taking you there too, not as a diversion or a prologue, or even as justification, explanation, credential; but as another originating layer, deep sediment.

I knew Simon long before he married Merle. In fact *know* is hardly the word. Or perhaps it is. I knew every tidal change of his body, the horizon of his eyes. In youth he was strikingly beautiful, so pale he seemed almost hairless, with long features and milky skin. It was a bleached look that suited him well, although in recent years it has begun to clash with skin that has grown blotchy and rather too red.

I met him quite by chance, travelling with my husband, fresh from sleepy, distant suburbs, on a series of slow, turbulent flights taking us across the high spine of New Guinea. I'd noticed him at the airport in Port Moresby. Or rather, I noticed him notice me. I looked up from the bags I was labelling and there were those eyes taking me in. I turned, in some confusion, to the arm of the man beside me.

At the next airport I felt his attention again, as if it were a disturbance of air before I stepped up to the bar and saw him. I ordered two lemon and sodas. He lifted his beer and smiled. Oh lordy. It was hot, steamy hot outside, the air rose from the tarmac in thick waves. I blushed, and this beautiful man remained pale.

It was the very last year of the sixties, just before the Christmas that clicked the calender over to 1970.

We were on our way into the Sepik, and so was Simon. Our business – or rather my husband's – was ethnography. Mine, back then all those years ago, was to be a wife. There I was carrying a bag packed with romance novels, high and low, and a kit of balsawood and glue, plasticine and tape, for the tiny buildings I liked to make while my husband worked, model villages and cathedrals to entertain me as I dreamed. Simon, like my husband, had legitimate worldly business. He was collecting local art, though the word that was used in those days was more often artefacts than art.

Always quick to make a deal, Simon shook my

husband's hand and, without a glance at me, offered a share of the jeep and driver he had already arranged.

Which is how the three of us came to be travelling those gravelly roads into the Sepik hills, through some of the most surprising country I have ever known. Feathery forest falling and fading, a soft light, streaky and seductive, silver ribbons of water, tall palms, birds with plumage of rose and amber, brilliant blue, chalky yellow. Gentle laneways transformed without warning into a twist of steep impenetrable cliff folding around the tributaries of the great river system of the Sepik, a web of waterways that lay across the land like capillaries across the retina of an eye. There were few fords and fewer bridges.

It was, literally, a landscape that took the breath, as the jeep nosed down steep banks into water that ran fast and choppy, accelerating against the sweep and tug of the current towards the dense green of the other bank where parrots flew and squawked at our approach, scattering in the sky. As we travelled deeper into this enchanted world, surrendering to the lurch of the road, Simon put his hand on my shoulder to steady me. Water lapped at our feet and streamed behind us as we lifted into the forest on the other side, and the road straightened itself out again. It was the sort of place that invites adjectives.

Along the ridges, where the roads were covered in grass as smooth as a lawn, we slowed to pass women in coloured smocks with billums of vegetables on their backs, families of pigs tended by small boys, solemn men carrying ceremonial yams, or a snake hung along a pole like the trophy of a hunt. Squat on these ridges were the villages where we stopped to drink the milk of green coconuts, or brightly coloured squash from the mission store. Children clambered over the car, and young men brushed them off so they could open the bonnet and inspect the engine; women gathered around with fruit to sell and requests to make: alka seltza, disprin, needles, cloth.

While they looked at the still-exotic machine carrying pale-skinned plunderers into their village, we looked up at the huge edifice of the tambaran – or spirit-house – which towered above us. Its huge woven front, thirty feet high and as wide as a sail, was peaked in a decorated spire as imposing as any cathedral. Fierce carvings gazed down at us, teeth bared, daring the imperial eye to fall with anything but awe. Inside the great whale-like sanctuary of the interior was the treasure – in the form of art and artefact – that Simon and my husband were after: the masks of the tambaran.

Sixpence, sixpence, the children called. Our meagre pockets swelled with wealth. A few cents here, a few cents there, our bags were carried, food appeared, and we were ushered to the *haus kiap* which villages were still, then, required to maintain as a place for the visitors and officials that a colonial regime inflicted upon them.

After a meal of vegetables and sago, bony fish from the river and trade-store rice, a little blackened pig, Simon and my husband, emissaries from a desired and moneyed world, arranged themselves cross-legged on the slatted floor, and waited for the elders. The voices of children, the running of small feet, announced the old men's arrival; the room hushed as they padded in on splayed feet that had walked the bare earth without protection of shoes.

Greetings were exchanged in wordless trills of sound, hands shaken, as the elders took their place with impressive intent. Simon and my husband sat square beside them. Spivvy interpreters who wore rubber thongs and spoke pidgin and a little English, opened more of the beer Simon had produced from the back of the jeep they'd spent the afternoon examining. The old men spat their betel.

Women, as I quickly learned, were excluded from the tambaran. Entirely and absolutely. There was no entering that sacred belly if one's own belly was able to expand with its own mysteries. The masks and gongs could be brought out to tantalise the women, to demonstrate the power of their owners, but they could not be worn, or owned, or danced with. Not if you had breasts. Which I did, and as a consequence found I was a liability. In the presence of the elders, Simon and my husband turned their attention from the demands of my presence. Half concealed in the shadows of the *haus kiap*, I became voyeur and silent witness to the negotiations that would, the next morning, bring the riches from the tambaran.

For Simon it was serious business: a good mask from the Sepik would fetch hundreds of dollars, even thousands, in Berlin or New York. His hoped-for profit came in obvious coinage, and a lot of it.

My husband operated a different currency. He didn't want cash, and he didn't want the masks: he wanted the knowledge, the stories, the powers they represented. For him it was the nature of the secrets themselves that mattered. His desire, his aim, his hope, was to dive into their mystery as if that way he could penetrate the origins of life itself, the secret of death.

We each had our template, and beyond that we saw little; appropriation was not a word I knew, and colonial was an adjective like any other. The words I used were from the vocabulary of the novels in my bag. I may as well have been in a moon country. As if to jolt me into a reality he wished me to share, my husband used words like sacred.

He explained to me that its meaning was not the same as secret, for the word secret came from *secretus,* the past participle of the Latin verb *secerno,* while sacred is a simpler move from the verb *sacrare.* My husband was like that, very precise, wanting exact meanings. *Sacrare,* he said, means to render holy, while *secerno* means having been separated or divided. It comes from the ancient art of sifting grain, separating the edible from the inedible. Good from bad. The valuable from the wasted. Masks for him were in this category, separating one thing from another, so if you grasped one possibility, the other was also within grasp: turn it around, and there you are.

Simon was quite different. He was slapdash and near enough. In all the years I've known him, he's never once offered the origin of a word, and tends if not to untruth, then to the slide of possibilities, so nothing is ever quite divided or separated. He lives with a sort of messy overlap, a lack of clarity, a maddening ambiguity. When he was young this was part of his charm; as he has grown older it has become a messy weakness. But back then, in the prehistory of this story, when his vocabulary ran to the tint and texture of ochre, soft impressions, his stories were always good.

While he piled his booty into the back of the jeep and talked to me of Picasso and Breton and Paris in the twenties, my husband would sit for an entire morning with a single mask as its legends were told, its provenance interrogated, genealogies taken. He would then accompany it, swerving to avoid the jeep, as it was carried ceremoniously back to the tambaran.

For me those mornings passed slowly. With no bargaining power, no status and no role, I'd sit on the verandah of the mission store and finish reading *East Lynne* – that was my taste in those days – or *Northanger Abbey*; or I'd paste together the struts for the tiny *haus tambaran* I had measured out from a plan I'd had to create for myself. The great cathedrals of Europe came boxed and scaled, ready for me, but if the cathedrals of Oceania were to succumb to my collection, I'd have to imagine them into existence from scratch.

Or else, fractious, I'd sit on the fender of the car, unbuckle my sandal and surreptitiously trace Simon's initials in the dust with my toe, his whole name, and mine, hearts entwined, daring myself to expose more, daring my husband to look my way, and looking, see. But when Simon came towards me, I quickly rubbed it all out, scrubbing with my foot in the dusty earth.

'You must be bored,' he said, squatting beside me, lifting my foot, dusting it, rubbing his soft fingers against the instep. 'Come back to the coast with me why don't you,' he said re-buckling my sandal, his voice as soft as a caress, so soft I could well have imagined it. I blushed another deep, rosy, blush.

As if that were the signal, my husband came towards us. But rather than hear my confession – which was what I longed for from him, more, even, than Simon's palm on my breast – the two men turned to each other as if they were the ones entranced, and the argument between them continued: a rising dispute that had accompanied us day after day, night after night, since we set out on this ill-fated journey.

Was it plunder, as my husband said, for Simon to collect and buy?

Was my husband trying to freeze a culture, as Simon counter-accused, into a form that suited his own nostalgia? It was his discipline, Simon said, not art, that had introduced the concept of primitivism, studying tribal societies as if they were a direct conduit to some daft notion of the sacred.

Not at all, my husband replied, it was artists, especially the French, who were the ones to make a fetish of the primitive, entirely for their own benefit, incorporating it into their work and claiming a heightened spiritual value as their own.

Neither man commented on my own clumsy attempts to carry Oceania away with me. My models dried unnoticed on the back seat of the jeep.

And so the days passed, layered with voice and emotion, and days became weeks and possibly even years. Time became elastic, at once too fast, dense with desire, and yet slowed-down, elongated. In a landscape enchanted by such dreams and memories, it is impossible to say what the reality was for those for whom it was a daily world. We borrowed their spirits, we traded in their art, we stripped their myths, yet I understood little of the art, or the buildings, let alone the lives, of the people whose voices surrounded me.

My husband and Simon had their certainties, but I doubt that they knew much more.

When the masks were brought out, I viewed them neither as items of trade, nor as manifestations of the sacred, but as something that could absorb the slippages of my own unmasked face. Instinctively, I wanted one.

My husband, as if to prove his serious intent, or to mark himself from Simon, refused to buy anything. Not a single mask. Not a gong, not a mortar, not the smallest strip of tapa cloth. He would leave the Sepik with clean hands. I, on the other hand, longed for a mask with a desire as covetous as any Simon was banking on in his customers.

As the veneer of my wifely persona became harder to hold in place, the masks spoke to the condition of my heart, not because they concealed a truth that lay hidden, a kind of opposite, but because, for all their elaborate ritual of concealment, they evoked the secret they hid. In my guilty solipsism, their truth – and mine – lay not in separation or division, as my husband had suggested, but somewhere between what was seen, and not seen. Another possibility, though I had no name for it.

I suppose what I wanted from a mask was to be able to give shape to my painful uncertainty. But under the circumstances I was not in a position to ask either man for money; as a wife, a dependant, a married woman, I had no currency to call my own.

In the last village, where Simon had agreed to leave us and return to the coast – and where we were to meet a geographer who was studying yams and would take us further up the river – I saw the judgement mask. When the masks of that village came out, the paintings on sago and bark, the gongs, the canoe prows, the spears and tools, among them was a small rather chunky mask, not elaborated as many of them were. A severe, modest mask. Its effect was additionally striking as it had been painted with European distempers. A long blue nose, round ochred eyes like spectacles, a white wisp that was barely a mouth.

Amongst all that was laid out for Simon's delectation – and cash – that one mask caught my eye. The movement came from it, not from me, and in response I could feel the caged flutter of my heart.

'Can I buy it?' I asked my husband. 'Please?'

'It's not a very good example,' my husband said. 'It's been contaminated with that paint.' But that was what I loved most about it: that faded midnight blue, the russet red, the smoky white.

'Shall I buy it for you?' Simon said, and I could see his hand reach into his pocket. It was a moment of weakness he came to regret, for he knew what I did not know, and nor did my husband: that the strangeness of the old distemper would increase the value of the masks on the commercial markets of the West.

'How will I pay you back?' I said.

'Accept it as a gift,' he said, and as he did my husband came to my side, and his hand, too, was in his wallet pocket. He took out twenty dollars – a lot of money in a place that paid grown men a shilling a day to carry the bags and equipment of government officials and other interlopers, but very little in western scales of art.

My husband's was the money I accepted. Of course. Simon shrugged, and perhaps – I am not sure – it was his turn to blush. Not blush exactly, more like a slight flush, or flash of emotion, hostile and proud, a hint I should have had the sense, or wisdom, to take.

My husband noticed nothing. Or rather, I did not notice him notice. He had turned to the grizzled man who squatted beside the mask and asked where it had come from. It was not a mask from the initiation ceremonies, it was not a mask used to conceal, or to conjure the spirits of the tambaran. It was a headpiece, attached, the grizzled one explained, to the stand inside the tambaran – a kind of pulpit – for the elder who spoke in dispute or debate.

'A judgement mask,' I said and lifted it level with my face as if it could offer me certainty, or balance, or knowledge.

Both men watched, and embarrassed, I wrapped the mask in a towel and leant it against my pack.

Simon went back to loading his booty into the jeep.

As the hour approached when he was to leave and I would remain in the village with my husband, I began to feel faint, and rather nauseous. I was caught in a vice of impossible impulses. Risk banged against safety. Desire against obligation. If I left with Simon I was afraid that I would lose every bearing. If Simon left without me, I would have no idea where to find him. Having refused his offer, several times as it happens, I had no address, no telephone number, no way of asking, no reason to know.

All morning, as Simon packed and bartered, my husband stayed close to me. It was he, not Simon, who was concerned for my health. He put his hand to my brow.

'You're very hot,' he said.

'Of course I'm hot,' I said, pointing up at the sky which was clear and hazy, with a huge sun hanging in it. 'Look where we are.'

'I think you have a fever,' he said, standing up to inquire about the mission, whether there was a nurse.

I closed my eyes and leaned into the shade of the store's verandah. I could hear footsteps, the murmur of anxiety, lowered voices.

'I could take her back to the coast,' Simon said, appearing with the pastor who'd come flapping into the village with his first-aid box.

'A doctor,' I said, opening my eyes.

'I should come with you,' my husband said.

But there was the geographer to consider, my husband's research trip, and I was no use when it came to yams, I couldn't even eat them.

'Fly straight back to Moresby,' my husband said.

'I'll take care of her,' Simon said.

And so the lie was told. With lies, in my experience, one should be careful, for it is often the case that the lie itself can make the excuse come true. Ask for a doctor, and you'll end up needing a doctor. Offer care and you'll be sure to have to administer it. But I didn't know that then, when my husband helped me into the car as if we already knew, which of course we did not, that it was a final gesture of a doomed marriage.

This part I remember, not clearly as if it were a film, but slowed down into an underwater sequence, an opaque dream: the crowd around the car, the men counting their notes, the children on the bonnet, the pastor sweaty and red as he ran into the village, my husband curiously pale, as if he was drained of blood, which I am sure he was not, the draining of him a figment entirely of my memory.

'That was a very girl thing to do,' Rosie said, 'swooning like that.' And I suppose it was. 'Pathetic,' she said.

'What would you have done?' I asked her.

'I wouldn't have been married in the first place,' she said.

'And if you had?'

'I'd have told the truth at once,' she said.

Rosie views secrets with a rather touchingly brisk good sense. She took a tough position from the start. Every secret, she said, is a betrayal. Or rather she put it first as a question, the little girl in her opening up, *can it be*, she said facing this hard truth, and then, yes, she reasoned, if there wasn't a secret there wouldn't be a betrayal. For her secrets are like rocks, great substantial things you stub your toe against, diversions in a life that should run smooth, frustrations she'd rather eliminate.

'I hate secrets,' she said.

'Don't you have secrets of your own?' I said.

'Not important ones,' she said. 'Not serious secrets.'

I also hate secrets, perhaps it's a gene we share, but I am old enough to admit that the secrets I hate are the ones other people keep from me.

'Don't you think,' I said to Rosie, 'that there are times when a woman needs to play her cards close to her chest?'

'I'd despise a woman who did that,' Rosie said.

'Then you'll have to despise me,' I said.

As Simon and I were driven back along those enchanted pathways, crossing the treacherous tributaries of the river we'd just left, I moved in a kind of trance, given over entirely to turbulence, awash in emotion, beyond thought. Neither masked, nor unmasked, I believe I trembled with the perverse pleasure that comes with erotic risk. In retrospect it's hard to be sure, and considering Simon now, it's hard to imagine; but I think I remember the trembling. And I remember that we reached the coastal town of Wewak as darkness fell – a sprinkling of lights, a tiny airport, trade stores strung like lanterns along a curling beach. And the Windjammer Hotel.

Shameless, we took one room.

There I was drawn into a realm of which,
beyond the trembling of that journey, I had no
forewarning. It was not so much the longing for
the tongue and pulse of the lover – sinew, muscle,
mucus, tear – as surrender to dark stirrings that
had no place in the clean suburbs of my youth, or
in the marriage I had made too young, or in the
novels that lay unopened in my bag. Beside them
the balsawood and glue was closed in its box.

Lying with Simon on a hard bed in a small
room with slatted windows looking out towards
the great belly of ocean sighing on the edge of the
monsoon, removed from daily inevitabilities, I
gave myself over to the dangerous swoop and fall
of sensation; all body, all murky interior, belly
rather than heart, perverse extremity, not centre.

Until the morning when the door opened and
my husband stood silhouetted in the frame. The
rain had begun during the night with a dull thud,
it was sheeting off the verandah; the slatted blinds
were angled in such a way that they caught the
movement of water into water so that the meeting
of sea and sky was obscured. We were enfolded in a
tear-grey world. There was no one to sing the alba,
the dawn song of warning that was sung in trouba-
dour Spain to alert illicit lovers. There was no one
to forewarn us, no one to guide. We were jolted, or
at least I was, not only back into the ordinary shape
of the body, but into consciousness, and reality.

Simon flew to Sydney the next day.

A week later a letter arrived from him. Full of protestations, promises, adorations, hopes. All of which would have meant more had not a letter arrived in the following mail addressed to my husband; I took it from his pocket that night as soon as sleep had claimed him. *I tried to stop her,* I read, *but it was impossible.*

Unlike Rosie and her rocks, or my husband with his sieve, I think secrets are more like waves. They crest, a perfect story rolling in, a powerfully perfect shape, green and curled against the sky – that smooth rush of pleasure, riding in. And then the wave breaks, and there we are in the foam and rush of swirling water, sand, weed. It's then that we lose our footing as sand churns through the water, no longer pure green. It's then that accidents occur, toes are stubbed, backs broken, children dragged out in the undertow. And one wave creates another. Before we get back on dry land another wave has formed itself and in its wake the struggling swimmer thrashes and gulps, a god cast low. It's a long way to the beach, all those people dreaming on their towels, soaking up the sun, opening the sandwich case, gossiping with their neighbours, turning the page of a novel.

Isn't that what secrets are like? Not solid like

rocks, an impediment life must go round, or something to push through a sieve, separated from the value of life, but as much a part of life as the wave is part of the ocean.

The Greeks peopled the deep with gods and demons. I went to the library and looked them up. Oceanus was the first of the Titans, and when he married his sister Thetis, she bore him three thousand children, each one a wave – enough to fill the oceans of the entire world. He also sired Metis whose name means either, or both, prudence and perfidy. Ambivalence has always been associated with the sea. Deep down under the water were the lovely nereids, that compassionate chorus of sea-nymphs; but flying around above were the harpies, evil spirits with the faces of women, who blew up storms and seized unwary travellers.

Larousse says that even the genealogy of the Sphinx of Thebes can be traced back to the ocean. The Sphinx, you will remember, devoured anyone who could not answer her riddle, and when Oedipus cracked it, she leapt in fury to her death. As is often the case with riddles, they tend to be more powerful when the answer isn't known; once you get them, they are oddly banal. There's the famous one about man walking first on four legs, then on two, and then on three. The one I prefer is *Who are the two sisters who give birth to each other?* The answer, also from the ambivalent realm, is day and night.

Which is why I say that every secret has an excess, a flowing wake, the capacity for undertow. Even if you don't believe in demons and sea-spirits, there are sharks and conger eels prowling that water.

As I churned in the sand, unable to get my footing, I realised that there was another player in a drama that until that moment had comprised Simon, my husband, and me.

I was the next to fly to Sydney, where a grim-faced Simon met the plane. He had made the arrangements, he had paid the money, and afterwards to his credit he sat beside me as, sedated, I wept over the little blob of blood which would never be the baby I was not brave enough to have. I tell you this, not because it bears upon the story – in truth it is tangential – but because it bears upon the telling of it. A motivation, a wound tended over several decades, an exchange: a loss, a life, a story.

A fair exchange? I'll leave you to decide.

To get an abortion in 1970, discretion was required, a good deal of money, and if anything went wrong it was up to you, the woman, to get yourself to hospital and tell the lies. But it wasn't like those novels of the twenties where women bled into the mattress ticking until they died.

What was shocking to me was the perfunctory way in which it happened, as if nothing more grievous than a tooth was coming out, so that even my despair and Simon's chagrin were flattened out, coarsened somehow. Leaving us nothing to say to each other.

What I took from the bloody grief of that day was the understanding that by letting the mask slip, revealing my treacherous self, I had tasted the salty tang of the deep. Something crossed over in me, and I knew that although I would struggle to the surface time and again longing for the veneer of rosy, surface narratives, conger eels would chase me back to keep company with the sea creatures.

My reading changed to Olive Schreiner, Doris Lessing, Katherine Mansfield. The stories I told were terse. For the most part I gave up my balsa-wood as childish, a diversion, an affectation of which, when I opened the box and smelt the plasticine, I felt faintly ashamed.

Simon, in contrast, bobbed to the surface and took good care to stay there. It was as if something in him became hidden. At the time I thought it was from me that he hid himself, but now I realise it was from himself that he took cover. Worldly success, a kind of chimera tantalisingly close, was the prowling shark that snapped at his toes.

Since then, I told Rosie, Simon has become a rich man. He owns galleries in Melbourne, Sydney and Brisbane, and through them he sells what is now unambiguously called the Art of Oceania. He writes monographs, curates exhibitions and, until recently when time seems to have stopped on him, he still managed to travel back into the Sepik where, twenty-five years later, the roads are liable to ambush and he is accompanied not by a girl, but by an armed guard.

When he began trading, in those first years when everything could have been scuttled by a careless pregnancy, his rival was Isobel Cullen; when he checked into that room at the Windjammer Hotel with me, he already knew Isobel. He did not yet know of the existence of Merle. And had he known, a daughter would hardly have signified. It was Isobel who ran the gallery, made the deals, commanded the authority, brought in the money. That's where his attention lay. He had hoped for a clear run. But the ground had been tilled before him, and Sydney claimed, and if there was an expert in Oceanic art, a commercial expert that is, it was Isobel Cullen. It was to her and her gallery in Victoria Street, not to the brash new Simon, that the dealers from Berlin, London, New York, turned for information, contacts, the objects themselves. The glories he wished for himself were hers.

Faced with this problem, Simon utilised his strongest resource to persuade Isobel Cullen into the role first of mentor, then of collaborator. He made himself charming; he made himself useful; he made himself indispensable. He used his eyes and the willowy bend of his body to good advantage, listening and amusing, offering his arm, holding the door. He had youth on his side, and good fortune, for the attentions of a man like Simon were exactly what Isobel wanted. Neither of her sons would play this role; and anyway she wanted a frisson that they could not provide. Simon and Isobel were, in a sense, a perfect match.

'How vile,' Rosie said.

'Yes,' I said. 'I suppose it was.'

But it didn't seem so at the time. Even, later, when he persuaded Isobel's daughter, the immaculate Merle, to become his wife it did not seem vile. I should know, for I watched it all as if it were a campaign laid out before me.

First Simon took me to meet Isobel.

It was late in the afternoon on a hot day and the door of the gallery was open. She didn't hear us come in. She was looking at herself in a mirror, adjusting an amber necklace. She smiled when she saw us – a smile, and then a slight frown. She put down the mirror, closed the gallery door, and took us through to the house for a bottle of wine. We sat on the verandah at the back looking across

to Woolloomooloo and the city, a view I've come
to know as well as any in Sydney, though that afternoon, as I listened to Simon and Isobel tease and
laugh, I regarded it with that slightly startled sense
of recognition as if it were a painting I'd seen only
in reproduction.

Next I met the boys, Merle's brothers – Brian,
who I adored, and Pablo, who I did not. You could
say that with the arrival of the Cullens into my life,
or the slide of mine into theirs, I fell further from
the love I'd once had for Simon. At any rate I felt
again the pulse of risk, and this time energy and
movement did not come from Simon. He moved
out of the house we had shared for a year down
near the canal, and Brian, briefly my lover, moved
in. It was the seventies, remember, and the fact
that I took Brian as a lover did not mean I gave
Simon up. Passion had died in that blandly sterile
surgery, but dependence had not, and with the
interweaving of both our lives with the Cullens,
the bonds that bound us loosened on one ankle,
and tightened on the other.

It must have been during this time that I first
met Tom Cullen, the father of Merle and the boys,
though he was so shadowy and insubstantial to me
then, that I realise I can tell this part of the story
without so much as mentioning him. He was so
unlike my idea of what a father should be that I
could not see that everything rested on him:

financially, emotionally. I wish it were not the case, but it was; for a long time I could not see him at all.

Last of all I met Merle. Isobel had kept her at a distance, locked up at school, and in their house at Mudgee, as if she didn't trust the city with her prized daughter. As if she were hers, and no one else was going to have the chance.

It wasn't until she won a scholarship to the conservatorium that she arrived in Sydney. It was the New Year of 1971, and there she was standing on the verandah at one of Isobel's Victoria Street parties, her hair alight in the evening sun. She seemed extraordinarily young, even to those of us who were barely less young. Perhaps because her skin had that strange translucency that often accompanies red hair, or because it fell around a face that was a perfect oval, or perhaps because she had been protected even against her own longings, we responded to her as vulnerably at risk.

Simon was not the only one who fell in love with her.

Five years later Simon married Merle. He had not courted her for five years, but he had watched her closely, and made sure she was in his line of vision, so that when it all blew up with Isobel – with Isobel and Merle that is – he was well positioned to make his move. With the ear of both mother and daughter, he could move between them with every advantage and confidence. It was a dangerous game he played, remaining the ally of one while not betraying, or seeming to betray, the other.

To Isobel he presented himself as the link that would hold her daughter to her. To Merle he turned his full attention, listening to her every word, so that by the time he took her to bed, she too had mistaken the intensity of his gaze for understanding and love. Oh Merle.

Within weeks of this sudden, explosive event – the details of which I will tell you when we come to Merle's secret – she had moved out of my house at one end of Glebe and into the old rooming house at the other that Simon was converting into a dwelling worthy of the dreams he had for her. There were sinks in every room when he bought that house, but Simon had what is called a 'good eye' and also good contacts. But although walls came out and windows were opened onto verandahs, Merle said she never liked it as a house. Perhaps the ghosts of those old men lingered on and dragged down the air; or perhaps it was because it was in the dip of Hereford Street with factories opposite and the fumes from Bridge Road sucked round the corner. There was something airless and stuffy about that house. Simon had ceiling fans put in – the sort you see across the Pacific –

which circled with their slow *thwack-thwack* above their disastrous, unhappy marriage.

For once in his life Simon was faithful. I believe that was true, though maybe I judge only by the fact that he made no overtures to me. In any case that wasn't the cause of the marriage breaking down. Breaking up. It was a simple, and pre-dictable case of a woman finding herself lonely in the company of a man in whom she had confused the reflection of her own depth for his; and a man who believed that all that was required of him when it came to the daily continuation of emo-tional life, was constancy and a supply of good sex. Simon never had any trouble providing the latter, and Merle did not complain of the former.

What he could not comprehend was that she was not satisfied by – indeed barely seemed to notice – the worldly successes which came to him and which he willingly shone on her. Or would have, had she let him. After those first whirlwind months when he'd said *Marry me* and she'd said *Yes, of course,* he returned to his accustomed ter-rain, and she learned to keep from him, as effec-tively as she revealed, those bone-deep longings she could no longer articulate, or name. *Talk to me,* she'd say. But she never said *Listen while I show you my heart.*

Their lives, it seemed to me, as I watched from a not entirely comfortable sideline, were, like their conversations, fundamentally at cross purposes.

In any case Simon was busy, always busy, pre-occupied with the gallery. Those brief years when he was married to Merle, ending as the eighties began, were the years when he made his name, his money and his reputation. Success built around him like a carapace: he wore it proudly, it shone in the photographs that reflected him back to himself in his splendid armour. Merle cracked open the armour, but the aperture she created was never sufficiently wide for her to enter, or perhaps when she glimpsed the loneliness of his heart, she found that she had no further interest.

She sat at the window of the gloomy house in Hereford Street, and taking out Britten's cello suites, she lifted her arm to the bow. If Simon had attended to her playing with the attention he had used to woo her, he might have heard in this choice – played and replayed – something of the condition of her heart as she leaned into the stretch of their intensity. Or their discipline and demand. He might then have been prepared for the graveness of the move she was leading herself towards.

But Simon rarely listened. He couldn't, for when she played he was at the gallery. When he was at home, she was silent, her cello in its case.

When Simon married Merle, he was already running the Victoria Street gallery.

At first Isobel did not give up her interest in the gallery; she simply made room for Simon to operate under its auspices. That this had happened, had been, on Simon's part, another form of seduction. It wasn't just that he made himself useful, taking over the tedious jobs. For that Isobel could have paid.

No, it was his attention to her private wishes that drew him into her confidence, and into the gallery. He understood the unsure nature of her vanity. When they took clients out to lunch, he'd pour the wine and, deferring to her knowledge of Oceania, he'd draw her out – for her own benefit, and for the benefit of the client – on the book she was writing about the early expeditions into New Guinea. *It's going to change the way we see Sentani, this book,* he'd say.

When he was alone with her in the gallery, Simon was cheerful and attentive. He had read up on Lake Sentani, and talked to her at length about the Sepik villages. He made sure he knew everything she knew, and besides, was a good addition at the dinners she liked to give in the large rooms above the gallery. He watched as she relaxed into her life around him.

So it is not so surprising that he saw the letters arrive. He was usually in the gallery first. He'd put her mail on the desk. He'd notice – of course he'd notice – where her letters came from. He knew which envelopes – which handwriting, which post marks – made her glance around at him in a gesture uncharacteristically furtive; a slight shrug, a half smile. He saw her slip the offending letter into her desk drawer and turn the lock.

Simon darling, Isobel would say as she let him take over another of her tasks, her clients, her shows, *You wouldn't give me the morning off to write, would you?*

It became an obsession with her, that book, and this Simon also knew. After all, it suited him well that she turned her attention from the gallery, and although he didn't entirely believe in the book, it cost him nothing to encourage her.

The book Isobel wanted to write was to be an account of the expeditions into the north-west of New Guinea. She wasn't interested in the brawn of explorers who had scaled the great mountain ranges of the centre. That wasn't the book she wanted to write. Her expeditions were of an altogether more neurasthenic variety: the journeys of dealers and artists into the northern river systems with the aim of bringing out the art that would find its way into the galleries, and, more significantly, onto the canvases of the West. She wanted nothing less than to reinterpret Picasso. It was a project conceived on a daunting scale, and its heart – its driving force, its reason for being – was the story Claude Ferraris had told her of the Surrealists at Lake Sentani. Simon was certain that it was Claude who wrote the letters, although any mention of his name – tentative and occasional – was confined entirely to the book.

Isobel gave years of her life to that book, and she never came near to finishing it. Simon's view was that in the end it sent her mad. It was too large, too difficult, too sprawling. And too tied to her conception of herself. My view is that the figure of Claude clouded her vision, and she was never able to make the story hers. But then Isobel did not have the stomach for too much reality. But what is significant here isn't that so much, but that because of the book and her obsession with it, she had the noblest and best of reasons for leaving the daily mundanities of the gallery to Simon.

In 1976 when Simon married Merle, the gallery still bore Isobel's name. Well, actually it bore Tom Cullen's name. *Cullen's*. The gallery was just called *Cullen's*. Tom ran the branch in the city which dealt in modern Australian art, and had by then become a cultural icon of a sort, leaving Isobel to take over the small gallery in Victoria Street where they had begun, and that now dealt only in her beloved Oceania.

The shops ran separate accounts. Isobel had insisted on that when Tom moved the last pieces of

Australian art; Simon told me so that day at the clinic, not out of some sort of proto-feminism, but – as you will see – for much more pressing reasons.

'God it's complicated,' Rosie said. 'You'd have to be an accountant to follow it.'

'Listen,' I said. 'Otherwise Simon's secret won't make sense.'

He is embedded in this story, and even if I wanted to, there's no move I can make to extricate him. And there's no move he can make to extricate himself. This is not something he'd admit. That's why he's in the clinic. At least that's what I'd say, but then as you will have noticed, I am not sympathetic to Simon. I'll drive across Sydney to see him, I owe him that much – or my conscience won't let me do less – but I'm in no mind to tidy up a story for his benefit. In this, at least, I will not follow Isobel's example.

By the time Simon and Merle divorced, the deeds of Isobel's gallery were in Simon's name, and the sign that hung outside said *Simocea*. It was a deal between Simon and Isobel. It had nothing to do with Merle, but she never forgave him. The price, it's true, was unusually low. To Simon – and also to Isobel – it was a deal. To Merle it was theft. That was the word she used. Biblical and judgemental. And she used it as fuel to the fury into which the frustrations of five years of marriage had erupted.

The ground was scorched for miles in every direction as that marriage came unstuck, and I was one of those who were singed. While the lawyers could negotiate everything else, they could not settle the bitterness that came, depending which way you looked at it, from this theft, Merle's fury, or Simon's humiliation. Merle knew no mercy. *Theft*, she said. And the word became fixed. So fixed that theft, I was about to find out, was the subject of the confession I was driving across Sydney to hear.

As to their parting, it is enough, I think, to say that Merle fought a hard bargain, and it was a bitter day for Simon when on the steps of the court, in addition to almost all the profit from the gallery, he settled on her the house he had found and restored; the house that he loved, and she sold just as the boom started: a windfall entirely for her own benefit, enough to set herself up in New York.

What does bear on this story is that while Merle was celebrating with her QC, Simon caught a taxi, broke a window – Merle had already changed the locks – and took from the house the Sentani figure that Isobel had given to Merle on the eve of their marriage.

It had been a staggeringly generous gift. Not so much because it was far and away the most valuable single item that had ever been in Isobel's collection, never offered for sale, but because it had been given to her by Claude Ferraris who had described the watery paradise of a lake spread out among the foothills of the Cyclops Mountains whose craggy peaks were the breeding ground of gods every bit as powerful as the gods of Greece. For her he had conjured the romantic version, with fruit falling from every tree, gardens of bamboo, honey-skinned youths diving from gently rocking canoes, old men wizened with the wisdom of ages, and the fineness of his own discrimination when it came to the collecting of art.

On the cover of her book, in tribute to this dream, and this man, Isobel planned to have this figure of the primordial couple that Claude had given her: stark, unadorned, magnificent. For nearly thirty years it had stood in Isobel's gallery; its commanding presence would have fetched any price Isobel had cared to name. The famous museums of the world had inquired. A note had even come from a dealer in Paris on behalf of a client that Isobel took to be Picasso himself.

'Can't you see what it means that she's given it,' Simon would say.

But Merle did not like the figure, and was not grateful. It loomed over her while she practised, she said, and dominated the small rooms of a house it was never meant for. There's not enough room for my arm, she said, lifting her bow.

Simon took the figure up to his study on the top floor.

If Isobel had been hurt that Merle did not like the figure that she had given, she didn't show it. There was compensation in the fact that Simon treasured that strange double-headed creature as if he had personally dived into deep water for it. To own the prize of the Lake Sentani collection was, for him, the apotheosis of every desire he'd carried since that first trip he'd made into the Sepik, when my life had so suddenly and dramatically bumped against his. That it meant so much had a curious effect – for with it, his hold over Isobel was strengthened. It was as if she, not he, was the one indebted by gratitude.

Rosie is right, there was something strange, and rather unpleasant, in Isobel's attitude to Simon. I think she loved him in a way that Merle never did. The hopeless love of the woman who, over the yardarm of mid-life, is still addicted to the allure of romance and the attentions of attractive men. She'd always been a sucker for glamour and she – not Merle – loved the fact that Simon was invited everywhere, and when openings and receptions clashed with the orchestra which Merle had joined before the marriage and refused to leave, then Isobel would take Simon's arm. In those days it was her face, not Merle's, that I saw in the glossy magazines I read at the hairdresser.

Now, of course, the face we see is Merle's. When we arrived at the clinic that morning, the paper was folded in such a way that her photo lay face up on the table, beside which the smooth-talking director invited Rosie and me to sit.

We had overshot the turning, concentrating more on the story I was telling than on the map, and by the time we'd twisted up the hillside and found the clinic perched above the bushy edge of Pittwater, looking out towards Scotland Island, we were stiff and thirsty. The director gave us tea of a variety I couldn't identify, and told us that Simon had been admitted when the symptoms that had taken him to the hospital in the city proved to be the harbinger not of the heart attack he had antici-pated but of a breakdown.

'It's often the case with men,' he said. 'They find it too hard to admit to a breakdown. It's still shameful, you know, in our society, so they prefer the route of a heart attack. That's how we get a good number of our patients.

'Which is why I wanted to see you before you see Simon. He's not yet able to say he's here for psychiatric reasons, but it's as well that you know so that if he becomes distressed you won't worry that he's in danger, though I do advise that you ring for a nurse none the less. Our staff are very experienced.'

And so on. He was orchestrating the visit, put out, I think, that Simon wouldn't, or couldn't, make his confession to him; and although he didn't quite say that I was to report back to him, he made it clear that he was *following Simon's progess carefully.*

'Be sure to see me before you leave,' he said.

When I suggested that Rosie come in with me to see Simon, he was adamant, his hand literally on her shoulder, as he showed her the way down to a beach and a small reserve at the bottom of the hill.

Simon, after all the fuss, was asleep when the nurse – to whom I had been handed on – opened his door. Tousled and rather unnervingly boyish, he held out his arms and I went to him as a mother does to a child. He was flushed and smelled stale, perhaps it was the medication, and his body was heavy as if he could not bear his own weight. The nurse took him from me, helped him out of bed, sponged his face and settled him into a chair beside french windows.

Outside was a courtyard with discreetly arranged seats, ugly paving around beds with too much blue plumbago, and quite a nice birdbath. The view we should have had was blocked by another wing of the clinic.

'I nearly had a heart attack, you know,' Simon said.

'So I gathered,' I said. 'But you're okay.'

'Just,' he said, a hand to his chest. 'I feel awful. Just awful.'

He told me about being taken to St Vincent's in the middle of the night. A rambling story about a very young doctor, two drunks still fighting, a nurse who he was sure he recognised, a taxi that didn't come.

He spoke in a voice that was, for him, unusually close to a drone. On and on he went, with stories that at first seemed disconnected, but which returned as the afternoon passed to the self-pitying complaint I'd heard many times over the years, about the fickleness of women. Of Merle in particular, and also of me.

What he seemed never to be able to understand was why, when seduction seemed so complete, the women who fell in love with him did not remain in a state of entrancement. For him this was the betrayal: that after the abortion I was no longer sure that I wanted him. And that Merle, once so completely his creature, would now not receive his calls.

When he was last in New York he'd stood outside her apartment and pleaded into the intercom, but she would not see him. He waited for almost an entire morning, he said. Charlie Quatrain came out with a child he took to be their daughter, tall for ten, with a lot of black hair. He watched them get into a taxi. There was no sign of Merle, and no response when he pressed the bell again. For Simon this was an uncommon humiliation. For all the girls who adorn his life – in a way that boys will never adorn ours – he is unsatisfied, and says it is Merle's fault because she stole something from him, though when I pressed he couldn't say what it was. In any case, as I pointed out, if one is to be literal about it, it is he who broke into Merle's house, not she into his. But in matters of the heart, literalism is always an error.

'And you're as bad,' he said. All these years later there is still something he can't comprehend about the capacity of a woman – in this case me – to pull herself up out of her thralldom; when she does, it is – for him – as if she rises as the spectre of the condemning judge. Which is why he had called on me, for who better to confess to than one who has already judged you harshly?

It was only as I became irritable and tired – imagine an orchestra tuning up for hours, that's what it was like – that he came to the point. The point, of course, was Merle. No, not even that. The point was Simon's conscience. The burden of his secret had become intolerable, all the more so as he felt himself aggrieved, and badly misunderstood. Guilt is not always alleviated because we have good reasons for our crimes.

The first of Simon's crimes was, of course, the Sentani figure. He'd taken it, he said, because after the disaster of the divorce, it was all that was left with which he could bring the gallery back to life. It had been stripped to the bone, and so had he.

What nobody knew – and this was at the heart of his grievance – was that when he had taken over the gallery, it had not been the triumph – as Merle had called it – of an eighties cowboy. The price was low, but far from making a killing, it had been part of a deal with Isobel in which he bailed her – not the gallery – out of private debts. Debts Tom knew nothing about, at least that is what Isobel said, and which would have been deeply embarrassing should their nature and origin ever come out.

'I don't understand,' I said. 'How could Isobel run up debts? They always had money, that family. The gallery was doing well, wasn't it?'

'She was lending money to Claude,' Simon said. 'She gave him more than $20,000 in a single year. It was a hell of a lot in those days.'

'But she hadn't seen him since Merle was born,' I said.

'That's what she said, but it wasn't true.'

'Did Tom know?'

'Of course not,' Simon said. 'That was the point of the deal.'

'Who does know?'

'Nobody,' he said. 'Isobel made me promise never to tell.'

And that was the nub of his complaint, that he had done this for Isobel – he'd saved her from disgrace, and therefore also Merle – and in return he was seen as some sort of raider, a barrow boy on the make.

'Are you sure it's true?' I said.

'Of course I'm sure.'

'Then you should continue to keep it as a secret.'

'What's the point? If Merle doesn't know, there's no point in it.'

'You mean it only counts if you've done something good if someone knows about it.'

'Not someone,' he said. 'Merle.'

'So she'll forgive you for taking the Sentani figure?'

'That,' he said. 'But not only. So she'll stop being so bloody proud.'

There is a Buddhist concept of Secret Good, the good that is done without attention being drawn to it, acts of goodness which work their way in the world though we never know their origin, acts of goodness we also should be able to perform, but rarely do, without seeking recognition; the kind of good that is brought by the hand of a god passing over our towns and villages, our tables and beds. I forebore to mention this to Simon.

'Anyway,' he said, 'I need it to bargain with.'

'What are you bargaining for?'

Simon looked at me, and from his look I knew my face was tight with disapproval. He knows, I thought, that I have stopped liking him. He slumped forward for what seemed a long pause, and when he sat back up his face, so recently flushed, was drained of colour. He was crumpled, and as pale as he had been as a young man.

From a standard-issue hospital chair overlooking an anonymous courtyard, I saw what I expected never to see: Simon's tears. He had not wept for the baby I aborted; he had not wept, as far as I know, for Merle when she caught the plane and left for New York. He had not wept for the child she had subsequently borne to Charlie Quatrain, the girl he'd watched get into a taxi. He had not wept when Isobel died. Merle, who had not returned to Australia in time to see her mother alive, sobbed, heavily pregnant, behind the coffin. Even Tom Cullen, usually so composed, seemed that day to have lost his buoyancy. Nothing about Simon's appearance was ruffled at all.

But that afternoon in the clinic he wept, and I did not. From my point of view, I'd say almost the oddest aspect of that afternoon was that I was almost intensely unmoved as he reached his unexpected cadenza.

'That's not all,' he said, groping feebly in the

direction of my hand. 'Will you keep it a secret if I tell you?'

'Depends what it is,' I said, accepting the pressure of his fingers in my palm.

'I took the letters. That's what I wanted to tell you.'

'Which letters?' But with the sinking of foreboding, I knew the answer before he spoke the words.

'Isobel's letters from Claude.'

'So it was you,' I said. 'Merle knows someone took them.'

'How does she know they exist?'

'I thought you must have said something.'

'Of course I didn't tell her,' he said. 'That's the point. She can't know.'

We looked at each other with that strange stillness that comes with a confession; though it was, I suppose, a moment of great closeness, it was still not one that drew me to him. On the contrary it was as if I were watching him through water. Which might simply have been the effect of a long afternoon, and no lunch. Outside the sky was almost dark. I was beginning to wonder where Rosie was.

'There's some awful stuff in them,' he said.

'You'll have to tell her,' I said.

'I can't,' he said.

'What did Isobel want with the letters?'

'I never talked to her about them,' he said. 'Or rather, I tried once, right at the end, but she was

ill. You know, almost mad. In any case I only knew
about them. It wasn't until after Tom died that I
read them. I knew they were there, that's all.'

'Why didn't she destroy them?' I said.

'I suppose part of her wanted it known,' he said.
'I thought Tom would have got rid of them. I wasn't
intending to take them, I was in the house on my
own, you know, that day Tom died, no one else had
arrived. Brian was in Melbourne. Don't you remember? I was just looking to see if they were there.'

'Where are they now?'

'At the gallery,' he said. 'In the desk drawer. I
want you to get them.'

'What for?'

'Maybe you can make Merle understand.'

Outside in the corridor I could hear the
advancing clatter of the meal trolley, and voices
coming our way. The nurse opened the door, with
Rosie behind her.

'There we are,' the nurse said, bustling over to
Simon. 'Time we got you back into bed.'

'And who's this?' Simon said taking in Rosie
with a glance that told me he hadn't entirely collapsed. In the presence of a young woman, he ral-
lied, insisting to the nurse that he was fine,
perfectly fine, and far from returning to bed, he
was going to walk us to our car.

'Now, now,' the nurse said. 'We can't have you
out in the cold.'

Simon ignored her.

'You look just like your aunt,' he said, addressing himself to Rosie. 'Or rather just like she used to look.' And then to me. 'I hadn't realised how old you'd got. Have you told her?'

'Some of it,' I said, taking him to mean his wrangle with Merle, his theft of the figure. With this admission he lapsed back into gloom – why did I feel guilty? – as if he'd quite forgotten his moment of charm. Maybe this breakdown was real after all.

We shuffled our way along the corridor, past the food trolley, with its bland cabbagy smell, past visitors with bunches of flowers, past the director's office at which I did not call, and into the foyer with its muted colours and piped music.

'No further than this,' the nurse said.

'I don't mind bringing the letters up to you,' I said as I opened the door to the cool evening air, 'but you're going to have to deal with this. I can't negotiate for you, and I won't lie to Merle. Not over this.'

'I told you as a secret.'

'There've been too many secrets,' I said.

'Who are you to decide what's secret and what isn't?' he said. 'Half an hour ago you were telling me to keep Isobel's secret about Claude and the gallery. You can't have it both ways.'

'It's a question of discrimination,' I said.

'A bit late for that,' he said.

2 MERLE'S SECRET

Merle, as you will have gathered, was the third child of Tom and Isobel Cullen. She was born in 1948 in London, and was registered at Australia House the following morning. Coming back along the Strand, on his way across London to St Mary's Hospital, Tom bought a small and extremely expensive spray of mimosa, which is as close as the English get to wattle, as a reminder to Isobel of Australia, and the life that was waiting for them both.

Tom Cullen was the youngest son of a family descended from squatters who'd picked for themselves several large shallow valleys up against the ranges behind Mudgee. His eldest brother, a solid

man with his hair parted in the middle like a pro-
hibition gangster, ran hundreds of acres, which
had once been prime sheep land, as vineyards.

His sister had married well and lived in the city,
a smart, rather shallow woman, vain of course,
who gave smart parties at her very smart house in
Bellevue Hill. She was the sort of person who
enjoyed the humiliation of others. The first time
she invited Isobel to one of her parties, she'd said
Don't bother to dress, will you. When Isobel had
turned up in one of Tom's shirts and tight black
pants, thinking it a bohemian thing to do, she
found a house teeming with women in strapless
dresses and expensive earrings. Her sister-in-law,
ostentatiously polite, had worked the room with
Isobel in tow, impressing her guests with the
calamity of Tom's choice.

Tom, the youngest of this brood, was out of the
mould, the cuckoo in the nest, so unlike his siblings that one would be forgiven for thinking he
had come from different stock. For a start Tom
Cullen was one of the kindest men alive. Where
his siblings were coarse, he was sweet. Not a tall
man like his strapping brother, he had thick
brown hair which, when he was young, had to be
lifted frequently – and most fetchingly – from his
forehead. His irises were as dark as melted choco-
late, with a shine that prompted everyone to com-
ment on their sparkle. Even when he had grown

older, a little stout, with the first signs of grey at the temples, they still sparkled – truly – and he still had the slender hands and fine wrists that protrude, almost shockingly, from his uniform in photographs of him as a young officer during the war.

But more than this, more than his physical attributes which were charming but not extreme, he was a man blessed with a kind of calm that seemed to come to him from nature. In a family of large, crashing egos, he did not push forward, and it was easy to miss his strengths and to overlook him as shadowy, as I did for many years, somewhere on the edge of noisier lives. Not a lot of drive, you'd have to say that. Vitality, but not drive.

Without Isobel I can't imagine what the gallery would have been like, where the scope, the determination, the success, would have come from. But then, without Tom's ability to turn his attention to the next task as if the doing of it was all that was ever required of him, the gallery might not have existed at all. He used to tell a story that irritated Isobel, about a Japanese student arriving at a famous monk's door begging for the secret of enlightenment. The monk took him in and with a certain ceremony served him tea. After a while he asked the young man who was straining for an answer, whether he had finished. The student

indicated his empty hands. Then, said his teacher,
you should wash the cup.

As a young man before the war, Tom had jettisoned Melbourne University where he was supposed to be reading law, and had enrolled in the
George Bell School of Art. In the company of students – who soon became friends – like Peter
Purves Smith and Russell Drysdale, he realised
very quickly the limits of his ability. Not his interest, but his capacities, calmly judged. As a result
he persuaded his father, a heavily bearded man I
have seen only in sepia, to finance him at London
University. It was a plain proposition. Schooled in
fine art, he would return to Australia and deal in
the paintings of others. Business, enterprise, was
comprehensible to his aged parents, and while
they would have preferred him to trade in something more dependendable – his sister Una had
married into porcelain: basins, baths, toilets and
such – it was all in all a relief, an escape from
unnecessary shame, something they could speak
of openly in the district and invest with a certain
seriousness.

When, shortly after this, Tom announced that
he was to marry Isobel, they entailed on him, as
encouragement and approval, the house at
Mudgee. She was not the class of girl they would
have hoped for, but they consoled themselves that
by the mere fact of her presence she would be a

steadying influence. The other brother had the living provided by the land. And although it was an unusual arrangement, Tom and Isobel were to have the house that opened on one side to a long shallow valley once given to sheep and now to vineyards, and that was closed on the other by the rounded hills and dry creek-beds that at dawn turned from gold to pink to silver.

Isobel was the daughter of a widowed Melbourne tram driver who had risen to the rank of inspector. He was a union man, a member of WEA and a believer in progress, education and betterment. It was on the small amount of money that he left her, in the hands of the union's lawyer, that, at four guineas a term, Isobel made a short exploratory foray into the George Bell School. When she left, it was not because she measured herself against the best, as Tom had done. What she took against was the absolute lack of glamour in the mainly middle-class women who wore smocks over their skirts and took up their brushes with a kind of cheerful amateurism. Whatever else Isobel would be – and she knew from the first that she would not make a painter – she would not be an amateur. When George Bell looked over her shoulder in the mirror one morning, and said that if she attended to her compositions with the same concentration as she did her hat, she might have some hope as an artist, she scarcely looked at him, turned on her heel and clattered down in the rickety old lift to the gritty air of Bourke Street.

Round the corner in Little Collins Street she saw Tom Cullen at the counter of Gino Nibbi's bookshop and went in to see what he was buying. Facsimile prints of Gauguin's Polynesian women, postcard-sized reproductions of Picasso's African period and a small monograph on Cézanne. 'Ah', she said. 'Why muddle around up there in the studio, when there are paintings like this in the world?'

In the presence of this sweet-natured imp of a man – who, naturally, she had noticed the minute she'd walked into the school – she felt a kind of hunger in herself. So when Tom said come and have lunch with me she said yes, and when a few weeks later he said come to London with me, she said yes. *Of course*, she said. *Yes.*

Tom had already put his proposition to his father: study and then trade in paintings. What he had not put to his father was his secret desire to change the landscape of Australia's art so that the name of someone like Drysdale would become as familiar as Streeton, say, or Heysen. Beyond that he had not gone. It was Isobel who conjured up the gallery and the parties to which the most elegant would come dressed, if they wished, merely in a shirt; it was she who imagined into existence the patronage of the powerful. And it was she who saw that as well as introducing modern art and

Australia's own artists to a nervous and conserva-
tive public, they could supplement it perfectly
with the sale of strange and exotic arts.

'Like what?' Tom asked.

'Like African art,' she said, looking at the
Picasso prints. 'Or Pacific art, even. Why not?
There must be some.' She'd once heard a lecture
from an ethnologist – her father had taken her to
it – and had a dim memory of wooden carvings,
abstract faces, dark masks. No, not dim, more
luminous than that, for though the memory was
not clear, it had entered her like a charm. For Isobel the gallery that existed in her imagination
would be the perfect way of finding the glamour
she had longed for in those seriously drab rooms
of the Brunswick Progress Association, while still
upholding its ideals.

She could imagine it all, way, way into the
future when not only would the rich ring for private viewings, but curators and librarians would
come – as indeed they would – to consult the content of the gallery's records and letters – and the
contents of their own trunks and storerooms. And
if she'd had any idea that such things were to
come, she'd also have imagined the TV cameras
and documentary films. Given half a chance,
there was no limit to Isobel's imaginings.

'Isobel, darling,' Tom said, 'there's a lot to
study first.'

But by the time they reached the other side of the world, Isobel was pregnant. So instead of taking the bus with Tom to the university each morning, she stayed in the flat in Pimlico, just round the corner from the Tate, and looked after little Brian who was named for his dead maternal grandfather, a victory, as Isobel knew, of considerable proportions. It was early in 1939 and Isobel was just nineteen years old.

By September she was pregnant again, and Tom had his name down, like his friend Peter Purves Smith – who was also in London, having retreated back across the channel from Paris – for enlistment in the British forces.

Living in London had not been such an exile. Several friends from the George Bell School were there, or in Paris, and with the war they converged on London. Russell and Bonnie Drysdale were not far away in Hampstead. Peter Purves Smith was round the corner in Warwick Square. In small rooms, crushed round small tables, they dreamed up the possibilities of art that would take the excitement of Europe to a new view of Australia.

These were the conversations Isobel pined for all through the long disruption of the war. For her the exile began when she heaved her pregnant belly back onto the ship for a reluctant return to Australia and the old house at Mudgee.

There in a room that backed onto the ranges,

she gave birth to her second son Keith, named this time for his paternal grandfather. But although this was the name on the birth certificate, right from the start Isobel called him Pablo in deference to her ambitions, if not to his, and in opposition to the weight of history she felt in the house that she came to, for all its welcome, as an interloper.

It wasn't that she disliked her parents-in-law. She didn't like them particularly, but she didn't dislike them; she regarded them with a tired neutrality neither antagonistic nor apologetic. She found them a disappointment, having assumed that glamour would come with a house, and a family such as the Cullens, as automatically as driveways and coach-houses. Instead she found frayed carpets and mousey parents who were given to reading Dickens aloud to each other, and considered ten-thirty a dangerously late night.

Reverting to the lessons she had learned in the self-taught circles of labour Melbourne, Isobel regarded her crusty in-laws as an irrelevancy. While she'd hoped for glamour, she'd also been imbued with the notion – very dangerous, she would later say – of the upper class as inbred and stupid, a sort of left-over buffoonery that would, in years to come, be as insignificant as Bonnie Prince Charlie.

But at Mudgee there was the one great advantage – even in wartime – of *help*, and while the boys ran happily in the garden under an eye other than hers, Isobel sat at her table on the wide verandah and read the books that she ordered from Gino Nibbi and paid for with the money that came to her from her ignored parents-in-law.

She missed Tom. She missed him so badly that there were days, weeks, sometimes even months, when she was restless and dissatisfied, her body a kind of force-field of longing. Unable then to settle to the books that lay in unopened packets, she walked for miles up the dry gullies, into narrow, shaly valleys where, until the war put an end to it, people had panned for gold, and where Chinese families still eked out an existence from wretched soil. Tom, she discovered, knew their names; and her father, she knew, would have expected her to make it her business to know the conditions of their work. But she walked up the creek without speaking and all that passed between her and the valley's inhabitants were nods, and slight, unconvincing smiles. She had her sights set on a very different future.

That was Isobel's story. That was the story Brian and Pablo told many years later when Simon introduced me to them, in a short-lived organisation called the New Workers Art Movement that consisted of no workers, few artists and not much movement. It was an affectation back in those days when everyone I knew lived in Glebe and no one locked their back doors and we all slept with whoever we fancied – which in my case meant Brian though not Pablo, whom it was hard to believe anyone would ever fancy. It was a time before life got real, before I discovered the Mitchell Library and my own worldly ambitions, before Brian finished the law degree he'd deferred for a revolutionary decade, and Pablo surprised us all by getting seriously married.

As if Brian knew that he was only the rehearsal, Merle was a kind of present that he left for me. It was his idea. After Isobel, who knew nothing of our sleeping arrangements, had made a tour of inspection, opening cupboards and tapping her heel on the floorboards, Merle moved into the front upstairs room of the house where I lived near the canal. She painted the walls an alabaster white, opened the doors onto the verandah and took out her cello.

Like this, she'd say, *use your arm.* But I could never master the sweep of the bow. Used as I was to the small movements and precise gestures that were needed to hold the frame of a miniature dwelling, I could not imagine that capacity of elbow, and arm.

I returned to my table and the model of the Victoria Street gallery which I was making in spare moments, and which, like everything else in the house, absorbed the querulous sound of Merle learning the expanse of her cello.

Day after day she practised Bach's cello suites. At first I heard only repetition, phrases and chords, as she struggled with their complex simplicities. It was a time of learning for both of us. She could judge my mood by the book I read. George Eliot. Proust. Rilke. I could judge hers by the doleful sarabande she chose, or the courante that danced in the air. On a good day she would play from the cheerful first suite, or maybe the heroic third. I was careful with doors on the days she played the second, her hair tied back, heels turned in towards each other and toes strained against the floor. On other days she surprised me with a snippet of Peter Sculthorpe, or a long sigh from Benjamin Britten.

In my room at the back of the house, I read *To The Lighthouse* and contemplated the impossibility of Lily Briscoe's quest to paint only what she saw. The ordinariness of life, and its miracle. Proust did it. Rilke did it. What stopped Lily? I knew what stopped her. Of course I did.

In the morning Merle and I would catch the bus up Glebe Point Road, along Broadway and down George Street. Together we'd climb the hill to the library where she'd stop for a cup of tea in the old tea room that used to be up on the fourth floor with a bumpy little parapet that looked out over the city. Then she'd walk across to the conservatorium.

In the late afternoon when I went to meet her I'd listen to the sounds mixing in the air outside the practice rooms and think rather unformed thoughts about how like life it was, the heat, the restless cacophony – as if each unsynchronised instrument represented a desire, a hope, a possibility – and why it was that despite the gloriousness of long shadows reaching across the gardens to the blue glimpse of harbour, there is always something hidden and grievous in our most private hearts.

Of all the Cullens, Merle was the one most loved. Ten years younger than Brian, and light-years younger than Pablo, who never got the concept of youth, she was, they said, the cherished one. 'The one condemned to be whatever they want me to be,' she said. 'That's what I am, the inheritor of their fantasies.'

She was born, as I have told you, in London just after the war. Tom had been demobbed, one of the few men of his regiment who (unlike his friend Peter Purves Smith) came out of Burma without TB. He was well, in that he was not ill, but shaken into a different, more sombre shape, perhaps more completely his own, when he cabled Isobel to pack up the boys and join him in London.

Isobel, of course, was packed already, champing

for release. But a berth out of Sydney had not been so easy to come by, and she had had to wait until she found one on an old troopship returning to Europe after unloading refugees. In the spring of 1946 she pushed the boys up the gangplank without a backward glance at the old man, their grandfather, who knew he would not see his son's children again, or indeed his son. There were tears in his eyes, and apprehension in the eyes of the boys as they threw streamers to the crowd on the wharf and strained to find the face of their grandfather. But nothing clouded the sky for Isobel that day. *Goodbye,* she said. *Goodbye, goodbye.*

At the other end she tumbled into Tom's arms. *Welcome,* he said, and they took two paces back to look at each other. It was then that she opened her eyes and saw the damage that had been done by the war, to her husband and a blitzed-out city. The small boys stood silent at their knees.

In this London, Isobel kept a more difficult house – actually two rooms and a shared bathroom on the edge of Earls Court – while Tom finished his degree. Washing hung in great loops from the kitchen ceiling. Milk, butter, eggs and meat were rationed. Cooking required a canniness that had been entirely unnecessary at Mudgee. Without practice in the arts of war, Isobel was reduced to tears and horrible meals of swede and turnip.

'It tastes fine,' Tom would say. But it did not. 'It's awful,' she'd snap back, leaving the table. 'Why can't you admit it?'

Before she knew it, she was packed again; that is to say, her heart was packed, and looking for escape.

As soon as she got the boys into school – another task that would once have been straight-forward but in postwar London was far from it – Isobel would sit in a lecture with Tom, or spend her afternoon in the libraries and galleries and auction rooms. It was she, as much as he, who scoured exhausted Europe for the paintings, the trinkets and the treasures, the stock that would set up the business until their friends got painting again, and bring into being the dream of a gallery that was to appease Isobel's longings and feed the children on their return to Australia.

It was of this future that Tom hoped to remind Isobel on that day after Merle was born when he bought mimosa from a barrow at Charing Cross on his way across London to St Mary's Hospital.

Merle was named after Merle Oberon. Her second name was Mary not after the Virgin – there was nothing Catholic about either of her parents – but after Mary Queen of Scots. During an uncomfortable pregnancy that seemed unnatu-rally long, Isobel had read a highly romanticised novel about the beautiful, fated queen, and did not consider the implications of giving her name to her tiny daughter.

'Why did she call me that?' Merle wailed. 'What cruel fate did she wish for me?' She made a point of reading up on Mary's bloody history: accurate – or at least historical – accounts that spared no detail.

Merle at times quite disliked her mother, though it seemed to me that Isobel was exactly the mother a girl like Merle needed. She was clever. She was sharp. She knew the world. What Merle refused, I took for myself.

Isobel was the first woman I had come across, back then when I was young, who gave me a clue about how someone like me – no longer married, awash with unfocused ambitions – might live in the world without despair or shame. She was the first woman of my parents' generation who spoke of a woman taking a lover as if it were natural, and a right. And she was the first woman I'd met with her own study, and the only person I knew who was writing a book. It was due to her example, I think, that I abandoned a submerged desire for architecture, and enrolled instead in arts. I looked upon her manuscript as a talisman, as if it were itself an object of rescued art. I took a certain, vicarious, pride in it, for amongst the photographs that the manuscript had accumulated was the one she'd taken of the judgement mask I'd bought in the Sepik. Seeing its dusty colours in this official form, separate from me, reinforced its presence above my desk.

Did Simon give you that, Isobel had asked when she first saw it, on her tour of inspection before Merle moved in. *He's got a good eye. Don't get rid of it.* So I never liked to ask her what it was worth, and for years secretly regretted that I could not, as I tried to scratch together enough money to move out of that house by the canal, which was pleasant in the summer, but prone to flooding during winter storms.

Which is how it was still hanging above my desk last year when Rosie lifted it off its nail and said *Wow, some mask.* I have that to thank Isobel for as well.

By the time I knew the Cullens, Isobel no longer lived with Tom. It wasn't that they'd separated exactly. When he was in town he lived above the gallery in the city, and although he was sometimes at Isobel's dinners, he rarely slept in the house that had been their first gallery. At Christmas and Easter Isobel would be at Mudgee presiding over the long table in the lugubrious room at the back, the least festive of rooms, used only for festive events, and she'd be in the kitchens fussing and giving orders which without servants – that day had long passed – fell to Merle and me or whichever of her itinerant friends had been taken home for Christmas.

Tom's domain was the verandah to which every-one retired as soon as the meal was over. There he presided over the bottles that tilted towards the glasses that passed their way. Sometimes there would be an easy silence out there in the after-lunch heat; more often a genial erudition as Tom spoke of Ian Fairweather or Peter Purves Smith, the least known of Australian artists; or if the mood was quiet, he'd read to us from Auden, maybe, or from Emily Dickinson. It was from Tom that I first under-stood that there was a hidden underbelly to our secrets, and when I responded with a gasp – half shock, half delight – he leaned across and gave me the volume from which he read. And that is how I think of Tom, straight from Emily Dickinson and the deep shade of that verandah. *His mind of man, a secret makes,* he'd read, *I meet him with a start/ He carries a circumference/ In which I have no part.*

Visitors would come, friends who knew, as I never would, something of Tom's mysterious cir-cumference: artists returning from Europe; com-posers from their sojourn in Japanese monasteries; old friends driving from Melbourne to Sydney. If the afternoon proved long enough, and the shad-ows reached across the valley before the bottles were finished, Tom would burst into raucous singing, quite shockingly out of character, and in a gravelly voice start a line of bawdy songs that nothing in my experience of him had prepared me for. His sister, the ghastly Una, would stand in the door with an expression on her face that could only be described as a wince.

The house in those days, twenty years ago, was shabby, even dilapidated, as if the walls themselves were fraying at the edges. Mould crept over skirting boards that had to be kept dry by roaring winter fires and wide open summer windows. But the great rambly sprawl of that house with its courtyards and verandahs, long corridors and tucked away rooms, had a spirit as generous as its host's. Merle loved it there, and so did I. We would settle in for the vacation. But two days after Boxing Day, Isobel would retreat, back to Sydney and the house with its gallery at the end of Victoria Street.

'I need more peace,' she'd say, though we all knew that she wouldn't be back a week before her table would be crowded.

'Is that so?' Tom would say, his habitual response to the changed and changing plans of his wife and family; and he'd make his own retreat, back across the yard to the workshop he'd created for himself from the old stables.

He still did all the gallery's framing although, by the time I knew him, the Australian artists he managed were successful enough for him to have afforded any assistance he liked. Even when prices boomed in the eighties to heights no one would have imagined a few years earlier, he still worked in the workshop. But he did give up the column he had written for the Melbourne *Age* and the touring lectures without which – along with the remnants of family money – the gallery would not have been able to stay in business during the lean years of the fifties and early sixties, when modern Australian art was almost impossible to sell – not so much unfashionable as a kind of embarrassed cultural secret no one wanted to mention. For mentioning it, looking at it, understanding its meaning, would rattle the old idea of itself that the Australian buying public had managed to cling to, long after it had dried to a useless husk. It was easier to stick with reassuring images of a nostalgic past than to accept the pressing discomforts of the present.

During those lean years, Isobel, inspired by her discovery of Claude in London, had consoled herself with her Oceanic art, and had even made a bit selling to dealers in Europe or New York.

Tom's consolation was taken in the steady rhythm of the workshop. There were windows along one wall that were open all summer, and an old black stove that roared all winter. Between them, on a shelf with oils and lacquers, was a small statue of Tara, the goddess who cups her right hand, palm up, in the palm of her left.

I paid many visits to that workshop before I noticed the statue, and when I did it was because Merle pointed it out. 'Look,' she said, pointing to the hands. 'One hand means wisdom, the other means compassion. Compassion held in wisdom.' She gave a dry laugh and turned Tara sideways so she was looking out of the window.

There was a story Tom liked to tell out there on the verandah after lunch, *a determining story*, he said, about a Japanese prisoner his unit had captured in Burma as they made their way, ridge by ridge, valley by valley, pushing the Japanese back through the jungle. Tom and another young officer had taken the prisoner, whose head was completely shaved, in a foxhole they were clearing out; but instead of meeting a hand raised with a sword pointing to the gut, as was usually the case, or a grenade ready to throw at his captors – which is what they feared – the bald and very young soldier sat in meditation.

It's only now as I tell this story, the story of the Cullens and Merle's secret, that I understand where Tom's capacity, so unusual in an Australian man of that generation, came from, and I suspect it was what Merle loved in him, that ability to be, simply to be, with whatever life presented to him. It was a capacity that drove Isobel to distraction.

She saw it as passivity, a refusal to act. She knew that it was her will that had brought the gallery – and the shape of their lives – into being, and she gave little credit to his steady presence in the workshop. And because the workshop was so thoroughly his, a retreat that took him into a realm that was beyond her control, she came to resent the hours, the days, the years, he spent in there.

It seemed illogical to me, as Isobel showed so little interest in Tom. But there was a lot, at that time, which I did not understand. Perhaps she wanted to feel him press against her, to know how his desires abutted hers, to feel a little push to her pull. Yet he would accept without the slightest trace of hesitation whatever it was that she wished to do, and he'd hold open the door of her smelly old VW as she loaded her bags and pointed back down the dust-white road towards the city.

It was in the impulse, so different from Tom's, to mould the world to her desires that Isobel clashed with Merle. With Tom Merle never felt badgered, or on display. It wasn't that Tom didn't have opinions or views or even urgings when it came to Merle's life, and the decisions she took. *What are you thinking of doing?* he'd say as they sat side by side on the verandah. What made the difference for Merle was that he had the capacity to wait for her reply, responding to her wishes and uncertainties without judgement, or expectation.

They would sit together on the verandah outside the kitchen where meals were usually taken: father and daughter together in a tableau without movement.

Waiting was not in Isobel's repertoire. Nor was silence. But while Merle could sit beside her father in silence for an hour or more, she also enjoyed her mother's noisy dinners. With the protection of other people, with Isobel focused elsewhere, she could admire the drive and flamboyance of her mother. And she liked the quiet Sunday afternoons when Isobel opened the doors onto the garden at the back of the gallery, rolled down her stockings in the sun, lay back in her chair and gave up – just for a moment – the attitude of fight.

What Merle didn't like was that whenever Isobel came to us, she'd open cupboards and drawers, and even letters, or say, lifting a lid on the stove, *What on earth's that?* I didn't mind; after all Isobel wasn't my mother. But Merle did. And she minded when Isobel seemed not to understand what it meant to have been accepted into the orchestra as deputy principal. *Nobody knows that*, Isobel said. *It's never in the programme.* And she minded very much when Isobel said that as it didn't seem likely she'd be good enough to be a soloist, was an orchestra what she really wanted? Or teaching? Had she contemplated the thought of years stretching ahead of her with nothing to look forward to but the next spotty youth farting and straining into her room as they both attended to the unwieldy instrument between his knees, or hers? Isobel's plan for Merle was that she should make a specialty of twentieth-century music. There'll come a point, she'd say, when the obsession with classical trills will have to give way to our century. Music is very far behind the other arts in the way it's appreciated.

'What about a quartet?' Isobel asked. 'A modern quartet. Have you thought of that?'

'Don't interfere, Mother,' Merle said.

'Why won't you call me Isobel,' Isobel said. 'The boys do. We're past the days of Mother and Father.'

'Is that so?' Merle, in the manner of her father, said.

When Isobel left, getting into that spluttering car which spewed fumes through our windows – I don't know why she didn't get a better car, in everything else she was stylish – Merle would come up to my room, lie on my bed and say *Why does she make me feel like this? Sort of empty. As if I'm not really me. As if she's got a plan, and I'm it.*

I'd sit on the bed, cross-legged beside her, and sometimes I'd let my hand rest in her hair, sometimes I'd lean forward until my own hair fell across her belly and I could smell the faint flowery scent of her skin, an edge of salt and vinegar; and for a long time the secret of my desires – which are incidental to the story I tell – remained mine with nothing but a slightly elevated pulse to give them away.

'I'm going to write to her!' Merle said, banging closed the door one Saturday afternoon, after Isobel had suggested that she go to London. Or New York. Or polish up her French and try for a teacher in Paris. *Do something, for goodness sake,* she'd said. *You're just like your father. Passive.*

But there Isobel was wrong.

You don't love me, Merle wrote to her mother on a piece of paper from my desk. *You don't love me at all. You want to be rid of me. You want me out of the way, because I irritate you and remind you of Tom.*

She added a couple more pages along these lines, they don't bear repeating, the sort of letter many daughters of strong women are tempted to write as they try out their own shape. 'Do you think you ought?' I said. She cast me one of those looks that novels describe as smouldering, although they usually contain as much apology as defiance, walked to the end of the street, dropped the letter in the box, and waited.

She waited more than a week. Banging and clattering round the house, she waited. Staring into the street at the children walking past on a short cut from the school on the other side of the canal, she waited. Furiously playing Kodaly – the first hint of things to come – she waited. I listened, astonished, to the wail of her cello that echoed through the house like a wild and electrifying force.

And then Isobel's letter arrived in one of the gallery's smart bond envelopes. *On the contrary,* she wrote, *my darling Merle, you were a child born of great love.*

And this is the story Isobel told Merle and that I am calling Merle's secret, though by now, as Merle says, it's hardly a secret any more, and if it were I wouldn't be telling you, would I? When I think about it I can see that it isn't really Merle's secret at all, but Isobel's. But as it was Merle's flushed and lovely face that I was looking at when she read the letter, her voice stricken and reedy in that alabaster room, it remains in my mind, and in my heart, as Merle's secret, and Merle's alone.

'On the contrary, my darling Merle, you were a child born of great love,' Isobel wrote.

'I've never told you this story. Tom has always insisted that I shouldn't, he says it's our secret, we shouldn't burden you children. But then Tom would. That's the problem, that's always been the problem. As I need hardly tell you, and you're old enough now to understand, it has not been an easy marriage.

'It began, all the difficulties that is, in the years after the war, just before you were born. We'd been separated for so long, the boys were used to me and not at all used to him. And he was in a state of shock, all the men were, and there we were suddenly expected to get on with romance which of course was what we all wanted. But how could we? We just sort of looked at each other. You can imagine. Can you? I hope you can imagine. I was in my twenties, the same age as you are now. Old by some standards. Young by others. Everything was so interrupted. Not even how we grew up was normal.

'So there I was in London, two small children, a husband who didn't fit the memory I'd hung onto all through the war, and how after all that can one admit to being disappointed? We didn't fight. Not at all. We were kind to each other. That's not true. Tom was kind to us. To me and the boys. I was irritable. Pablo was wildly jealous. Brian made a fist of it. He was old enough to be chuffed by the notion of a father and spent a lot of time going over the medals. He'd pin them onto his school shirt and I'd have a hell of a fight to get them off.

'So there I was in London, in those ghastly rooms, and we were lucky to get them, you people have no idea, stuck with the children and ducking under the washing that was drying inside. England.

Always the same. Wet and dingy. At least if you have money you can get the clothes dried somewhere else.

'Once Pablo was old enough for school, things improved a bit, and sometimes someone would come and sit for me, and when they did I'd escape. I prowled round London like a cat. I'd go through sales, anything from Portobello Road to Bond Street, from barrows in the street to galleries. I was looking for stock for the gallery, for the stock we'd bring back to get started with. I'd go to lectures. Sometimes at the university, but less and less often as Tom was there. Not that he minded, on the contrary he was welcoming, but as much as anything I needed to be alone. I'd go to the School of African and Oriental Studies and slip into the back of lectures there. I'd scan the notices in bookshops in Charing Cross Road. Looking, always looking. For what, I don't know.

'But I found it one afternoon in a tiny gallery up a steep flight of stairs in Soho. *Oceania.* The word attracted me, just the word, that's all. And up there in that dingy room was the gallery owner, rather a crumpled little man, French Polynesian I think, wrinkled and small, not at all what one would expect. And with him, selling some wooden figures, was Claude Ferraris. You will recognise the name. Though his name is all I have ever told you.

'He was, quite simply, the most attractive, the funniest, the most wonderful man I have ever met. I looked at him, blinking into the dark, waiting for my eyes to adapt, and there he was, it was like looking into my own eyes.

'He took me downstairs to coffee at just about the only French patisserie there was in London after the war. Not that there was much in it. He bought me café au lait, which came in a bowl, and a tiny bit of gaufrette. It was the first moment in my life when I understood what sophistication meant. Before the bowl had cooled enough to lift, I was in love with him. And, my darling Merle, he, your father, was in love with me. Yes, do I spring it on you, the truth I've kept hidden all these years, that Claude Ferraris was your father. How else am I to tell you, if not baldly, like this. Or did you see it coming?

'For weeks Claude and I would meet during the day. He was in London trying to rustle up some money, as he put it, and he put up excuse after excuse to stay. He had a room in Pimlico, just round the corner from the rooms your father and I, that is to say Tom and I, had when Brian was born. And therein, for you, must lie the confusion. Who should you call Father. Do not think badly of Tom. He has loved you as his own, and if he had his way, that's all you'd ever know. But I'd rather you knew the truth.

'For weeks I didn't tell Tom about Claude, not a word, and then at last I couldn't bear it, I couldn't bear to be in the same room without telling him. Which is what I did, and needless to say, being Tom, he encouraged me. Go to him then, he said, and discover what you do feel. Milly had just arrived in London, you remember, my friend from Melbourne, she died when you were little, and she took over the care of the boys and I went to Claude.

'We spent a month in his room in Pimlico, and I doubt that any woman has ever been happier. We ate in cafés and pubs when we could, and the rest of the time he cooked, he was a wonderful cook, even on rations, I'd never known a man who cooked. I think that's what really did it. You know what Tom's like in the kitchen and it gets you down in the end. In the evenings we walked for miles along the river. We told each other everything, and he confessed to me his great desire to paint.

'As a young man he'd been one of the English expatriates in Paris in the twenties. Well, not really an expatriate. His mother had been French so he was technically half French and he spoke it fluently. But he'd been to school in England, grown up in England; he was very English. Despite his beret, you would never have known. He'd studied cubism in the twenties, and had joined the Surrealist group. And that's how he came to Oceania. It was through him that I first heard of Lake Sentani,

I know I've told you that, but now you'll understand the importance? Do you? Please do.

'Please Merle, try to understand. He'd been
there, can you imagine, with Viot, in 1929. He
described it all to me, the villages strung out over
the water, the low mists which hung over the lake
early in the morning so only the crest of thatched
roofs and the carved buttress roots of the great
upended trees rose above it, the masks shining
with silt as they came up from the bottom, the
huge wooden figures.

'And it was I who cautioned him against selling
the figures. Prices were rock bottom, no one had
any money in 1947, he'd be giving them away. We
had dreams of travelling through the islands
together, through New Britain, Rabaul, the
Solomons. Oh we had such dreams.

'But neither of us had any money. He had
inherited an old farmhouse in Devon, a kind of
minor manor, but had no money to fix it, or get
the land working again. In any case what he
wanted, the only thing he wanted, was to paint.
And for that he needed support. Even if he had
sold the figures they wouldn't have brought in
enough. Not nearly enough. The solution, it
seemed, was for him to marry his second cousin,
which, before he met me he'd reconciled himself
to, and use her money – which was considerable –
to get the farm working and him painting.

'You can imagine how I felt. But I had no money. And in any case there were Brian and Pablo to consider. I couldn't stay in England and send them back to Australia with Tom. Well, I could have, but Tom would have drawn the line at that. There are limits, even with Tom. And I couldn't bear the thought of leaving England if leaving meant leaving Claude. We dreamed of meeting every year somewhere in the Pacific. We dreamed so many dreams. And then in the middle of it all, while I was sort of shuffling between Pimlico and Tom and the children, I realised I was pregnant. You, Merle, my greatly loved Merle, were about to make your entry. The date was set for Claude to marry Jessica. Tom was preparing for his exams. I was pregnant.

'There is nothing like a pregnancy to sharpen the lines. Claude went to Devon. I went to Tom.

'Tom said at once that we would raise you as our own, and no one would ever know that your start in life owed itself to anything but his love for me. Almost the worst bit of it all – I wonder if you're old enough to understand – was Tom's unfailing loyalty. But I had no money, I had no choice. I had two children. I was about to have a third. And I had ambitions. I had ambitions as much as Claude ever did, and I don't see how raising chooks in Devon would have satisfied them. Not that I saw that then. Not really.

'Which is why, Merle, you must think about

your future, do some more training. You don't
want to end up in an orchestra. Or teaching.
Stretch yourself. I was almost going to write that
you are too like your father. But of course you're
not Tom's child. You have a father of great vision,
you should think to that too, and find it in yourself. He's never had his due as a painter. A friend
of Ben Nicholson, all that lot. But somehow never
taken up. Tom doesn't think he's much good, but
then Tom wouldn't.

'I only saw him once again after I went back to
Tom. He came to the hospital to see you. There
were tears all down his cheeks. And just before we
left for the boat he sent me the large Sentani figure, the one beside my desk in the gallery. I will
never sell it now, though when he gave it to me, he
said if I needed to I was to sell it in order to edu-
cate you. If you ever have a child I'll give it to you,
so that whatever happens she will be safe.

'I hear from him now and again, through inter-
mediaries, and I send messages back with details
of all the children so as not to arouse old feelings,
but to let him know what a fine daughter he has.
So you can see, Merle, why it matters so much
what you do, that you make something of yourself,
that you rise out of the Cullen propensity for
doing enough, but never any more than enough.

'There. I've told you. And I've told Tom I'm
telling you. I hope that will put an end to your

nonsense about not being loved, and that it might even propel you into some suitable action.

'Think, my darling girl, of the fate of a woman if she cannot generate her own wealth and favour. I was fortunate, you might say, in the kindness and decency of my husband. But I warn you, good in a man can be as great a burden, and the price you pay is always the loss of love. If I'd been rich. If I'd been free. But I wasn't. So make sure that you are. This is my message to you.

'Your loving mother, Isobel.'

Merle was furious, distraught, gulping air. I thought she'd hyperventilate, and running round the house after her, trying to get her to sit still, I surreptitiously took the first-aid book from the shelf in the kitchen, and looked up revival methods. Heart attacks, epileptic fits, even strokes and spider bites. But nothing on furious panic attacks. I suppose they could cause any sort of fit, and it was as well that I was prepared.

She rang Tom at Mudgee.

'Is that so,' he said, when she railed against him, against Isobel, against her very birth.

'Don't crap on,' she said. 'Tell me if it's true.'

'It's true,' he said.

'Then why didn't you tell me?' she said. 'Why? Why?'

'Because I didn't want you to have to face unnecessary pain and confusion,' Tom said. 'Whatever happened during those years doesn't change my heart, and it doesn't make me any less your father.'

'Yes it does,' Merle said. 'You can't be my father. Not if someone else is.'

'Is that so?' Tom said.

'I can see why Isobel gets so furious,' Merle said, banging down the phone.

But such sympathy as she'd had for Isobel evaporated with the fateful letter, and in its place came a harsh unforgiving fury. Merle, hands on hips, interrogated her mother. Over and over again she wanted the story. Had Isobel seen Claude since? Ever? At all?

'No,' Isobel said. 'I told you. I haven't seen him since you were a few days old.'

'Why should I believe you?' Merle said.

'Because I'm telling you.'

'Do you have his address?'

'Yes.'

'What is it?'

'Fenton Farm, North Molton, Devon.'

'England?'

'Of course, you know that.'

'I'm not assuming anything,' Merle said.

Next Merle rang directory inquiries. Then she rang Qantas. Then she wrote to Claude leaving him no option, and he, taking no chances, cabled back that he would meet her in Paris. They could have four days together, all expenses paid. Once she got there, that is.

Merle was in full flight to a new future.

Isobel rang her at our house by the canal, and she refused to take her calls. I made the mistake – the serious mistake – of taking the phone and saying to Isobel that *Yes, I'd try;* try, that is, to mediate, to soothe, to soften. And Merle, already wild with anger, said that I too had joined the ranks of the betrayers, could she count on nothing?

'You can count on everything,' I said.

'Oh yeah,' she said. 'Like you wouldn't betray me to my mother?' she said.

'Merle,' I said. 'That's not fair.'

But Merle was gone, a swish of her skirt, the slide of her shoe on the stair, a bang of the door. Reason, explanation, sense. These are not words that can be used of that time, and in those last weeks before she flew to Paris, the words that were spoken in that house pricked and bled.

There is one small detail I haven't told you. Secrets, it seems, are rarely told all in one go. What I didn't tell you – or Rosie in the car that day – was that when Merle came back from the post, from dropping the letter to Isobel in the box, she walked upstairs – I heard her sandals on the boards – but instead of going on up to her room at the front, she came into mine. She was wearing a shirt of a very pale blue cotton several sizes too large. I was lying on the bed reading. She came and lay down next to me. *Oh Merle*, I said, and she took the book from my chest where it lay, and sitting up leant across to put it on the shelf next to the sketches for the balsawood model of our house that I never got round to making. This time it was her hair that fell across my belly. I could smell the shampoo we both used. She undid the buttons of my shirt, one by one, she undid them, and in response I barely breathed as her hair swept up and down, and she bent lower, and the texture of hair gave way to the smooth blush of skin, and a tang, risky, a roll like the ocean, a strange sensation of being rocked over deep water.

Outside the wind began to heave in the trees, we could hear the scuff of milk cartons blowing along the lane by the canal. When Merle got up to close the window, she said the clouds were coming in from the south. *A front*, she said, *I should have known*, and she wrapped herself in her faded blue shirt and was gone.

That's what happened. A minor incident in the course of this story, but you will see from it that though my part was slight, it was not without heart.

There was an again, it is a word I can use quite

truthfully, but it was not the same. Sameness is not a word I can use, though I would like to. Once Isobel's reply arrived, the words we spoke were harsh and ungiving, for it was then that I made the mistake – the first of my mistakes – of lifting the receiver from the ringing phone.

With every step Merle took away from me, I pressed harder against her, as if by holding to everything that was slipping, I could reassure myself, if not her, that the ground we both stood on was more than a crust over deep mud. The house by the canal became tear-stained.

Simon visited and sighed. On the few nights that he stayed, I lay beside him and wept.

Isobel rang every day, making everything worse.

Tom did not ring. Brian went down to Mudgee and reported that his father spent the whole day in his workshop and had nothing to say on the subject.

Merle dragged suitcases down from the roof, and as she did clouds of dust came floating into the house.

All in all it was a relief of the most miserable and regretted sort when, on a fare paid for by Tom, she finally got on to that plane for London. And Paris.

It was some time before any of us heard what happened, and my account of it is pieced together from scrappy postcards, the little she said to me, and the version Simon shouldn't have given of those night-time secrets with which on her return she allowed him to woo her. What is clear is that during those four days she fell, predictably and thoroughly, in love with the romantic figure of a father who could show her where the Surrealists' studios had been, walk her round museums with a story for every painting. And be shown to the best table as soon as he opened the door to the Café de Flore.

For four days Claude listened carefully as Merle spoke, drawing from her an account of her ambivalent responses to Isobel – which she would not have expressed even to Tom. In short Claude gave every indication of understanding her most secret thoughts. What a father! What a man! If Isobel wanted something more for Merle she had certainly produced it. Another life opened up, like a speech balloon in a cartoon, the great fantasy of being restored to one's princely origins, plucked from the drab realities of ordinary life.

When the four days in Paris were up, Merle had no intention of relinquishing a single jot of this fantasy. She'd got it from Claude that Jessica, his wife, knew of her existence, even – contrary to the story Isobel had told – that Isobel had been to the farm when Merle was a babe in arms, and there'd been a tearful scene. That Claude had driven her to Taunton for the train. Beyond that, on the subject of his affair with Isobel, he was not forthcoming.

And so it was that Merle spent a month in Devon. She stayed at the farm. Jessica welcomed her. Claude, losing focus if not interest when days stretched into weeks, drove into town, and didn't always come back in time for dinner. Their children, two boys a little younger than Merle, arrived to give this half-sister of theirs the once over. *One of them is called Hamish,* she wrote on a skimpy postcard to me. *Can you imagine.*

What happened at Fenton Farm exactly, I don't know. Simon's version was that she was there long enough to experience the normality of Claude, and didn't like it. He was being uncharitable, and shouldn't have been telling me anything. But she was certainly there long enough to discover that far from the glamorous creature she had fallen for in Paris, Claude was a man much given to indigestion, with a tendency to gruff irritability in the mornings.

As part of the family, in that she was connected by blood and was therefore allowed behind the face that was presented to those who were not, and yet at the same time as a stranger who would soon be gone, Merle found she was in the uncomfortable position that Anne Eliot complained of in *Persuasion*, the strange role of *being too much in the secrets of the complaints of each house*. In her case, of course, there was only one house, but as many squabbling inhabitants.

From Jessica she heard of his tetchy domestic complaints – there was no evidence of his cooking – and his easily disturbed sensibilities.

From Hamish she heard the details of long, rather tedious disputes about money.

And, for herself, she feared that the paintings – the production of which required that the entire household bend to his needs – would be indifferent.

When she did go into his studio – which she had avoided for the whole of the first week – Claude gestured to canvases piled thick against the walls, thirty years of work unsold and unseen. He gave a slightly embarrassed shrug. *A foolish old man*, he said of himself, and Merle felt the stab of his disappointment. In response she spoke too fast, reassuring him with a rush of words. She said the colours were clear, and she liked the effect of ambiguity in the landscapes, as if everything was seen through deep water. She rushed and hurried. There was neither space nor silence between them.

When, later, in the house, Merle turned the subject to herself, to the stories of her life, she found that he turned away just a little too quickly, before the point had quite been reached. After that she kept her distance, retreating into the kitchen and the garden, where she discovered from Jessica that he had made several trips into the Pacific during her childhood.

'Did he meet up with my mother?' she asked.

'I didn't ask,' Jessica said. 'The less I knew the better when it came to Claude's women. Why don't you ask your mother.'

'She says he didn't.'

'There you are then.'

Merle was disappointed. The fantasy emptied out. She discovered inconsistencies, contradictions, sleights of hand. She didn't discover any shameful secrets, Claude made sure of that, but she did discover the ease with which a man imbued with kingly qualities by the desires of women can be reduced to rags and tatters, a beggar on the street. Had she not expected so fine a creature, had she not been as caught by her own dreams as she was by Isobel's, she would have been less disappointed.

But her disappointment was the least of it. What she could not bear was the painful encounter with his. What pained her was not the limits of his talent, for his work was indeed tolerably good, but that he had lived for so many years by a hope that was never realised – and that without the world reflecting back an image of himself

as successful, he was without success. He was not
equipped for life of private success, or private satisfaction.

Worse still, she saw in him, as if in a distorting
mirror, the fate – hardly considered before this
moment – of her mother, and this she deeply
resented, and feared.

After a month at the farm she could take no
more, and having come to stay for the rest of the
year, found she had no interest in remaining, no
interest at all. Jessica drove her to Taunton and
saw her off on the train to London where she studied for a month with Jacqueline du Pré, and without returning to Devon, just a phone call to say
goodbye – and with only a few days' warning to us
– she booked an early return to Australia.

When questioned, as inevitably she was, by Isobel,
by Brian and Pablo, by me, she simply said, *Tom's
my father.*

Which, in any real terms, he was. If she told
anyone the whole story – other than Simon – it
was probably Tom. But I never heard him speak of
it. As to the rest of us, all we got were scraps, little
bits dropped here and there with great reluctance, and eventually we gave up trying. That I
know as much as I do is due, as I have said, to
Simon.

Simon met her off the plane.

That was the second of my mistakes.

The cable announcing her early return had been addressed to me and I asked him to go in my place, as I was booked to go to north Queensland. Not on a holiday, nothing frivolous like that, but for research. It was a decision I thought – stupidly – that Merle would understand, even approve.

Merle and I had always spoken of our ambitions in the frankest of terms. Mine, quite ludicrous really, was to become a journalist, to convert the lives I'd taken to researching in the library not into essays for the university, but into stories for magazines and newspapers. Hers, though she never admitted it to Isobel, was to stay in the orchestra until she'd learned enough to make a mark. That was the phrase she used. *What kind of mark?* I'd say. *I don't know yet,* she'd say, irritated if I pressed. Though she did not hesitate to press me. *You should go for broke,* she'd say. *Give up those stupid models and write a book,* but I couldn't imagine a life with sufficient scope for that.

The National Times *seems interested,* I wrote in my note on the kitchen table. *I think I can do it. Darling Merle,* I wrote, *you gave me courage. Simon says he'll pick you up and I'll be back in no time at all. I've left a bottle of champagne in the fridge. Drink a toast to me.*

But a toast was not what she drank. This I have not forgotten.

'Merle,' I called, when I got home. 'Are you there?'

The back door was closed, the house was still and quiet. My room was as I had left it; Merle, as far as I could see, hadn't been in there. I pushed open the window. Motes of dust danced around like tiny sprites. Merle's room was messy, there were clothes everywhere, a sweater I recognised as Simon's, a pair of shoes much too large for Merle, and a well-used bed. My body, my heart, the blood squeezing round my veins, took in the information before I did, that is to say, before my mind did.

When, late in the afternoon, they came in through the front door calling my name, filling the house with energy and life, moving the air so that the sprites that had settled after my arrival danced again, I had to sit down to accommodate the weight of information that had just reached my brain.

Perhaps if I'd met the plane I would have regained the role of intimate and confidante, and she would never have married Simon. But when the delicious story is ripe to tell it runs the risk of overripening, and falling rotten to the ground if it waits too long to be heard. Merle had no interest in waiting. And she had no interest in the letters I'd read in my northern library. Far from praising my ambition she said, rather tartly, *Don't make a fool of yourself*, as if the ambitions, the hopes she'd encouraged – insisted on – counted for nothing.

So she had told her story not to me, but to Simon. This I have not forgotten either.

I sat in the kitchen and listened to the murmur of their voices that slid down the stairs, a slippery waterfall of indecipherable words, soft murmurs, long sighs. In that heady exchange of secrets that are sometimes the most compelling part of falling in love, and the most bitterly regretted when things go wrong, Simon won, and I lost her.

'I'm telling you,' she said to him. 'But I'm not telling anyone else.'

'Shouldn't you tell Isobel?' Simon said. It was not me that he considered, only Isobel. I know this because I stood outside the door and heard.

'No,' she said. 'Especially not Isobel. Isobel lied to me, and anyway she lives a fantasy about it, it's embarrassing, and I'm not going to be part of it.'

'That's not fair,' Simon said.

'Too bad,' she said, leaning forward to kiss him. 'Promise. Just promise.'

'I promise,' Simon said.

It was a promise he regretted, and didn't keep. He told me some of it, in bed as it happens, the last time we ever slept together. He told me enough to be convincing, and my vigils at the late night door told me the rest. Whether he told Isobel, I don't know. If I'd been him, I would have been tempted, for he had now come to occupy that most uncomfortable position of being too much in the confidence of the secrets of both.

Between Isobel and Merle nothing was right again.

On Merle's side there was an increasing distance, a shrug of dismissal, a refusal to comprehend, or to forgive. And on Isobel's there was a kind of perpetual complaint which bled into paranoid pleading. Merle seemed not to notice, though to everyone else it was painful to watch.

It's hard to know in retrospect whether Isobel's erratic behaviour was the result of the illness that killed her much too young, not much over sixty, or if something had twisted in her, as if the little grain of bitterness and disappointment that had been fought down for all those years had exhausted her, getting a hold on her until it had risen up first in anger, then paranoia, and finally in a series of small strokes, as the blood vessels in her brain popped – *pop, pop, pop* – until there was nothing recognisably Isobel left.

Every overture she made to Merle was rejected. Merle would not talk to her of Claude. She would not read her attempt at a manuscript about Lake Sentani. She would not leave the orchestra. She would not discuss her future. She was resolute in her refusal to allow Isobel the satisfaction of success:

either her own, or her mother's reflected through her.

When she married Simon, I thought – foolishly, erroneously – that at least with Isobel she would relent. But Merle would not give any ground. She did not like the Sentani figure. She refused a Mudgee wedding, and nothing Isobel did – either cajoling or hectoring – could change that resolve. She rarely went to Isobel's dinners. She was not rude, she did not stop Simon from going, she was simply absent. She never complained when Isobel rang asking Simon to come to her at once, there was something urgent at the gallery that needed sorting. She made no complaint, and she made no inquiry. She did not object when Isobel, shining with pleasure, accompanied Simon to receptions and opening nights. As the river swept her and Simon apart, Isobel was washed with her daughter's disaffected husband onto the other bank.

Merle's capacity to hold herself at a distance was awesome, her capacity to withhold herself, to hold her own counsel, to hold her grievance and give no ground. I think it had always been there and I missed it, tricked by that mass of red hair, and that air of vulnerability, which all of us had rushed in to assuage. She was, if you understand my meaning, too lovely to doubt. That perfectly balanced oval face conjured up desires that deceived us all. I never saw her determination as ruthless. Instead I was hurt and bewildered when I too, once loved, became the target of her scornful fierceness.

By the time she left for New York there were few that she was talking to. I mean really talking. Tom. Possibly Brian. Certainly not me. It was a lonely departure, and she didn't return until Isobel was dead. She wrote to Tom, and from him we heard that she had met Charlie Quatrain and that they had formed the quartet. By then Isobel was in hospital, her brain and her personality shot full of leaky holes. Simon told her about the quartet, news she had waited fifteen years to hear, and also about the pregnancy when it came. But whether she took it in I don't know. Whether she took it in and kept it there.

'Will Merle come?' Isobel asked on her last day of life, in an unexpected flash of lucidity.

But Merle did not come. Tom rang her with news of the death, and only then did she return.

That was 1985. A long time ago. Since then, until Simon rang from the clinic and I came to ponder the subject of secrets, months, even years, have elapsed without me giving the Cullens a thought. Even Merle. The last time I had seen them all together had been at Tom's funeral, which seemed at the time to mark the end of an era, though I should have known from the tug of my heart that there was much left undone.

Tom died of a heart attack one autumn afternoon five years ago while he was in his chair on the verandah, after a lunch of bread, cheese and a glass of wine – which he had taken with a neighbour's son who was helping in the workshop. After lunch Tom had stayed in his chair, while the neighbour's son went back to the workshop. When he returned in midafternoon – coming into the kitchen from the other side – he didn't think anything of it to see Tom still sitting there, nor did the tilt of his head seem so surprising in one known to enjoy an afternoon nap. It wasn't until a brisk wind had chased the last of the sun from the house and a chill was gathering around the verandah chair and its silent occupant that the neighbour's son realised the tilt was more like a slump, and that Tom was indeed cold, stone cold, and had been for some time.

The funeral was a quiet occasion, befitting a man like Tom; the crowds and, as it turned out, the cameras, were kept for the memorial that was held later in the city. He was buried in the graveyard of the church which had been built in the valley by a pious great-grandfather giving praise for the birth of a son. In that small stone church, backed against ranges bleached drought-dry, a ghostly silver, Merle played Peter Sculthorpe's *Requiem* for solo cello. Brian read from Kenneth Slessor's 'Five Bells':

> *. . . You have gone from earth,*
> *Gone even from the meaning of a name;*
> *Yet something's there, yet something forms its lips*
> *And hits and cries against the ports of space . . .*

The ceremony itself was a curious mix of West and East, a juxtaposition encompassed by the life that had been Tom Cullen's and exemplified by Merle's choice of music. Una huffed with disapproval, but for the rest of us it seemed not strange at all. And, in the event, even Una was silenced, possibly even tearful. How could she have not been when, as the coffin was carried from the church into that burnished valley, Merle played again the plainsong 'lacrimosa'. A lament for the passing of a man whose life had encompassed the tension between a deep knowledge of impermanence, the inevitability of change, and a transforming faith in a consciousness as wide and as empty as the Australian sky. Merle's cello sang of forgiveness, begged for forgiveness, acknowledged the ending that comes with death and pressed against that knowledge.

It was, in a sense, her funeral. That is to say, a funeral of Merle's design.

Beside a grave hacked from hard ground, under the dome of a dry ancestral sky, she wept, unabashed, for the father he had been.

Afterwards Merle stayed on in the house for two days, and rather to my surprise asked me to stay on with her. That sort of intimacy had ended when she moved out of the house by the canal. I had visited the house in Hereford Street often enough, usually when Simon wasn't there, and there had been a moment, I remember it well: she was at the sink, I walked up behind her, put my arms around her, and she leaned back into my shoulder. We could have unbent then, relented, but as I say it was only a moment. *Trust me,* I'd said. *Why?* she'd said. *You don't trust me.*

So when this invitation to stay at Mudgee came, I accepted warily.

'I could do a story for *Vogue,*' I said.

'Don't even think about it,' she said. And though I was beginning to think a lot more than that, I made no reply.

As it was we were cheerful together, not close, I wouldn't say that – we each held a great deal in reserve – but familiar. Maybe it was just that there was no time for sensibilities or misgivings. She set us the task of going through the desks, the bookcases, even trunks stored in the old servants' quarters.

After years in which she had shown no interest in the secret, she was anxious, certain we'd find diaries, letters, something that would tell the story of Isobel and Claude. She didn't believe that it had ended with her birth.

'Why not?' I asked.

'It doesn't ring true,' she said. 'And anyway, Simon hinted.'

'That there were letters?'

'That there was something. I thought at the time he was trying to bribe me, you know what he was like, always manoeuvring. So I never took him up on it. But I remember it.'

And so we looked. Looked and looked. We found Tom's letters from the war, Brian's first attempt with paint – a semi-abstract house – her own baby shoes. Boxes and boxes of papers about the gallery, exhibitions, more boxes of letters from friends and artists and colleagues – was there anyone they didn't know? – from anthropologists on Easter Island, publishers, curators and collectors. Brian had arranged for someone to come down from the Mitchell Library to price them, and it turned out that Tom had already had him there and had discussed terms and possibilities, including the possibility of embargoes were there to be any documents that, in his, or the family's view, should not yet be made public.

But there was not a word about, or from,

Claude. Not a hint of Merle's secret. There were diaries of Isobel's from earlier, just one or two, many from later. And one great absence.

Could a record be so thoroughly expunged? Can there be secrets that involve something as major as the birth of a child without leaving a material trace? These were the questions we asked. It's all very well, we said, to say that those are the secrets we don't need reminders of, every day we see the flesh and blood, but that doesn't take into account curiosity, and dreams that are clung to even after they have passed, the great human resilience of hope. *It takes a very strong head,* she quoted to me from C.P. Snow, *to keep secrets for years and not go slightly mad.* Tom had a strong head; Isobel, as we know, did not.

We went through every trunk, but found nothing. Perhaps Sara Paretsky would have done better, or Ruth Rendell. As it was we weren't the FBI, or even V.I. Warshawski, and short of ripping up the floorboards, there was nowhere else to look. In the workshop there were ledgers recording every repair, every frame, every order, every sale. But no personal papers. A few books of poetry – Auden, Rilke, Douglas Stewart, Gwen Harwood, and the Dickinson Tom had read from – but otherwise it was given over to the austerity of tools and wood, the fine smell of oil and sawdust. On the shelf between the windows and the stove,

where she had always been, was the figure of Tara
with her hands cupped, one inside the other.

'If there had been letters, would Tom have got
rid of them?' I asked. He had brought everything
to Mudgee when he'd cleared out the flat above
the gallery in Victoria Street after Isobel's death.
He'd have known what was there. I couldn't see
him tampering with the record, but I thought it
was possible that he could have wanted the private
to remain private when the records of his life were
carted to Sydney, to be laid before the eyes of
every PhD student the library cared to send their
way.

'I asked him once if he'd destroyed anything,
and he said no,' Merle said. 'Once I knew, there
was no reason for him to. Tom never lied.'

'Not even to protect you?'

'Maybe if she hadn't told me,' Merle said. 'But
then I would never have known to ask. I don't suppose,' she added as an afterthought, 'anyone else
has been through here?'

Once we knew what we were looking for, we
could see that they had. There was no dust on the
trunks that held the letters, while those full of old
clothes, Christmas tree decorations, tablecloths,
even the one with the last of Isobel's Pacific artefacts, were coated in a silver-grey film of dust deep
enough for our fingers to trace our names. My
name and hers.

'Look', Merle said, drawing a heart, 'our names are linked.' She laughed, tied her hair back – it was still long and billowy then – and wiped the trunk clean with her sleeve.

We went through the possible candidates, and with one exception – Simon who, not being part of the family, neither of us thought of – we eliminated them all. Pablo didn't get to the house until the morning of the funeral, and by the time Brian arrived on the day after the death, the house was full. Tom's brother was dead and his dork of a son, Merle's cousin, usually only a matter of miles away running the vineyard, was in Adelaide. In any case we couldn't imagine him mustering the gumption, let alone the spirit, to rifle anyone's drawers. There was Aunt Una, Tom's horrible sister with her pretensions and her daughters in the social pages and on the smartest of charitable committees, who hadn't been able to come down the day he died but had rushed down the next morning to take charge of the house. Could it have been her?

'All she'd want would be first go at anything worth money,' Merle said. She looked around to see if there was anything missing from the walls, a Drysdale drawing perhaps, a Fairweather watercolour. But there were no obvious gaps, nothing to suggest concealment.

Simon escaped our scrutiny. By going through an inventory of the family instead of following the logic of who arrived at the house when, we didn't so much as consider the visit Simon made on the evening of Tom's death: a memory that was jolted into me like a bang on the head that afternoon in the clinic when he made his confession. He'd come down on the evening of Tom's death, and had left again the next day.

When the boy found the body cold on the verandah, he tried ringing Brian, but he was doing a case in Melbourne. Pablo was in Cairns, even further away. The nephew was at a winegrowers' convention. Una said she couldn't get down that night because she had a function, would you believe. She told the boy to try Simon. He'd have been alone in the house for several hours, plenty of time to go through the trunks; knowing what he was looking for, he had taken the letters with minimum disturbance. I know this now, and so does Merle, but we did not know it then.

Unaware of what we'd missed, we spent our last day at Mudgee – before we returned to Sydney and she flew back to New York – walking up the gullies behind the house, above the dry creek-beds where city weekenders, unaffected by the drought, have taken over the old huts of the Chinese and extended them with skylights and fancy decks. We could hear their stereos as we passed. We swerved to avoid them, and clambered to the top of the ridge, a hard climb that had us breathless and sweating.

At the top we frightened a tiny snake that was stretched out under a fallen branch. We all jumped in the air, Merle, me and the snake, up there above the plume of smoke that we could see rising from the chimney below us.

The house is a guesthouse these days. I stayed there recently. It is run by an open-faced New Zealand couple in gumboots and Fair Isle sweaters. They've polished it into submission. Not a speck of damp dares appear on the skirting boards, the windows roll open in smooth silence, the floorboards no longer creak, the frayed runners have been replaced by grey berber, each room is decorated in a different colour and the names of the colours are affixed to the door by way of identification – as in *You're in the green room,* etc. – and the mantelpieces that once had photos of Merle as a tubby baby, Pablo getting married, and the old grandmother I never met and Isobel said was as dry as a stick, shushing Brian when he told the story – surely apocryphal – that she'd been pregnant for nearly a year with Tom. (Could it possibly be true? Not the year, the implication of the adjustment required.) In their place are china shepherdesses and kleenex tissues in fluffy holders.

Staying there was a mistake. I thought it would help me write this story, as if I might stumble on something, a dropped slip of paper, a diary tucked behind a chair, a bundle of letters tied with ribbon, something that would reveal the truth, the real truth, about this complex and difficult story, a kind of ultimate secret that would lay bare not only the secrets of this story, but all mysteries, all ambiguities, all shadowy realms, all secrets.

The doors still open onto the verandah (scrubbed within an inch of its life, without dogs, cats, leaves) and the hills still change from pink to orange to gold as the light dies, but now the garden is trimmed and neat, ready to be walked in by wholesome couples on a weekend without the kids. There is an air of respectable good sense about it. Not even a newspaper is to be found tucked behind a chair.

But surely it can't be that none of these people come trailing secrets with them. Perhaps they're not there long enough for their secret lives, their secret selves to mark the place. Even if I didn't know about Isobel and Tom and Merle, it's their presence that hovers there. I am being sentimental. But then I've come to think that without secrets, without complications – those luxuries – without the tug and pull of shadowy realms, life is rendered monotone and uninteresting. Secrets, dangerous and damaging though they may be, take us into our own depths, and the depths of life. Without them there would be no mystery, no frustration, no challenge, no charge.

3 ISOBEL'S SECRET

I have spent a lot of my life reading other people's letters. Not private snooping. I've only done that once, and it didn't tell me anything I wanted to know. That's not what I mean. I mean letters in libraries. Research. A respectable activity and one that I enjoy, if that's the right word, not so much because it's respectable and makes me feel serious, with a book under my arm, but because in letters you sometimes come across the secret shapes that few of us reveal easily. Nor, necessarily, should we.

There are queasy moments in this line of work, when the words in a letter that is now numbered and catalogued leap from the page with long-distant and very private pain. Few of us write letters, at least not personal letters, with a view to their future in a library. Politicians maybe, but even writers who know in some rational part of their brain that this could well be the fate of their correspondence – especially these days when everything has a price and it seems to be going up – still take up that blank addressed page and mark it in a moment as intimate and as private as if the person to whom we speak was there with us. *My love,* we write, *why do you do this to me?* There are things we say on paper we might never admit to face to face; it's as if we're in the company of an intimate, but of course we are not, we're alone in our room with only a pen, seductive as a lover, our secret selves sliding across the paper as silky as ink. Yet despite the years of work I have done on other people's letters, this is not something I have thought much about, at least not in an intimate, immediate way, until it came to the unravelling of Isobel's secret.

The letters I was reading in north Queensland when Merle came back from seeing Claude, had been written during the late thirties and the first years of the war by Marjorie Barnard in Sydney to Jean Devanny in Townsville. They were both writers, one rather better than the other; on the face of it an unlikely friendship. One woman was a communist, the other a librarian for whom it was a large leap of faith to change her vote to Labor.

What united them was that they both had unorthodox emotional lives. By which I mean that their experiences of love fell outside the restricted expectations placed on the women of their time. I read their letters in an official capacity with a letter of interest from a newspaper and a valid reader's ticket.

This was how I came to be in Townsville when Merle arrived home to our house in Glebe. While she took Simon to her bed, I was innocently reading of Marjorie Barnard's secret affair with Frank Dalby Davison. Marjorie Barnard was in her forties, a single woman at her professional prime when she fell in love with a man who evoked in her desires that he, being married, could not meet. In her letters to Jean Devanny I followed the arrangements they made to meet at a time when such a liaison could have ruined them both, or at any rate certainly her. And I read the letters she wrote when he dumped her, moved to Melbourne, divorced his wife, and married another woman; letters that are the private accompaniment to her finest story, 'The Persimmon Tree', in which a woman recovers in a Sydney flat from a long illness. There were few people to whom she could admit the nature of this sickness, and certainly not, in 1943, the reading public of Australia. Not, of course, that the sickness in the story was hers, or, in any literal sense, the narrator her. We like to read autobiography into fiction as if, by demanding that particular form of authenticity, we can sidestep the contingencies of life – our own as much as others' – and shore ourselves up against the dangerous slippages we all make into imagination and disbelief.

Marjorie Barnard could manipulate the veils of fiction, letting them lift and fall on her own life, but she also held to the view that letters are a private act of communication and should be destroyed on receipt. This was a practice she adopted; there are no letters in libraries from others to her. The people she wrote to had a different ethic, or at least a different practice. They saved her letters and passed them on until eventually they made their way into libraries, where they survive in neatly cata- logued folios for the likes of me to find.

Until I read Claude's letters to Isobel, Marjorie Barnard's were the most disturbing I had cast my official gaze across, and even as I stripped the veneer from her life and showed her as stark as a body on the mortuary slab, I knew exactly the chain of betrayals that had brought not only her words to me, but mine about her to the magazine reading public. Given my trade, I am glad that this is so, and I lament the letters, the other side of the correspondence, that she destroyed. But as a per- son with blood in my veins I stand accused. Of what, I am not sure.

Maybe Rosie is right when she says that every secret is a betrayal. We shouldn't call ourselves human if we are not able to shoulder that reality; as to writers who take it a stage further and turn secrets into stories, blurring the lines between what was and what might have been – well, it's no task for the squeamish.

I make this preamble by way of washing down the slab before the next corpse is brought in. And though I never seriously doubted that I would lift the sheet and show you Isobel lying there, naked and cold, this time I do not have the imprimatur of official sanction.

There are no catalogue numbers for Claude's letters to Isobel. Simon had taken them from the house at Mudgee the night Tom had died. I took them from the desk drawer in Simon's gallery and without consulting him about what to do next, I read them. Of course I read them. What kind of lily-livered wimp would I be if I hadn't? But I didn't read them straight away. I held off for a couple of days. To prolong desire? To extend the moment of titillation? To delay the betrayal? Or because I had a bad feeling about them?

Rosie was similarly restrained.

The gallery, when we let ourselves in, was stuffy and dusty. Unopened mail was piled behind the door, and there was a foetid, unused smell about it. Damp, I suppose. There were specks of mould on the ceiling. The gallery had only been closed for a week, but judging by the mess in the office – papers everywhere, unwashed cups, half-empty glasses of wine, a focaccia curling with mould – no one had been attending to it for longer than that. The woman who had worked there all year had left in an unexplained wrangle – sex, I suppose – and Simon possessed none of the lowly skills required of office keeping. Filing cabinets were open, there were books out of the shelves, and everything, when we looked, had to do with Lake Sentani.

There was Jacques Viot's account of the expedition, *Déposition de Blanc*, which he wrote in 1932, and a few pages of scrappy translation. There was the monograph – in German and with no translation as far as I could see – of the adventurer Paul Wirz's visit earlier in the twenties. A Dutch monograph from the fifties, mercifully in English, or perhaps not as it was written in deadening ethnographic prose. And a recent American publication which succeeded where Isobel had failed in accounting for Viot's expedition and its impact on French Surrealism.

In the corner behind the desk loomed the Sentani figure itself: wide-grained, dark, sombre and insistent. In the gloom the primordial couple stood there tethered, their feet bound together as if by a macabre manacle. The male figure, touchingly slender, drops his chin to his chest, while his mate leans away from him, her stubborn chin straining forward in a gesture of eternal frustration. Their oddly almond-shaped eyes do not meet each other's. Their outside arms hang loose by their sides, while their inside arms, which could be linked in an embrace, are held across their separate wooden hearts. When you look closely you can see these arms are spindly, fragile, even withered. The grain of the wood is oddly coarse, rather ugly; damaged, we'd always supposed, by those years on the floor of the lake.

Rosie clicked on the lights and sat at the desk.

'This place needs a good clean,' she said.

Which is how she came to be there a week later when Merle opened the door. I'd put it to Simon, and he could hardly refuse, ten dollars an hour and Rosie would clean the gallery through, open the mail and answer the phone. If nothing else she would keep the air circulating.

'It could do with a coat of paint,' I said to Simon on the phone.

'What's the point?' he said. 'What's the point of anything?'

His voice was rough, as if something had gone out of him, there was a flatness that I hadn't noticed at the clinic where, despite brinking into tears, he'd been labile, with every lapse matched by a surge of emotion. It was with this desolate tone that I realised it was not just Merle – or rather his long battle with Merle – that had brought him crashing up against this wall, but the greater, deeper shock that comes when one is confronted with the collapse of all meaning – the definition I suppose of that much maligned and underrated phenomenon of the midlife crisis that seems the province of those whose successes are as ruinous as defeat.

'Listen,' Rosie said the next day when I joined her in the gallery, 'I've been reading up on Jacques Viot. He was a sleaze-bag, if you ask me. He cashed in on the Surrealists, traded on them, but he never even signed their manifesto. Everything about him is on the nose. A couple of years before he was in New Guinea, he took a job as a magistrate – do you think it can be possible? – in Tahiti under a false name. He'd gone there to meet – listen to this – *a beloved face*, a boy I should think, as he was drummed out on criminal charges at the end of the year.'

'I thought he was wanted for debt in Paris,' I said.

'Looks dodgy to me,' Rosie said. 'Anyway do you know why Loeb went into partnership with him? In the hope he'd recoup his money, that's why, and to get him out of Paris. Like when

Claude teamed up with him, it wasn't a great moment with Breton waving them off. They sort of crept out of Paris. Shit, they didn't even like travelling. Listen to this, it's the first line of Viot's book: *Journeys are very unpleasant.* How pathetic. Third-class tramp steamers and grubby hotels. So much for Isobel's grand fantasy!'

'Poor Isobel,' I said. 'No wonder she never wrote that book. I suppose she had all that material?'

'Most of it,' Rosie said. All except one of the books on the desk were from shelves that had once been hers. Simon had bought the glossy American *Art of North West New Guinea.*

'The place wasn't even that isolated,' Rosie said, turning its pages. 'There was a Dutch settlement on the lake. Viot never mentioned that! But it was beautiful,' she said. 'Look.'

The photographs of Lake Sentani – lavishly coloured in the American book – show an intricate waterway surrounded by neat round hills. Just as Claude had described, knolls of land lie across the lake, reclining promontories of hips and breasts with bushy shading in the crevices beneath smooth grasslands. Indented into the peaceful cover of these hills are the coves with villages built out on trestles over the lake. *An enchanted fortress,* Viot called it. *An enchanted castle.* I could see the enchantment, but nothing about it appeared to be fortified.

'He was seriously weird,' Rosie said. 'He loathed the colonials and the missionaries. Well that's not weird. He said the Dutch,' she flipped through the pages, 'had *vague minds and large bellies whose sole exercise consists in playing bowls and drinking beer.* I can't see the bowls. All those hills. Anyway he was scornful of them, they were probably awful, and he was paranoid as well. He'd have been a shit of a companion. He never mentions Claude, and despised everyone else. He even hated people who'd come for the art, like some poor bastard of a professor who'd come down the coast with them and had taken whatever he could from the bits and pieces the Dutch had already collected. Never even went into a village. He was a snob about how you got your art, it had to be drastic like getting it out of the bottom of the lake. I wonder how they did get it out. I mean look at that figure, it's not small. And the lake was deep.'

'Silty, Isobel said.'

'There you are then. They wouldn't have had dredging equipment, all that stuff police drag things out of lakes with. I don't see how they could have got it out by diving. It'd have been waterlogged.'

'More than one must have dived,' I said. 'Two men could have got it up.'

'But look at the photos,' Rosie said. 'They're not men. They're boys. This is where it gets weird. He calls them *the last saints,* really over the top, I think he means all of them. *They go naked,* like they are innocent and noble, all that shit. I keep thinking of his boys.'

'Rosie,' I said, 'his boys might be a figment of your imagination.'

'Or they might not,' she said. 'Come on. What do you think? Look at these photos.' Sleek young boys, wet from the lake, glistening like young seals, smile up at the camera's salacious eye.

'They were *in an enchanted fortress,'* Rosie read, *'that no white man could penetrate.* Ha! Do you think he looked at anything? Anyway the bloke who wrote this,' she gestured to the glossy American book with the seductive photos, 'reckons Viot read detective stories the whole journey, and after he got back to France began writing them. They went a whole lot better than *Déposition de Blanc* that the critics said was romantic crap. It was. Kind of mad. He reckoned primitives and Surrealists were different versions of the same – down some opposite end of the spectrum till they came back and met. I don't know how he worked that out. I mean, just as well he switched to detective novels.' She laughed. 'I like this story. It'd make a great novel.'

'What about the boys?'

'Oh, well, the boys,' she said. 'That stinks. But if you're going to have a novel, I suppose you have to have boys.'

'Or girls,' I said.

'Girls are out of fashion,' she said. 'Not much shock value in taking a girl to Lake Sentani.'

'I suppose,' I said, kissing her on the cheek in the sort of gesture admiring aunts ought to refrain from.

'I'm trying to sort these bookshelves,' she said, rather crossly I thought.

Why is our culture so hungry for the secrets of other cultures? Why do we need to possess their objects? Their art? I think of Simon and my husband bickering all the way along that road into the Sepik. My husband resented everything Simon took out, every mask, every inch of tapa cloth. And he resented every change that was taken in, every pot of paint, every sheet of paper. He dismissed Simon as self-serving when he argued that change was in the nature of art; and Simon counter-accused my husband of policing the borders of culture according to his own definitions. But neither of them doubted the power of the objects they squabbled over.

These days cultural historians don't go in for the romanticism that was possible for Viot in the 1920s. You're unlikely to hear talk about saints, or enchantment; these days academic talk is more likely to be of a materialist bent, and arguing that the men of the Sepik, for instance, gain power not because there's anything secret in the tambaran, or magical about the masks and gongs that are brought from it, but simply by the fact of secrecy. They hoodwink everyone else, that is to say the excluded women, into believing in a power which they know of only in that it is kept from them; the men make that power theirs by sleight of hand. Perhaps there's an element of truth in that as a parable for other forms of masculine power.

But it still strikes me that there is something powerful in the meaning of the tambaran with its great belly, that archetypal female place where men, protected against the contingencies of the feminine, are taken into myth and ritual. Viot was batty, Simon was looking after himself, my husband was effacingly responsible, today's ethnographers are, as Rosie would say, seriously sophisticated, and yet it seems to me that for all of them the Sepik, or Lake Sentani, is an idea they hold to as if the key to the ultimate mysteriousness of life, on the one hand wanting all secrets explained and penetrated, and on the other drawn to the masks and figures as symbols of states of being, levels of consciousness that our empty sophistications block us from. Which of us does not think somewhere, sometime, if only secretly when we wake alone in the still night hours, that there must be another way. A simpler way.

Consider Tom. He wasn't interested in Oceania particularly; his eye turned to a more traditional East. But like Isobel, he had also walked along Charing Cross Road in those years after the war when he was reunited with a frustrated wife and two squalling children; not at all the image he'd carried through the jungles of Burma. He was walking off his own frustrations and misery, a tide of rising panic made all the worse by a sensibility that was attuned to the needs of others, a kind of natural courtesy.

As he walked through Soho one damp afternoon he saw a notice, scruffy and handwritten, advertising a meeting to discuss Buddhism and its application in the West. He remembered the young Japanese prisoner they had captured in prayer, a moment of luminosity that seemed true, somehow, in a way that very little about his life in London did, except when he was in the work rooms where paintings were restored and framed. In the detail of that work, in the alignment of canvas and frame, he was at ease.

So where Isobel had climbed the stairs to a dingy gallery and the immediacy of romance, Tom clambered down a flight of stairs into an equally dingy room where a number of men spoke of esoteric philosophies and sat in self-conscious meditation. Tom didn't tell Isobel. She knew nothing of these forays, so different from her own, into

DRUSILLA MODJESKA

other cultures and other realms. It wasn't so much
a case of tit for tat, more that whatever it was that
Tom was beginning to grasp there, a way of living
that was anchored in the mindfulness of the present, was inexpressible to a woman who preferred
romance as a way of dealing with the separations
of life, the longings that are born into the world
with us.

After Isobel died, Tom told Brian that he was
grateful to Isobel because the terrible shock of loving her when she clearly no longer loved him hit
him with the same force that others are taken by
with news of a serious illness, or some terrible loss;
it was a crisis that reoriented everything, realigned
him. With the children, he'd been careful not to
indoctrinate – that was Isobel's word – hoping
that curiosity would be aroused by his example.
But of course, as children do, they just took it as
the natural face of the father. Some fathers drink,
some work in city offices, others have worksheds
with statues and meditation cushions in them.
That's fathers.

Brian told me all this a few years ago when I ran
into him at a talk by a Vietnamese Zen teacher. It
was a horribly hot night in February and we were
squashed into a hall in Devonshire Street. There
weren't enough chairs; we were fanning ourselves
with flimsy sheets of paper advertising forthcoming events; children lay on the floor and wailed. In

amongst the crowd and the din, I spotted Brian; that's what I remember, the unexpected jolt of seeing him, the heat, the crowd, and then, suddenly: the presence of the teacher. He – the teacher – walked into the room and the temperature dropped. It could not have dropped, I know that, but it was as if it dropped. The room became still and comfortable, children quietened, chairs fitted, people without seats found places to sit. It was, I think, the only time I have felt certain that I was in the presence of a man who was holy. The shameful thing is that all I remember from that night were the strange aphorisms he used, and although I cannot say what context he intended for them, or even the context in which they arose, I would still say something entered my heart that night. *The clearness of the mirror,* he said, *has nothing to do with dust.*

After the talk I stood at the bottom of the steps in Devonshire Street and waited for Brian to come out. He kissed me, a warm rather slow kiss on the cheek, and pulled me towards him in a long hug.

'I've been thinking about Tom,' he said.

He came home with me and we took a tray and two chairs into the small wedge of air that in the inner city is classified as a garden. We were still there at two. We began with green tea, progressed to wine and ended, still quite sober, with brandy.

'After Isobel died,' Brian said, 'I went up to

Mudgee and spent a week with him. I took the time off, occasionally I get things right, though at the time I remember feeling sort of resentful, you know, I should have been working, and it felt like duty. Not the right motivation, but at least it got me there. Now I see it more as an attempt to save my own life. It was the first time I talked to Tom about his spiritual life, whatever you want to call it. He was very low, uncharacteristically so, and full of doubt. He said he feared he'd taken the path of meditation selfishly, even vindictively. It infuriated Isobel, she never understood it, he never explained it, just retreated into it. It saved him but it didn't save her.'

'Why do you suppose he stayed with her?' I said.

'People did in those days,' Brian said. 'They weren't like us.' Brian's second marriage had just collapsed, I suppose that's why I ran into him that night, why he was there.

'How much did he know about Claude?' I asked.

'A lot more than he let on,' Brian said. 'I think that's why he was so upset when Merle went hurtling over to see him. He knew what sort of man Claude was.'

'What sort of man was he?'

'There are some confidences I must keep,' Brian said with one of those prim looks people adopt when they shelter on the moral high ground. 'But I'll tell you this. It was Tom who took him to the hospital to see Merle when she was born. He had to be dragged there. Tom wanted him to see the actuality of Merle, see what was at stake having a baby, and he wanted Isobel to see the actuality of Claude. It didn't work.'

It certainly didn't.

'We've had enough for one morning,' I said to Rosie when she'd finished with the bookcase. 'Let's go out to lunch.'

We closed the gallery, and walked past the brothels and the smart houses that are bunched up together at that end of Victoria Street, but instead of turning into one of the cafés, I took her to Mezzaluna, a ghastly extravagance. We sat on the terrace looking across to Woolloomooloo again, and the city, a slight shift of angle from the view we get at the back of the gallery. It was tamer, somehow, an easier line for the eye to the smooth grass of the Domain.

'Are you up to the letters this afternoon?' I asked her as we walked back along Victoria Street.

'Yes,' she said. 'I think I am.' Her voice was sombre. 'It's odd, though. I mean I know we must. And I wouldn't think of not. But there's a bit of me that thinks if I don't know, then I can keep it kind of how I'd like it to be.'

'Save Isobel, you mean?'

'Not much hope of that,' she said. 'More like keep it a dream, I suppose.'

'That doesn't sound like you.'

'I think Sydney's changing me,' she said. 'You never know what's real here.'

'You mean you're getting a taste for secrets?' I said, and she laughed, and took my arm.

'Let's read them,' she said.

And so it was that Rosie knew Isobel's secret when the door of the gallery pushed open the next morning, and a woman in an elegant coat, loose and swaying to her ankles, the sort one is more likely to see in Europe than in Sydney, walked in. Her shorn pelt of hair shone in the light from the street outside. With her was a child about ten years old, tall for her age, in rolled-up jeans, a white T-shirt, Ray Bans and blue baseball cap. Her skin was the colour of milky coffee, and under the cap was a halo of dark hair in marked contrast to her mother's elegant, but shorn, head.

'You must be Merle,' Rosie said.

'And who,' Merle said, 'are you?'

'I am Rosie.' She gave her surname, her mother's maiden name, which with her move to Sydney she had decided to adopt. A name which is, of course, also my name.

'Ah,' Merle said. 'So where's your aunt?'

'She's working,' Rosie said. 'At the magazine.'

'Still?' Merle said. 'And Simon?'

'He's in a clinic.'

'What sort of clinic?'

'One of those places people have breakdowns in and pretend they're recuperating from something, or slimming. A rich person's clinic.'

'And well may he be rich,' Merle said, gesturing her arm round the gallery. Her eye came to rest on the Sentani figure. 'God it's hideous,' she said. 'By the way, this is Dili.'

'Hi,' Dili said.

'Hi,' Rosie said.

'So,' Merle said. 'What's the story?'

Which story was she referring to? To Simon in the first instance, maybe. In any case that was the story Rosie told Merle, exactly as it had happened, how he'd rung the morning her photo had been in the paper, how he was crumpled in a clinic, aggrieved and guilty in equal parts. And why should he be aggrieved, Merle wanted to know? So Rosie explained. Without speaking for him, or against him, she gave an account, quite factual and in a calm voice, of the story Simon had told to me, and I had told to her.

Afterwards she said that it just happened, it wasn't because of her position against secrets, and in any case she wasn't sure that she still held it; at that moment, in the stillness of the gallery, it came naturally to her. If betrayal was involved, it would have been a greater betrayal to have lied to Merle, to have dissembled; it would, she said, have made her a child, and anyway children shouldn't be lied to either. Perhaps, at twenty, she is still near to childhood, sensitive to the ploys of adults, and not yet old enough to have fallen prey to them.

'I did worry about Dili,' she said. 'But I asked Merle and she said, *It's okay, there've been enough secrets, I wouldn't have brought her if I hadn't told her.* So I pressed on, and Dili looked okay. All she said was that she didn't like the look of the figure, it spooked her, and she didn't want Merle to take it back. *It shouldn't even be here,* she said. She's a cool kid.'

I think Brian must have hinted to Merle about the debts, because she took calmly information I would have expected to undo her. She was even calm when Rosie gave her news of the letters.

'Of course,' Merle said, thumping the heel of her hand against her forehead, as I had done at the clinic. 'How stupid of me. It had to be Simon, he was the first one at the house. The bastard. He came down that night, rang the funeral people, did all that stuff, and drove back to Sydney before Una turned up in the morning. There wouldn't have been anyone else in the house. No wonder he looked creepier than usual at the funeral.

'So where are the letters now, do you know?'

'Here,' Rosie said. 'In the desk.' She took them out. 'I warn you,' she said, 'they're pretty upsetting, even for a bystander like me.'

'Some bystander,' Merle said. 'You know more than I do.'

'But I don't care,' Rosie said. 'At least not in the way you do. I just think what a great novel they'd make.'

'Don't you dare,' Merle said.

'Shall I read them to you?' Rosie said.

'Thanks.' And then to Dili: 'Do you want to hear them, or shall I read them quietly?'

'Read them quietly,' Dili said. 'That's how you're supposed to read letters.'

Merle sat herself at the desk which had once been Isobel's in the gallery to which the letters were addressed. She switched on the desk lamp, fished in her bag for her specs – she had reached the age that blurs the print – and while Rosie closed up and took Dili down the street for an ice-cream, this is what she read: the letters from the man who some, dignifying the act of ejaculation, would call her father, to the woman who received that dollop of sperm and brought Merle to life in her dream-filled womb.

I won't reproduce them all, they do not make pleasant reading. The earliest date from the mid-fifties when, contrary to Isobel's avowal, Claude arranged to meet her in Rabaul, where she was to be on the legitimate business of collecting, and travel on together to the Solomon Islands. It was not a successful trip as far as one can tell from his slightly scratchy letter afterwards. *No,* he wrote, *you can't come to Devon. Don't be ridiculous. I'll try to get up to London.*

The letters I offer to you here begin much later, just as Merle left Devon, and continue for a year, during which time Isobel ran up the debts that Simon would bail her out of a few years later when he bought the gallery, wrecking in the process his marriage to Merle. As if to compensate herself for this impending loss, Isobel pressed Claude to tell her the secret she sensed behind the story of Lake Sentani. Not that she suspected anything in particular; it was more that she credited Claude with knowing the *essence* of the story, as it were, some essential grain that she needed – as if the writing of the book lay not with herself, but with Claude and the figure from the lake. And her need, of course, was great. She might lose her lover, her gallery, even her daughter, but there was glory to be gained in the black and white of print, by conjuring a fortress enchanted against disappointment: a grand justification for a life lived in dream.

NORTH MOLTON. JUNE 22, 1975

Dear Isobel,
I did give you the Sentani figure, in a manner of speaking of course I did, but can you not see the context? There was no knowing if Tom would look after

you, I had a responsibility, I'd asked Jessica for all the money I could, she was adamant. It was the only thing I had that could possibly offer you any security, and I admit that what it could offer then wasn't much. Can't you see it as security for us both, for us all. As things have turned out you and the child have been well cared for, and you have made a living from Oceania which I, after all, introduced you to. I don't think you can trade on that old lecture in your progress hall. I was the one who told you where to go, where to look. And gave your shop credibility with the Sentani figure. I would have left it at that if things had turned out better for me. But I have been hounded by the critics, and I've never had the prices I deserve and that Ben and Frances have always had. Our fates have proved very different from what we might have expected. So please, old girl, don't be difficult. I'm not asking for the Sentani figure back, just for a small loan to be advanced against it. There's a dear. Last year's £1500 was greatly appreciated.
Your Claude

NORTH MOLTON. JULY 10, 1975

Dear Isobel,
You're a sport. I knew you would be. You always were. I remember you in that hotel in Honiara, do you remember? I'm an old man now and I'm glad to have known the glorious flesh of Isobel. My love.

The money made all the difference. Merle seemed to

like my work. Not that it matters, not at all, what she thinks, but she does have a good eye. It is strange, a daughter after a life raising boys, but of course she is your daughter, not mine. You are a generous woman, and I am moved by your offer. £3000 will make all the difference.
Your loving Claude

NORTH MOLTON. SEPTEMBER 15, 1975

Dear Isobel,
Of course I'll help you with your researches, though frankly, I'm not sure that this book is such a good idea. I know people go on about that expedition, as if the Surrealists were great adventurers. But at the time no one took that much notice, and it was hardly exacting. The real expeditions were through the mountains like Karius and Champion. They crossed the mountains from the Fly to the Sepik for God's sake. In 1926. So don't make a deal of our efforts. There was a Dutch outpost on the lake, Viot never mentioned that. He liked the tag of adventurer but in reality he liked his comforts. If there weren't enough on the lake there were certainly plenty in Hollandia. He took whatever he needed with him. Don't you realise it was as much an attempt to live the life he felt constrained from in Europe. Paris was hedonistic, but not that hedonistic.

In the pages you sent me you make our venture sound romantic, and in your letter you say you wish

you'd been there. Let me tell you, dear girl, it was
damnably uncomfortable. Mosquitoes, snakes, all kinds
of skin infections. Horrible food and those sour-faced
Dutch, I've never liked that culture. And yes, it was
beautiful I suppose if you like that sort of thing. I
suppose with antipodean eyes you see it as more
beautiful than it is, that sort of exoticism attracts. Like
Africa. But I've lived in the most beautiful county in the
best of countries, I'm a European through and through,
I knew Paris as a boy and London as a man. How
could I see it as romantic? The houses hung out over the
lake, and the latrines emptied into it. Pigs rooted around
in the mud and eels came out of it. It was rather vile. I
am becoming quite cross writing about it.

Take care with this venture, dear girl, the public
gaze is not kind and I wouldn't wish to see you
disappointed. I do care for you, you know.
Claude

NORTH MOLTON. NOVEMBER 22, 1975

Dear Isobel,
A note in haste. Glad to hear the child is to marry.
She needs stability. You must be proud.

Your gift is greatly appreciated, and your
confidence in me. £1500 is generous, but you know
what these exhibitions are. Does Merle mention it?
Sweet girl.
Claude

NORTH MOLTON. DECEMBER 13, 1975

Dear Isobel,
Of course I'm proud. Don't be difficult, it's not as if
she's marrying a fortune or anything. I explained, or
if I did not, let me now. I was writing in great haste
because I was taking some canvases up to London the
next day to see that dealer Ben used to use, I told you.
I used a short hand, I thought you knew me well
enough to understand that. You've always said there is
an ease between us, and you know how much I value
it. So, my sweet, don't be difficult, you're not married
to me. As to the money, it was generous, and it's not a
lot more than I could do with. I wouldn't ask if the
gallery wasn't doing so well. From what you tell me,
it'd only be one sale, two at the most. You always said
your role was to support the creative mind, not
compete with it. You've still got the Sentani figure
remember. You're quite secure.
Your admiring Claude
P.S. Christmas tidings.

NORTH MOLTON. JANUARY 6TH, 1976

Dear Isobel,
I thought you had that husband of yours as wound
around your little finger as you have me. Surely you
can get him off the trail. I thought you said you had
separate accounts. Not much sense in that if you have
the same accountant. Just conceal a sale. You're not

being your usual sweet-natured self. Is it the change?
I'm trying to think how old you'd be.
As always, Claude

NORTH MOLTON. FEBRUARY 3, 1976

Dear Isobel,
Years ago. Surely not. You were such a young and
lovely creature last time I saw you. And so receptive.
You made a man feel like a king, you were so sure
there was nothing you wouldn't do for me. The foolish
things girls say when they're in love. Have you
foresaken me? You must understand the importance of
this exhibition to me. I can't let it be known that I've
financed it. But if at last my work takes off, then I'll
repay it all, dear girl, and never mention the Sentani
figure again. Your offer is generous, and I wouldn't
ask if it didn't matter. This way we both get our dues.
As you suggest, £5000 should see me through.
Claude

NORTH MOLTON. 6 APRIL, 1976

Dear Isobel,
The crits were disappointing. But if one considers the
history of great artists damned by the press, even
though I am no longer a young man, one could say
the company I keep is good. No return on your money
I'm afraid, old girl. Not at this stage. Just as well
Tom's such a brick. Now there's an expression to take

me right back. To Pimlico. Do you remember Pimlico?
Of course you do, sweet Isobel. Did Merle ask, did she
say anything? Perhaps you could soften the blow a bit,
I don't like her to think her old father is a failure,
she's too young to understand the vagaries of artistic
fortune. Is she happy with her Simon?

My next letter, I swear, will be about Sentani. But
right now I have comrades to meet.
Claude

NORTH MOLTON. JUNE 2, 1976

Dear Isobel,
You always were a severe task mistress. I'm sure I've
written since Easter. But all right, the woman must
always be satisfied. I know you have always cared for
me, and I am touched by what you say. But is love
the right word? I don't think I've experienced the sort
of thing you describe. Maybe when I was younger.
But I don't put myself in that position. I do not like
to be vulnerable. Not that that's quite the word I'd
use, but you know what I mean, and it'd be better if
you were a little more the same. You are very
emotional, I know you women often are, but Jessica
doesn't let herself say that sort of thing. She's very
dignified. It's because she's English and we are
brought up to appreciate a certain control. So buck
up, dear girl, and if the book is so much part of our
story – which of course I value, you have been a

solace on so many occasions – then perhaps it would
be best to reconsider it.

So let's talk about Sentani. You're right when you
say I resist it, for the bald truth is that things
happened there of which neither Viot nor I have ever
spoken. Maybe if I tell you, you will understand why
I'd prefer you not to go on with this book. To do so
would be a breach of faith and if you care for me as
much as you say, I know you would not wish to do
that. Not that it's so very shameful. In those days it
wouldn't have mattered at all, merely a youthful
prank, but the world is changing and people take
things seriously these days which they didn't at all
before. We don't want to go stirring things up. It was
a long time ago, what happened, but with all this
black rights business going on in America, that sort of
attitude is bound to spill over in time. I believe they
have their own university in Papua, though mercifully
Sentani is under Indonesian control so that's some
protection. Not that I need protection. Not at all. Of
course not. But there are certain discretions.

There was an incident, nothing worth mentioning,
the Dutch arrived, we were escorted out, and in the
melee – well, some of the figures we took weren't from
the lake. It was a prank really, nothing more sinister
than that, but we told the tale, you know how it is
when you're young, just a bit of exaggeration here,
another bit there, and well, not everything we said
came from the lake actually did. Some of the pieces

weren't as old. Some weren't even from Sentani at all.
So one doesn't want to put them up for too much
scrutiny, wouldn't you agree?
Claude Ferraris

NORTH MOLTON. JULY 13, 1976

Dear Isobel,
I'm deeply touched and a little humbled by your
confidence in me, and if I thought you really had an
artistic temperament I wouldn't let you bow to mine. I
have given this considered thought, and I want you to
know how much I value your lively mind. Indeed it is
what I have always responded to in you. But you
yourself would agree that first and foremost you are a
mother, and you've done well with your gallery. Is a
book necessary to your happiness? I ask myself this
question, and consider the fortunes of Merle, and I
am satisfied that I am right. For us men there is a
different urge, and we do not live by love as you do. It
is not to say we do not love, and in my way I have,
but we need to express ourselves in the world, the man
has always done that, and it is for you that we do it.
So I am touched that my success means so much to
you, and I am pained that I cannot offer more. I felt
sure that this time something would have been
recognised, and there has been the occasional
encouraging sale. Reason to let me believe.

Looking back I can see the exhibition was badly

timed. I am not a bitter man, but the fates have been cruel. I have been born into a century that cannot recognise its own. So do not chivvy Merle to leave the orchestra. It is better that she finds happiness with Simon, for that is where she will be best served, and best able to accept her limitations. Striving for more could be unnatural in her, and will lead to great disappointment. It is not to be despised, a career in an orchestra. Did she ask about the exhibition? Be tactful in your replies. Dear girl,
Claude

NORTH MOLTON. AUGUST 17, 1976.

Dear Isobel,
You're quite right, I got off the track of Sentani and didn't give you the details. If I give them to you now, it is in the strictest confidence that you will not let them go any further. Maybe it'd be best to destroy this letter. In fact destroy them all. Letters are not meant for posterity unless posterity invites the query. Which for us I fear it will not. And do we want Merle to know how it has been for us? I am franker with you than any other, and wouldn't want her to see me as the failure it seems I have to be. Not of course that I would consider myself in such a way, not at all, but she is young and it is possible that she would.

What Viot never wrote about, and I never spoke of – it was a kind of pact – was the cargo cult that had been simmering away in that part of New Guinea for several years. Quite a bit of the stuff in the lake hadn't been thrown in by the missionaries but had gone in much more recently. There was a belief that if the sacrilegious offerings to their gods were thrown away, if they were repudiated, then the god of the white man would reward their tribes with cargo. People came out of the hills from miles around to throw away their graven images. We didn't know any of this when we set off, or even when we arrived, why would we, though of course the Dutch administration should have warned us.

So when we arrived at the lake, two white men with a string of bearers bearing patrol boxes full of paraffin lamps and tins of food and blankets and axes and coins, some of the people – they weren't very sophisticated – thought we were there as a reward for their sacrifice. The old men wanted the artefacts back, but the younger men were afraid it'd break the charm. And then, when we paid for the figures, there were many claims on the money; there was a lot of bad feeling, especially when the old men realised we were taking the pick from the lake with us. We didn't speak the language, we had to rely on interpreters, it was very difficult, and we tried giving mirrors and axe heads, that sort of thing, but somehow it all went wrong.

And then there was an incident with one of the boys Viot had brought in from Hollandia. He was *diving, and he was a coastal boy and swam well, but he got snagged on something, and when he came up he was streaming water, they thought he was dead, which he wasn't, but he got some kind of lung problem, and there was more bad feeling – that there was sorcery, that it was because Viot flaunted his interest in him, you know, all that – and in the end a huge row broke out, there were people with spears whooping down the hillside, brawls. It looked like murder, or warfare, or a riot, or something.*

The Dutch came and in the scrum we were sheltered in a patrol shed on the edge of the village. In there they'd stored a lot of old art, confiscated in the cargo cult business, bits and pieces they'd picked up from all over, from along the coast as far as Humboldt Bay. Some of it was only half carved, commissioned I think, and then jettisoned. In amongst it all was the figure, our figure, and as a prank I said Let's take it. And these too, *Viot said, picking through the masks, canoe prows, gongs and bowls. A whole lot of stuff. Tapa cloth. It was easy. There was so much movement, we could pack them in with the things from the lake, no one was any the wiser, and it increased our haul. We needed all we could manage as we obviously weren't going to get any more out of the lake.*

At the time it felt like a prank. Now I can see it skews a lot about our knowledge of Oceania, mixing up styles. To make it worse we had the figure doctored up a bit in Hollandia. A Chinese carver touched up

*the faces for us, they'd been a kind of blank, with only
a gesture of expression. I'm not sure if it was
intentional, a god or spirit figure, or if it was
incomplete. And we soaked it in water. I didn't think
when I gave it to you that Australia would become a
centre for Oceanic research, let alone that New Guinea
would do its own.*

*Not that it was such a bad thing for us to have
done, and if my own art was better understood, if I
had the clout of someone like Ben, then I could admit
it, make it a story, entice people with my eccentricities,
a colourful youth and so on. As it is, it will confirm a
view of me as lesser. And we know that is not true,
and because I know your belief in me is true and real,
I can admit this to you, which I would to no one else.
Dear Isobel, to think what our lives might have been.
CF*

P.S. There's no need to trouble Merle with any of this.

'I told Dili what's in them,' Rosie said when they
came back, clattering open the door and breaking
the spell in which Merle sat, the silence of the
gallery. 'She asked. I told her. And she's figured
out the answer.'

'The answer to what?' Merle said.

'The answer to the question of who should
have the Sentani figure,' Rosie said.

'Oh?' Merle said.

'Why can't we just give it back?' Dili said.

'Yes, see. Lake Sentani should have it back,' Rosie said. 'It's theirs.'

'And who do you propose to give it to exactly?' Merle asked.

'To the Free Papuans,' Rosie said.

'They're fighting a jungle war,' Merle said.

'So,' Rosie said. 'They'll win it one day. Or they could sell it and use the cash.'

'Come on,' Merle said. 'It's a fake.'

'That might make it more valuable,' Rosie said.

'I doubt it,' Merle said.

'We're serious.' The girls looked serious. Solemn. Merle reached out an arm, but Dili did not accept the invitation.

'Look,' Merle said. 'It's a wonderful idea, it'd be neat, and we'd all feel good about it, but there's a war going on, no one other than us is going to be sentimental about it. Some middle-man will make a packet – and they still won't win the war, they're fighting Indonesia for goodness sake. Or else it'll end up in a back room of some Javanese museum. Is that what you want?'

'We could do better than that,' Rosie said. 'We could try some embassies.'

'You're just kids,' Merle said. 'They'd make mince meat of you.'

'That's not fair,' Rosie said. 'Why don't you let us try, and see?'

'No,' Merle said. 'This is a ridiculous conversation. Still, it's stopping me slitting my wrists.'

Dili looked at her.

'Joke,' she said. 'A joke. When I think how horrible I was to her. All those years. You don't understand until you have a child yourself. Are you going to have them?' she said to Rosie.

'Children? No, not if I can help it.'

'Helping it's not the problem,' Merle said. 'You'll learn. Come on Dili, let's go back to the hotel. I told Charlie we'd be back by four.'

'But what are we going to do with the figure?' Dili said. 'It's hurt people here.'

'It hasn't done anything,' Merle said, turning the desk lamp to shine on it. 'It's just an old lump of wood. Look.' She ran her finger across the figure as if she were reading braille, running her fingers across the ridge and dip, the rise and fall of the grain. Then she snapped off the light, put the letters in her bag and opened the door. 'Talking of letters,' she said, 'is your aunt still turning other people's letters into magazine stories?' She laughed. It wasn't really a question. Then: 'Are you coming to any of the concerts?' she asked. 'Is she?'

'The last one,' Rosie said. 'We've got tickets. She asked Simon, but that stupid ponce of a doctor up there says he shouldn't go.'

'Why not?'

'Because you stress him out, I suppose,' Rosie said.

'Cowering in a clinic's not going to help,' Merle said.

'Brian thinks he should do meditation.'

'Useless for someone like Simon,' Merle said. 'Not a hope.'

'Better than prozac,' Rosie said. 'Or gin.'

'I don't know,' Merle said. She leant forward and touched Rosie's cheek, just the lightest brush with her fingers. And she smiled. 'It's so simple really,' she said. 'Isn't it.'

Meaning? Meaning what, I asked when I interrogated Rosie at home after this extraordinary meeting. What's simple? 'Just saying it, I suppose,' Rosie said. 'Having the idea. Doing it's what counts. Living, I think she meant. Sort of.' She poured herself a whisky and drank it down in a single gulp like a gangster in a movie. 'I'm going for a swim,' she said. 'Then I'm going out. You'd better ring Simon.'

The house, when she closed the door, seemed terribly quiet, a little cold. I didn't ring Simon. I did later, but not then. I didn't have the energy for Simon and his graceless determination to suffer. I needed to return to that private ground from which raw feeling can become reflection; that secret realm that belongs to each heart, and that our language once called sacred, a usage we have lost, leaving us with no word to describe an inner space sacred to us alone, without the consecration of church but with perhaps the blessing of a god. The ground that transforms reflection into understanding, and brings rest, a ground that paradoxically connects us back to a life steeped in the lives and loves and stories of others.

The question for me that afternoon was what obligation, what debt, do we have to the secrets of others. What does it mean to know someone's secret as I knew the Cullens'? Does it remain theirs and theirs alone? What happens when, by knowing it, the secret becomes mine?

It is in the nature of secrets that all that is allowed is a glimpse. *Getting to the bottom of it,* as they say, is usually impossible: a conceit, a literalism, a pompous hope. It is, after all, only in the face of God, *at the dreadful day of judgement,* if it comes, that *the secrets of all hearts shall be disclosed.* In the meantime, here in the mortal realm, the fact that we get a glimpse and no more, doesn't make the knowledge of a secret any less powerful in our hands. Even a fragment of a secret can be used to tell a story, to change a story, to alter the course by which someone else lives.

Thinking all this, I took the judgement mask from the nail beside my desk and held it level with my face. I wanted an answer. I wanted to lift the mask and see the truth beneath it. I wanted moral certainty, justification, the impossible disclosure. As a girl I'd wanted the mask to protect me against the confusions of an infidelity, as if there was a way of sidestepping consequence. Now, as a woman, I wanted its protection against a much greater treachery.

Impervious, the mask rested in my hands, a carved hunk of painted wood. There was no answer there. Beauty, ambiguity, risk – but no certainty. And precious little protection.

Secrets, as Rosie has been known to say, *they cause so much trouble.* It's a word that seems to carry a certain negative connotation. To call something private gives it an aura of respectability, legitimacy, goodness, in a way that to say it is secret does not. Perhaps my husband was right with his sieving metaphor, and negativity is embedded in the word, as if in our language a secret is rather like a shit, discarded waste matter. One lets them out, or they leak out, or they are sniffed out. Or one holds them in. Little nuggets of waste matter which we use as counters in the complex game of life.

This image, of secrets as shit, assumes that it is the waste matter that is discarded through the holes. Yet if you think about the action of sifting grain, it is the edible seeds that pass through the hole, and the stones, the stalks, the husks, that are left behind in the sieve. It is an equivocal image if we are to try to pin a defecating function onto secrets. I have come to see that it is a fateful literal-mindedness to discard all secrets as necessarily impure. Of course dreadful things happen in their name; but then honesty – that other shining word – can have its punitive, destructive side. There are examples of it in this story, and in life one does not need to look far to see the havoc either can wreak: dangerous secrets or inappropriate confessions. The question is not one of separation – good from bad, secret from private – but of discrimination.

Even in a gesture as simple as sifting grain, we must be able to discriminate. In the complexities of moral life the discrimination required is much greater, and the art of life – and the art of art – is to know when to speak and when to remain silent, when – and what – to reveal, when – and what – to conceal. Secrets are not shit; or if they are there's gold in the waste matter that comes from the nourishment we put into our mouths. *Our compost,* the Zen teacher said that hot February night, *may become a rose.*

Such talk is cheap. It is not hard to find a position on a subject as complex as secrets when one speaks in generalities. Generalities are a fine thing, but when I sat alone with the judgement mask in my hand and listened to the silence left by my beloved niece, it was the particularity on which I reflected. Not the particularity of the figure, or of the letters, or even of Merle. In that silence I knew the nature of my own secret, as if everything that had happened pointed to this moment. With the clarity of an annunciation, I knew that I would tell the Cullens' story, breach the secret, breathe another life into that figure from Lake Sentani, and by doing so breathe life into myself, lift out of a rut small repetitions by which I had warded off loss and kept myself small: safe, skin deep, page long.

I rang Simon. He accepted the news of Merle and the letters as if it were all he could expect: another perfidy in the name of woman. When I told him what I was going to do, my own treacherous intentions, he sighed and made little moaning noises. All he said was that he wanted a guarantee that I'd never reveal that he'd been the source of anything. *Don't be ridiculous,* I said, and he became quite tearful, complaining that I always asked for too much, and that Merle hadn't invited him to the concert. *Just come,* I said. *It'll be fun.* Refusing anything less than an embossed invitation, railing against her, and me, and life itself, he said he wouldn't, he couldn't, and anyway why should he.

When I told Brian what I wanted to do, he

shrugged and said he supposed he should have predicted it and told me less. *Oh well,* he said, *at least you could make us New Zealanders or something. And give Merle a flute.*

'A flute,' Merle said. 'No. Absolutely not. If you're going to tell it, have the guts to tell it as it is. This business of fictionalising the truth is much worse. A cover for moral cowardice. Having it both ways. If you're going to betray us, let's be clear that that's what you're doing.'

We were at the party after the quartet's last concert. Rosie and I had gone with Dili. The two girls had united in their defeat and had spent the week at the movies. There had been a certain sulky tone, but by the night of the concert their spirits had recovered, and walking into the concert hall that night, I think it could be said that we were all buoyant in anticipation.

It was to be a concert of last quartets. Years later people would remember it. Beethoven. Janáček. Britten. Beethoven, the programme said, had written his epigrammatic last quartet, no. 16 in F, so prescient of the modern, at the end of 1826. It was performed in Vienna the following year, two weeks before his death on March 26th. Janáček wrote his second, and last, quartet in 1928 at the age of seventy-four, during the last year of his life. And Britten wrote his third in 1976, and died just before its first performance in December of that year.

It was, as you can imagine, quite an occasion – reviewers were sharpening their pencils – and with no other role to play, the three of us were dressed for it. Dili was wearing billowing overalls of silvery stripes that shimmered as she moved. 'I like Merle to know where I am,' she said, 'so I always shine at her concerts.' Rosie looked gorgeous in a little black number she'd bought on the promise of her earnings from Simon. I wore my usual black with an amber brooch that Isobel had given me. At the party afterwards, when I told her my intention, Merle unpinned it, lifted it to the light, said that she hadn't thought I had it in me, and pinned it back again.

We were outside, leaning on the parapet, looking down into dark oily water. She was glowing from the success of the concert, I could feel the heat of her in the cool air, as if her body was still working for that instrument of hers, conjuring the deep note that grounds the dash and display of the violins, the tetchy viola, with the power of memory, or of the heart, or of consciousness itself.

It was a tough concert – that was the word Merle used – tough in the sense of uncompromising, calling up eels in the audience, and glorious nereids, a concert from the deep. The three quartets they had played were held together less by biographical circumstances than by a form of knowledge, or wisdom, that comes late in a life, the sound of the heart approaching death when it is almost as if life has never been more exquisitely present. The fruit in the moment before it falls. A poised moment in which past and future are held in a tender elegaic.

Brian told me later that in the score of the Beethoven, at the top of the fourth movement, is a motto which reads in German *Must it be?* with an answering refrain *It must be*. Biographical literalism ascribes this to the pecuniary demands of Beethoven's landlady, but to us, of course, knowing what was to come, its resonance is entirely metaphysical. Not resignation, but an incantatory acceptance.

'I'm taking the figure back to New York,' Merle said. 'There you are, I've given you the end of the story. Unless you're tempted to let the girls do the right thing and send it back. That'd be a very Australian ending.'

We laughed, but there was no laughter in it. Just a noise that approximated laughter.

'It was a wonderful concert,' I said.

'Wonderful,' she said. 'What a word. It was a tough concert.'

'Yes,' I said, 'but don't refuse the compliment.'

'What matters aren't the compliments,' she said, 'but that now when I play I know it's me.'

'Do you still get angry?'

'Not much,' she said. 'But I do get sad.'

'I saw that,' I said. 'In the Janáček.'

'I should have thought of what it would mean,' she said, 'playing that in Sydney. Did you know it was written for a young woman who he was hopelessly in love with. She was married, you know, the usual thing. That's why he called the quartet *Intimate Letters*. He wanted more than anything to make glorious music out of great love, and he feared the banality of weak music in the name of great love. His feeling for Kamila, he said, was so strong that *the notes hide underneath it and flee.*'

'So hopeless love is only redeemed by great art?' I said. 'That'd leave most of us uncovered.'

'Oh, even weak love can make a difference,' she said. 'To the person who makes it, if not to anyone else.'

'Isobel,' I said.

'Of course,' she said.

'That book wouldn't have saved her.'

'It might have saved her from the fantasy, and if it'd done that, it could have redeemed Claude's cruelty.'

'Was it cruelty?' I said.

'You've read the letters,' she said.

'They're more ambiguous than cruel,' I said.

'It doesn't alter the fact that she sacrificed everything for a weak and debased love. Everything.'

'So why are you keeping the figure?' I said. 'You never liked it.'

'There's no why,' she said. 'An impulse. I suppose it has to do with Isobel. All those years I rejected her because I couldn't bear her pride, that thin skin over so much failure. I couldn't stand it. I suppose I thought I'd be the same. I'd like to have been able to be like Tom, but I knew I couldn't. It was Claude's genes I had, and it terrified me. I don't know. Anyway I like it better now it's a fake.'

'I don't suppose it cares if it's a fake or not,' I said. 'I mean it's only ever been itself. It's us who've loaded it up with stories and values.'

'It's a reminder,' she said, 'of some sort of fundamental reality. The energy of male and female, the energy of birth, the cycle that has produced us, and demands of us, and that is us. From the point of view of the figure it doesn't matter if there's success or failure, if we live this way or that. All that matters is that life continues.'

'A bleak view,' I said.

'Not necessarily,' she said. 'It was Tom's view.'

'His view was that we should live well,' I said. 'Not just continue on.'

'You talk soft,' she said, 'but you're like me, not like him.'

She turned towards me and put out her hand as if to shake mine, a strangely formal moment, and I found that I had no urge for more, for the gesture of a kissed cheek, a cautious hug, an ambivalent smile. Then she reached into her bag and took out a chunky bundle of letters I recognised at once. I thought she was handing them to me, and reached out to take them.

'I'm not giving you this story,' she said. 'If you want it, you must take it. I won't help.' And she swung back towards the water; pressing forward against the parapet rail she stretched out her arm and held the letters perilous above the dark lap of the waves.

'Don't,' I said, reaching out after her. Our fingers locked. I could feel her nails, blunt and certain, the rope of muscle, taut as a string. I could feel the strength of her. And the brittle strength of envelope and paper. It was then that she smiled, and in that smile I felt a strange surge of emotion, not the pang of so many years, but a kind of resignation. Or maybe exposure.

She let the letters fall into my hand.

'So,' she said, raising her hands in an ironic imitation of the bow Tom would have made, 'we'll see what you're made of.'

In response I put the letters in my pocket and bowed to her, all the way to the waist.

I watched as she walked back into the party. Through the great panes of glass I could see Rosie flirting with a man I didn't recognise. He had a cute little bunched ponytail. And I saw Dili nip her father's champagne. And Charlie Quatrain stretch out his arm, like a promise, to welcome Merle into the light. Behind me I could hear the lap of the waves against the steep side of the Opera House; in the distance the drone of ferries, a wire clanking, and the sharp whirr of water police skimming over the water.

Standing in the dark salty air, for a moment it was as if I existed only in a fragmented mosaic of other people's memories. And yet the ballast in my pocket kept my balance firm. I might be awash in memory, but I also knew as I watched the party going on inside, that how we remember is as much determined by the teller of the tale, who gives us the moment to be remembered, the view, the shape of a head, the possibility – the silent voyeur who all along has sucked on the image, creating life from the juice of secrets, the invisible teller of stories, betrayer of secrets.

Through the glass I watched the pairs swaying backwards and forwards towards each other, keeping their feet moving, longing for one sort of union, and dodging the manacles of another. Perhaps this story would have been different if the figure from the lake had been carved in such a way that the faces turned towards each other, and their feet were free. In the Britten quartet Merle had played that evening, the instruments had been paired; not in conflict, or a macabre dance of romance, but in dialogue, a rich, sometimes disturbing conversation which ends in a serenity paced by the cello, like a tolling bell, the pulse of inevitability.

I have always thought of this story as Merle's, that all of us have circulated around her, loved her, and in loving her been orchestrated by her, so that she is the one we will return to, at a certain corner, glancing at a shirt worn in a certain way, a heel turned just so, a bend in the road, a chord, a shine of polish on wood.

But you know, and I know, that Merle lives only in this story. She is ours.

AUTHOR'S NOTE

In writing this piece I am indebted to the following books: Suzanne Greub (editor), *Art of North West New Guinea* (New York, Rizzoli, 1992), in particular to the chapters by Philippe Peltier and Elizabeth Cowling; Nicholas Thomas, *Oceanic Art* (Thames & Hudson, 1995); Sissela Bok, *Secrets: Concealment and Revelation* (Oxford University Press, 1984); and Antoine Prost & Gérard Vincent (editors), *A History of Private Life: Vol V. Riddles of Identity in Modern Times* (Harvard University Press, 1991).

Acknowledgement is due to HarperCollins Publishers for permission to quote an extract from 'Five Bells' by Kenneth Slessor from his *Selected Poems*.

I would like to thank Judith Lukin-Amundsen for her good editing. Also, Jeremy Steele for his musical advice, Maisie Drysdale for checking domestic details of an era I know only from books, and Hilary McPhee, the best of readers.

I would also like to make it clear that it is in the nature of secrets that real ones cannot be told. At any rate not publicly like this. Although my characters rub along beside names you will recognise – Jacques Viot, for instance, or Russell Drysdale – the stories they tell are entirely fictional. However, when it comes to these historical bit-parts, I have to the best of my ability kept within an accurate chronology and hope that the surrounding liberties I have taken are plausible. The Surrealist Jacques Viot did visit Lake Sentani in 1929, but the nefarious inclusion of Claude Ferraris in his party is a figment of my imagination. As far as I know, none of the figures that Viot rescued from the lake were fakes; certainly none that are now to be found in our galleries. Russell Drysdale, of course, showed with the Macquarie Galleries, not with Cullen's, which he could hardly have done as it did not exist. As to myself, you will not find my name on the staff of any magazines, and I have never had the eyes for making models of anything, although I have travelled (briefly) in the Sepik (unaccompanied by anyone even faintly resembling Simon) and I have read the letters Marjorie Barnard wrote to Jean Devanny. 'I' is a slippery creature, much given to ambiguity and prone to an almost chronic state of contingency. This too is in the nature of secrets, and increasingly I find that it suits me well.

AMANDA LOHREY

'The clear voice suddenly singing'

For Marnie Rogers

PART 1
SACRÉ ÉGOÏSME

1

I am standing next to Bridie and she is singing too loudly. We are standing in a circle of twenty or so women in the Trinity Church Hall on top of Trinity Hill in Hobart. The hall is old and draughty and some of us are wearing coats. Outside is the city's red-light district, decaying terraces with iron grilles. Across the road is a small park on the steep side of the hill, facing the mountain. Once the Trinity Church graveyard, the park is now a well-known haunt for drug dealing: syringes lie under the park benches; shadowy figures hover in the side alley beneath the autumnal sycamores. And we're inside the

Trinity Hall singing, with the door wide open to the cold night.

> *Soon . . .*
> *Soon . . . death comes creepin in my room*
> *Soon . . .*
> *Soon . . . death comes creepin in my room*
> *Hush . . .*
> *Hush . . . somebody's callin my name*

At least, some of the time we sing. For much of the time, however, we vocalise. This means we stand in a circle and improvise on a note, pitching our voices to the centre of the circle into a column of sound. Is this sound column purely metaphorical? It depends on where you're standing. If you are at the centre of the circle with your eyes shut you feel the sound vibrating across your shoulders and chest, the base of your neck begins to tingle and you begin to sway a little, forward and back . . . and you become aware of someone quietly moving in behind you, in case you fall.

But tonight I'm not in the middle, tonight I'm on the rim of the circle and I'm standing next to Bridie and she is singing too loud, that is, her strong, pure soprano voice is soaring above my hoarse, insipid contralto. She is purposeful and at ease; she is a soprano and she knows it. As usual, I am confused. I have two voices and I don't know which one to sing with. Why can't I just open my mouth and let my voice fall out? Like Bridie. Instead, I have to think about it. There is my chest or throat voice that is like my talking voice; deep and conversational with a slightly abrasive edge and good volume. But the problem with this voice is that after a while I get a sore throat. I rely too much on the muscles of the neck, forget to breathe in the right places, close off the base of the throat, and suffer. Then I switch to my head voice, my higher and lighter and more effortless voice, but with no top notes. Above a certain range the voice disappears, cuts out altogether or gives a light, high-pitched squeak. My resonating chambers in 'the mask' (nose, forehead, sinuses) fail me. And I don't like the sound of myself. This is a prim little folk-singing voice; plaintive. I sound like a timid female. I like my resonant chest and throat voice, the strong one, but that's the voice that tires. Head or chest? . . . throat or mask . . .?

Bridie is soaring. She is up there in the rafters, she is wafting across to the furthest corners of the hall, past the basketball hoops and above the chequered stage curtain. Next Tuesday evening I will stand next to someone else, someone who is . . . well, *less of a natural.* No one who knew me would ever accuse me of being natural. If I were a *natural* would I sit behind a computer day after day shuffling words around on the page, devising the various masks of fiction to hide behind? No, I wouldn't. And I surprise myself by even being here. I have been coming to this group for nine weeks and for the first three sessions I hated it. Now I am becoming addicted. But I don't know why I'm addicted, or what it is that I'm addicted to.

When the session is over we troop out into the frosty night air and I wait for Beatrice to unlock her car and give me a lift home. Driving down the precipitous Glebe hill, past the many mansions of Victorian gothic, we begin to talk about why it is that we come, especially on bitter nights like this, and I recall an encounter in midair over the Pacific.

2 *The secret self*

It is August 1986 and I am flying to the USA to spend a year in Berkeley. My husband is already there, looking for a house. I and my two-year-old daughter are on our way. In the long dim cocoon that is the cabin of a 747 cruising at night, I croon some lullabies to my daughter, at that moment stretched out across two seats, her head in my lap. Beside me, a handsome middle-aged man dozes fitfully. As the last of my muted lullabies trails off he opens one eye and says: 'Do you do requests?'

'Not here,' I murmur.

'In that case, I'll just have to count more sheep.' Before long, he too appears to be asleep, his head lolling to one side, his dark beard grazing my shoulder.

In the morning we exchange some pleasantries over our plastic breakfast trays. He tells me his name is Aaron and he is a professor of psychology at Stanford University where he is doing research into the nature of the work people do and how it correlates with their sense of self. What were their ambitions when they were sixteen? Are they doing at forty what they'd planned or hoped to do in their youth? And what do they see themselves doing in their ideal or fantasy life? Then he tells me the surprise of his findings so far. 'Everybody wants to be a singer,' he says. 'Not a baseball player, not even a movie actor, but a singer. On stage at The Met, headlining at Vegas – if the genie with the lamp appeared tomorrow, that's what they'd ask for.'

Somehow this doesn't surprise me, although I can't say why. Had he, I ask, arrived at an explanation?

No, he says, he and his team haven't got to the follow-up, but he is looking forward to interviewing a sample of respondents to his survey and 'coming up with some answers'.

He is of course exaggerating, as one does to frame a conversation point. What he has found is not that *everyone* wants to be a singer but that a surprisingly high number of respondents and interviewees have given this as their secret ambition in life. And why, he asks, do I think this might be?

I wonder if it isn't obvious? Doesn't everyone want to be noticed, and admired?

Yes, he says, but why singing? There are other ways of seeking the limelight.

3

I first fell in love with unaccompanied singing in the pubs of Norfolk and East Anglia. It was the seventies, and I was studying at Cambridge and living in a small village called Waterbeach in which there was no water and no beach because Cromwell had long ago drained the fens. On Saturday nights my boyfriend and I would often drive out into those mysterious fenlands with their endless dark horizon, and spend the evening in one of the dour village pubs. I was intrigued by their character, the way in which the public bar was like an extension of someone's living-room and the patrons on a Saturday night ranged from small children with dummies in their mouths to old men who could barely stagger in on a stick. And quite often on these evenings, several among the drinkers would sing, solo and unaccompanied. 'C'mon, Bert. Give us a chorus of "Black Velvet Band".' Bert was quite likely in his seventies, short and wiry and wearing a cloth cap, and if he were in the mood he'd rise from his table, wait a moment for a respectful silence to fall and give us the full version in a quavering voice that was quite hypnotic in its effect. Why I became addicted to these turns I can't say. As I got to know the various pubs I became aware of how the singing for the night would reflect the mood of the community. Feuds, ill-fortune, an impending election, anything could and did influence the tenor of the evening; who sang what, who stolidly refused to oblige; who turned her back on the singer of the moment.

I was reminded of this many years later when I went to see Terence Davies' lyrical cinematic portrait of working-class community, *Distant Voices, Still Lives.* Some of the most luminous scenes in this movie take place in the local pub where Davies lovingly captures the importance of community singing in the life of his family. Singing in the pub is one of the few times the family is free of physical and emotional violence. This is its moment of peace, of expressing unconditional love, of being free from resentment and recrimination, from the burdens of history or anxieties about the future; of being, simply, and for the moment, free. It resonated with times in my own childhood when some tribal event – an anniversary, a wedding reception – would be transported on to another plane by an outbreak of song. I remember still how the faces of the adults would suddenly soften; the expression in their eyes change.

Bert was a different thing altogether. To strangers like us he was the resonance of the landscape itself. Though I have several photographs taken at that time, none can evoke the quality of the fens like the aural memory of Bert's voice and the merest phrase from his song, its strange link to my own origins . . . *'It's over the dark and blue ocean/Far away to Van Diemen's Land'*. A callow twenty-year-old, I became aware for the first time how much the singer reveals of himself, how undefended an act of self singing can be; how impossible it is to fake almost anything. Nothing to hide behind, not even an old piano. This is what gives the amateur his grip on my attention; the sense of him walking a tightrope, that anything could happen. Even a mediocre professional has the assured mask of training and 'technique'. In professionals, in all trained singers, the voice is more separated out from the person, almost an entity in itself, something you can insure in its own right. Advanced technique can mask rather than reveal the self. When an amateur sings, he seems to offer up his whole body; just the pattern of his breathing can tell you so much; where he looks, what he does with his hands.

4

Another dark space. This time I'm sitting in Hobart's old Theatre Royal, with velvet seats and ornate boxes and portraits of Handel, Bach and Mozart on the roof framing an extravagant chandelier. It's the annual eisteddfod and I've come to watch someone I know sing. That someone is a friend whom I'll call Caroline, now warming up in a backstage dressing-room before coming on to perform two songs from the Schumann song cycle, *Frauenliebe und-leben* – 'A Woman's Love and Life'.

I've known Caroline since the day she was born. Once a pretty, bright-eyed child with flaming red hair, in adolescence she had become stooped and round-shouldered, hunched almost, and some muffling blanket of self-consciousness had descended on her. Often praised as a 'responsible' girl she seemed, as she grew older, to carry the weight of the world on her shoulders. In her late twenties she was treated on and off for depression and I knew her at one stage to have been on Prozac. At the age of thirty-two, she and her husband divorced and she was awarded sole custody of her two small boys. On her thirty-third birthday, out of the blue, her mother suggested she take singing lessons.

I had recently returned to Hobart to live and immediately observed a change in her: she stood up straight and the fire had come back into her eyes. Often over coffee she would talk about her singing class and her teacher, a woman called Helen to whom she told everything about herself.

'When I sing it makes me feel . . . relaxed. And it makes me feel important. It's partly to do with the breathing, I think. At the end of a lesson I feel high and clear and calm. Not like I used to feel. I used to feel stuck. Now I feel I've broken through.'

Broken through to what?

'It's hard to describe. I feel like I'm in another space.'

When she was at school, she said, she was told not to sing in the choir, just to stand and mouth the words because her voice wasn't good enough and it 'spoiled the sound'. The rebuff stayed with her; she felt as if her voice had been confiscated, like a piece of flamboyant jewellery that violated the uniform code. For the rest of her schooldays she didn't even sing in the shower.

'I went along with something I should have rebelled against. I should either have insisted on singing out in the choir or refused to participate at all. Instead of that I stood in the back row and mouthed the words, every year until I left school. Can you believe that?'

Yes, I could believe it. From other stories I had been told, it wasn't all that uncommon an experience. In fact I've heard this story, or some version of it so many times over the years that I've come to think of it almost as a kind of urban myth, internalised. And one of the most memorable accounts comes from, of all people, Tito Gobbi, who recalls the following episode in his autobiography, *My Life* (1979). 'At one of our rehearsals (for an end-of-term performance) our teacher, Maestro Bevilacqua, started going round the class muttering to himself. Finally he stopped in front of me and exclaimed: "You're the culprit! You're shouting like a mad dog – it's terrible. You keep silent. But as we don't want (anyone) to know you are not singing, simply open and shut your mouth and pretend to sing." '

In the year following her first lesson, said Caroline, it began to feel as if she were undergoing a transformation. She had gone along to her first appointment with some nervousness, expecting to be asked to sing. Instead, her singing teacher asked her to move around the room, making sounds.

What sort of sounds?

'Any sounds I liked. Oooohhh and aaaahhh, mostly.' After a few minutes of a kind of crooning, she started to cry. 'I felt as if my jaw was locked, and that it had been locked for years. And then I felt it open. It was a weird sensation.

'I had, then, what we, Helen and I, call my "little girl voice". You know, that high piping voice. You know how when you're nervous your voice goes up, like this. Well, mine was up all the time. I was too scared to let the little girl voice go. But somehow, through doing all the exercises, and the scales, and learning to stand differently, hold my head differently, breathe differently . . . Helen used to tell me things, about technique and so on, and after a while I realised that what she was really telling me was that it was okay to grow up. And from that moment on, my voice began to change, it got a deeper tone. And it got louder. Much louder. Now my voice just seems to get bigger and bigger.' She laughed, half apologetically. 'Some days it's so big it scares me.'

And I'm thinking: how come my voice isn't big enough to scare me? What am I missing?

Listening to Caroline I think I recognise something both remote and yet familiar, some faint echo of the ineffable; something, maybe, to do with awe. *Awe.* It's an old-fashioned word, a biblical word; a mixture of fear and reverence, a sense of benign mystery, a glimpse of the terror of the sublime. On a more prosaic level, I also recognise something else, something my own daughter is alerting me to – the difficulty of making the transition from girlhood to womanhood. This is an experience that can take you two ways; either the dissenting path or the compliant one. Much of the literature about adolescence focuses on the 'difficult' girl, the rebellious one who gets into sex and drugs, precipitates an emotional storm in the house and clears out at the age of fifteen. But then there are those other girls. In the presence of parents, in deference to their love and their idealisation of childhood – or sometimes, even, in sublimated recoil from maternal envy – these daughters are inhibited. Their secret selves have been camouflaged (stooping shoulders, piping voices) for so long that they feel self-conscious – foolish and absurd even – when they perform. For what is performance but a sudden flourishing of the bold and ambitious self; the hungry ego; a ruthless eros. This, I think, explains the phenomenon of why, contrary to the sentimental view, many young performers are more confident performing when their parents are *not* there. And yet, in order to make the most of their talent, they need some nurturing figure; if not the parent, then someone else.

For Caroline, that someone else appeared to be her singing teacher, Helen, a woman whom she frequently cited in conversation, chapter and verse – 'Helen says . . . Helen suggested' – and who seemed to figure in her landscape not so much as a second mother but as a first muse. I told her this.

'What does the muse do again? Remind me.'

'Opens the throat and enables you to speak. It's a Greek myth. The gods created the world and then found they had no one to sing its – or their – praises, so they created the Muse. The Greeks believed the existence of things was not complete unless there was a voice to express it.'

'I thought only poets had a muse.'

'Anyone can have one.'

It was somewhere around the time of this exchange that I told Caroline that I thought I would like to write something about why people sing. It wasn't only her own enthusiasm that had aroused my interest and she was not the first of my friends and acquaintances to take up singing. I knew a number of people in Sydney who, since the late eighties, had joined a cappella groups or community choirs and some who had arranged to take private lessons, not with any view to pursuing a career but simply for the sake of it. Everyone seemed to know someone who was 'into it' and inevitably the boom in new-wave singing groups had begun to attract the attention of the media. Clearly something was afoot in the *Zeitgeist*, something Stephen Schafer, Musical Director of the Sydney Gay and Lesbian Choir describes as 'a new renaissance, a new generation of singers'. I had just completed a novel which examined some of the more idiosyncratic ways in which troubled individuals go about getting themselves into a state of grace and it now occurred to me that singing might be one of them. I rang Helen, Caroline's singing teacher. Could we meet, and could I put to her the simplest of questions (Aaron's question on the plane to Berkeley): Why do people sing?

5

Helen Todd's studio is a pale blue room at the back of an historic sandstone cottage on the northern edge of the city. On entering, the first thing I notice is an enormous Japanese fan over the empty fireplace, and nearby, a Korg keyboard on a black iron stand. Against one wall is a large desk with many books and papers and a ceramic oil-burner that gives off a hazy scent of cedar wood. Next to the desk is a huge mirror that hangs from floor to ceiling. In the early lessons, Caroline told me, the mirror is disconcerting. To see all of yourself looking back at you in a strange room can be very confronting.

Helen is seated at her desk. She is a woman in her forties, slim with blonde hair to just below her shoulders. Perhaps because I know her to have trained as an opera singer I am struck by her resemblance to a more svelte and romantic version of a Wagnerian heroine. During our conversation she will sing to me in order to demonstrate a point and in a few days' time I will hear her sing in recital. She has a strong soprano voice with warm, dark tones, and a sexual charisma that is attractive to both men and women.

At this, our first meeting, I begin by reciting Aaron's research findings. I tell her that when I ask people like Caroline why they sing they find it difficult to give me an answer. Helen frowns, politely.

'I suppose they would find it difficult to answer that,' she says. 'You might as well ask them why they breathe.'

Why then, I ask, did she sing?

'When I was a child, if I didn't sing I'd feel desperate. I just had to do it. But each person will give you a different answer. Perhaps you need to ask more people.'

'Supposing,' I say, 'I were to offer myself as a student. What then? How should I go about preparing my audition?'

'You wouldn't,' she says, with quiet emphasis. 'I don't audition.'

'No?'

'No. If you can talk you can sing. That's the point I start from. It's the *desire* to sing that matters, at least at the beginning.'

Well, then, how would she describe her method?

'I don't have a strict method. My method is constantly changing, but the essence of it is the Italian method, *bel canto*, beautiful sound. I do use some of the Melba method – exercises and vocalises – but her great words of wisdom are in her simple advice.' She takes up a book from her desk. 'See, here. Here on page one, right at the top: *In order to sing well it is necessary to sing easily. Melba's first law, if you like. But how many students are prepared to accept that statement? Very few. They smile and say, it may be easy for you but it's not for me.* She closes the book and hands it to me. 'That,' she says, 'is when I talk to my students about poise. Poise is critical in singing. When we're poised we're balanced, and when we're balanced, we sing easily. When we're tight and restricted, we sing hard. I wince when a student says, Oh, I'm trying so hard. Don't try hard, I say, try gently.'

Take me, I say, through the first lesson.

'First, you have to hear the sound you would like to make, in your head, and then you make that sound. And that assumes that you are motivated, you are some way along the path of changing from being self-conscious to being conscious of self. Self-consciousness is crippling and you have to get rid of it.'

How?

'Simple, you work with the body. You don't

stand rigid and statuesque, that's the old stance, the one I was taught. You learn to loosen up so there's a sense of stretching to the heavens as you sing rather than locking your body.

'I might begin with this exercise. I'll ask you to call out; in the studio, at a sports oval, at the beach. "HEY!" (Yes, sorry to startle you.) The point is to make people realise that when there's an alarm, when there's something urgent, you will automatically breathe well and then you make a big sound which is absolutely on top of the breath. So singing is no different. HEYYYY! It's out! So what we're really doing, very quickly – and I usually do this in the first lesson – is getting people to call something out, and usually we stand on our toes and imagine that we're calling out to Mt Nelson. Some people find this difficult. Good children are seen and not heard, a lady is never loud, and so on. Once they've done that, shouted HEY! then straight away I must get them to sing, without any further talking, because that's a new imprint.

'There's a critical question in singing, as in life. Who judges me? Whom do I *allow* to judge me? This is a big issue for us, isn't it? *We* decide who judges us, *we* appoint other people our judges. So I get them to shout. And in shouting, learning to make a big sound naturally, they're usually becoming so engrossed in what they're achieving they're not giving themselves time to judge. I often talk to the student about who's judged them in the past – you have to be very careful about this – and inevitably they come back to saying: I'm always judging myself, I need to judge myself before I let anyone else judge me. So we go through that, and there are a number of stories I've got, little rituals, games.'

We talk about self-consciousness for a while, and inhibition. 'Inhibition,' says Helen, 'is partly an Anglo-Saxon thing. I suspect it happens a lot less in, say, Italy where everyone's expected to carry a tune. And I also think it's something to do with our religious background, the rigidity of the worship, the denial of the senses. Formal, dour. A lot of the people who are working with singing have got those church connections. They're not interested in sensual sound, in full romantic sound, they're interested in what we used to call the sexless, pure sound. And so we're encouraged to make that sexless, pure, piping soprano sound. I've got a bit of a thing about this sexless sound. They feel this is the spiritual sound. I can't go along with that.

'When Caroline came to me and sang, it was just beautiful, and pretty, and she hardly breathed in two minutes. I mean, enormous restraint. But I had to ask, where's the warmth? where's the woman? You have to help them say goodbye to their little girl voices. There are women of fifty still carrying these around.'

'How do you develop this warmer voice inside?'

'Vibrato. The vibrato appears when it's ready, when the tension drops away. You make long swooping and humming sounds, and you start to get a tremendous buzziness or vibration in your voice, and hopefully the larynx is not caught right up and you'll notice that when you go, Eeeeeeeeeeh, it's not tight and screechy any more, there is a warmth in your voice. It's to do with trusting yourself, deep down. It's all about having the guts to open your mouth and just let out what's there to be let out, at the given time. So once you get the mental set right you work on this other stuff, the exercises, the vocalises, the technical side. Singing is not just letting it all out. You have to emote, but emote with control.

'Of course, some people come to me for therapeutic reasons above all else. I see people come in who've been stifled, people who talk through their teeth and who can barely get their mouth open. They come in and they tell me their story. There are hundreds of stories, every person has their story. So they come in, they express this, they get here despite their fear, and off we go.'

6

On my first visit to the eisteddfod to hear Caroline I turn up on the wrong day. Late, I fumble my way in the dark theatre, down perilous wooden steps to the front stalls. Once seated I peer at my programme and discover my mistake, but by this time I am beginning to find the spectacle on stage so intriguing that I decide to stay. A young girl, no more than ten and dressed in top hat, white tie and tails is tap-dancing and flourishing a cane. An androgyne Fred Astaire, shuffling in the spotlight, 'Puttin' on the Ritz'.

It's the children's song-and-dance categories and according to my programme we are up to the Under Elevens. Watching these children perform (they are almost all girls) I become aware of the ways in which the performing child is there not merely to please her teacher, and her mother, but more importantly to act out a repertoire of possible selves. Eliza Doolittle . . . Madonna . . . some long forgotten vaudeville comic . . . Liza Minelli ('New York, New York'), anyone, in fact, you want to be. Absurdly fat girls do ballet solos; self-assured little stage brats point their toes, throw up their arms and belt out a tune off key. And the best thing is, at this age no one expects you to be able either to sing or dance. Or even to look the part. Just to hold your nerve.

As the afternoon sings and dances by I feel as if, uncannily, the history of a musical culture is being laid out for me; endless quotations from, and quaint embodiments of a living past. A group of adolescent girls revive Lancashire music hall in the 1930s with a rendition of the George Formby classic, 'When I'm Cleaning Windows'. Dressed in football socks, shorts and builders labourers' T-shirts they cart a ladder about the stage, strutting through a series of exaggerated male gestures, gawping and leering and sticking their thumbs up at their bemused audience. A chorus line of eight tots, four of them Chinese, step out with precision drilling, in transparent yellow raincoats and umbrellas, and sing and tap-dance their way through 'Singin' in the Rain'. And this is just one afternoon, one genre of performance. If you hang around any eisteddfod for long enough you'll hear German lieder, 42nd Street, Banjo Paterson, English art song, Jim Morrison, Mozart, Tommy Dorsey, Negro spirituals, Cole Porter, Techno, Acid Jazz and many, many renditions of Andrew Lloyd Webber.

Far from being stifled, many of these small girls seem to have been launched into a precocious maturity. Of a kind. It's true that some children are stifled, but there are others who are over-coached. They sing and dance in a lighted space, the lights go out and then what? I recall a piano teacher who had been a child prodigy telling me how her mother entered her into serious competition from the age of five and how, if she failed to win every section she was in, Mother wouldn't speak to her for days. She was pushed onto a treadmill and the performance space became a place of terror.

It reminds me of Alice Miller's idea of the true self and the false self. The false self is a compliant self, the self that an over-directive mother or father wants the child to be so that the child may enact the parents' own thwarted narcissistic needs. The so-called true self can only emerge if the parent acts as a supportive (open and flexible) nurturer who 'mirrors' the natural narcissistic impulses of the child, including aggression, in a way that expresses unconditional love. Since none of us has perfect parents, all of us are left with a carapace of false self that at some moment, like a dead skin, demands to be shed. What this means at any particular age will depend, perhaps, on whether we were stifled or over-coached. For the stifled, the voice of the true self has to find a way of speaking out and being heard, and it occurs to me that singing might be one of those ways.

It also occurs to me that there must be more to it than that.

7

Caroline comes second in her section at the eisteddfod, a remarkable result, much better than she or anyone else expected. Afterwards I offer to take her to supper. She is worried about the baby-sitter but she also knows that she is too high even to consider going to bed. She rings home, says she'll be late but not too late and we adjourn to a hotel next to the theatre. There, in celebratory mood, we order a couple of absurd cocktails and try to shut out the miked-up sound of the singer in the piano bar behind us. I want to ask Caroline about her ambition to sing in the eisteddfod. I know she has no desire to be a professional singer, so why compete?

'It breaks down a barrier,' she says. 'It's not so much the competing but the singing in front of an audience. Once you've sung in front of people you feel you can do anything.'

What about making a speech in front of an audience, or acting?

'Not the same.'

Why not?

'I don't know. Can't explain. All I know is that you don't have a sense of anything but the moment. There's no past, there's no present . . . I mean, it's almost like a revelation. Just everything being perfect and right and proper and in it's place. The thing's there as a whole. It's ecstasy.'

'Ecstasy?' I raise my eyebrows.

'Yes, ecstasy.'

'So you sing to get high?'

'Yeah, I sing to get high. I know about the physiology of endorphins, and the need to get a hit – probably about once a week is a good idea – and I know I can rely on singing to give me that. I could smoke dope instead but it doesn't work for me. When I'm down, dope only makes me feel worse. Singing, you might say, is my drug of choice. And the beauty of having lessons is that after a while you start to get a . . . well, a stretch. At first you're thrilled just to be able to open your mouth and get a good sound out, but then you want more, you want to develop. It's a stretch, you're not just repeating the same thing over and over again. You feel like you're progressing. Sometimes I think it's better than sex. With sex I never feel I'm progressing.'

8 *Masterclass*

On the following Sunday afternoon I find myself sitting in the recital hall of the Conservatorium of Music. I have come to observe a visiting maestro tutor a class of promising students.

The hall is a steeply rising auditorium with walls of grey concrete block, grey carpet and dark green seats; as blank and characterless a space as all the other institutional auditoria of low-grade modernism. On the front wall, behind the performance space, is a pale blue curtain of thin silk. The space itself is a glossy floor of polished boards on which stands a black grand piano. Out of the corner of my eye I can see Helen Todd sitting two tiers above me, watching the stage intently and waiting for the first of her students to appear.

The atmosphere here is quite different from the preceding Wednesday evening. The eisteddfod had been a kind of festive free-for-all with a slightly lurid and be-sequinned quality. The masterclass is a much more rarefied and, in a sense, poignant space. It's the space of possibility, of true promise, where the young singer is poised between the private devotions of the amateur and the public acclaim of the professional. The master, Ron Maconaghie, is a distinguished former baritone with the Australian Opera, now in his sixties. He is a short, broadly proportioned man who could be your local bank manager with glasses and receding brown hair; avuncular and relaxed in grey trousers and a green polo shirt under a navy reefer jacket with gold buttons. His singer's chest gives him a misleading appearance of being stocky so that it is mildly surprising when he first climbs out of his seat in the audience and moves onto the performance area to reveal, with a few large but graceful gestures, a lightness of foot, an ease of movement that betokens the kind of stage performer he once was. One can imagine the master dancing across the stage.

First up is Anna Carmichael, soprano, short and slightly built with her black hair pulled back in a knot. She is eighteen; half-girl, half-woman. As she waits for her accompanist to settle at the piano she smooths her long floral skirt that sits just above a pair of black Doc Marten boots, then girlishly scratches her knee. I remember Anna from the eisteddfod the Wednesday before, an exquisite little singer of great poise and wit.

Under Maconaghie's expectant gaze she begins now to sing Zerlina's aria from *Don Giovanni*.

> *Batti, batti, o bel Masetto,*
> *La tua povera Zerlina;*
> *Staro qui come agnellina*
> *Le tue botte ad aspettar.*
> (Beat me, beat me, my Masetto.
> Beat your poor Zerlina.
> I'll stay here like a lamb
> And await your every blow.)

Suddenly, when she sings, this girl seems so much older, so much more worldly and sophisticated. A moment before, she was shy and uncertain, now she is coquettish and mocking. Now she has authority. There's that secret self again, the one that pours forth, loudly, boldly, the one that knows things that you don't know, or don't think you know, or didn't know you knew until, just then, when you opened your mouth and heard yourself ('my voice is so strong, sometimes it frightens me').

Maconaghie listens for one verse and then pulls her up. 'Ba*tt*i, Ba*tt*i,' he says. 'The double *t* is almost like a *d*. Let's hear a good Italian *t*.'

She nods. 'Okay.'

A few more lines and he interrupts again. '*Bel Masetto!* Don't drop it between phrases. The Italian *o* – work on that. You'll find that if you get the Italian right you'll sing better.'

'Okay,' she says again, quietly. Her singing voice is loud and thrilling, her speaking voice barely audible, low and deferential.

'And don't rush. Think of the Italian as one long piece of chewing gum, stretching it out. Use your womanly guile, wheedle and sing to your boyfriend.'

'Okay.'

> *Batti, batti, o bel Masetto*
> *La tua povera Zerlina*

Once again he cuts her off. 'Come forward, come forward. Don't be frightened.' He guides her with his arm: 'Come forward, here. We have to make sure people can see us.' And then, turned half to her, half to the audience, he holds the flaps of his jacket open, exposing his chest. 'Here's my heart, here – here it is, don't be afraid. See.' And he opens his arms out wide. It's a charming gesture, from an old pro.

She smiles. 'Okay.'

'And again.'

Batti, batti, o bel Masetto,
La tua povera Zerlina;
Staro qui –

'What are you doing down *here?*' In one fluid movement he has crossed the space and put his hands on her hips and diaphragm. I am still novice enough to register, each time, the familiarity of singing teachers; they adjust the body almost as they would an inanimate musical instrument. Without preamble, inhibition or fuss, they handle the goods. Are the shoulders back? is the spine straight? are the knees too stiff and locked? is the diaphragm free and not pushed up under the ribs? are the ribs collapsed down on the diaphragm? And the hand on the crown of the head: 'Feel it here, here, *here.*'

I've imagined how I would feel under these conditions. Invaded, ill at ease; encircled, embattled, coralled?

'Visualise that your voice is actually here –' he gestures '– a foot or eighteen inches in front of you at mouth level.'

'Okay.'

'And remember, step forward. Don't be afraid.'

'Okay.'

'Good girl. Again.'

'*Ah, lo vedo –*'

'No, no. *Ah, lo vedo . . .*'

'*Ah, lo vedo –*'

'Plant the words more. Like a bad Shake-spearean actor. Overdo it. We can always pull it back. What is the first virtue in a singer? Courage.' Always, to demonstrate, he holds his arms out wide, exposes his chest and lifts his chin. 'Here I am, shoot your arrows at me. This is the sound I'm coming to make, warts and all, like it or lump it.'

'Okay.'

'From the beginning.'

'Okay.' *Okay, okay, okay, okay.*

She starts up once again. *Batti, batti, o bel Masetto . . .* How many times is it now? She's visibly tiring, waning before our eyes. As if in response to this, he steps across, moves behind her, takes hold of her hands and lifts her arms into the pose of The Pride of Erin. Then he begins to dance her forward, gently . . . one and two and one and two . . . and as they continue to dance he begins to sing along with her, in a contained, lilting duet, pausing to say, at intervals, 'Don't be frightened', or, 'Take a breath there, take a breath there, very good.' Then he lets go of her, drops his arms, stands back a little. 'Very good,' he says quietly. 'Alright, okay, we'll stop there.'

And I want to say, no, no, go on singing, please. Good as she is, his singing is something else. It has a quality of surrender, as if he has long since let go of whatever it is she still clings to. Of course, he is much older, and has none of her nervousness. But still, there is something else there and one day, if she is blessed, she'll have it too.

'Very good,' he says again. 'Well done.' He puts out his hand to her and they shake hands.

And the girl walks off, as if in a daze. As she begins to climb the steep aisle of the auditorium he calls up at her. 'These are just thoughts, Anna, just thoughts. Now go home, and think about being a little more on the front foot. Open up the chest and the heart.'

He looks down at his paper, looks up again. 'Next?'

9

Seduced by the subtle couplings of the master-class, in the weeks that follow I sit in on several of Helen Todd's lessons, each time with an increasing sense of the absurdity of my project. I'm an observer making notes, but they're the wrong kind of notes, designed for the eye not the ear, and a poor substitute. The voice creates sound waves which penetrate the body in such a way and with such startling and immediate effect that no other sensual experience even approximates it. Moreover the dynamic between teacher and pupil is an elusively aural one; a kind of duet, sung in code.

The only way I could crack the code would be to have a lesson myself, and then my code would only be my code and no one else's. And that's not enough. We all want to know everyone else's secrets, not just our own, if only to discover what it is that binds us together – or keeps us apart.

I arrive one morning at Helen's studio, just before ten. The student this morning is Wayne McDaniel, thirty-six and formerly a professional basketball player with the NBL, now a journalist and commentator with the ABC. I had spoken to Wayne on the phone the night before and sought his permission to come along. Now I sit in a corner of the studio, near the window, and try to be unobtrusive.

Wayne is already there and loosening up. Tall but not freakishly so, he throws his arms in the air and can almost touch the low ceiling. Accustomed to being watched, he is easy and relaxed with my presence. He is a slender, good-looking man with a kind of lithe elegance, even in old jeans, a loose blue striped shirt and stockinged feet. His black head is shaved. With her blonde hair and gently imperious manner there is something Nordic about Helen and in this small room together she and her pupil make a striking pair.

The lesson begins with some scales. Helen explains that while Wayne is a bass baritone she wants him to work on developing his baritone upper notes, on getting rid of the falsetto he is apt to lapse into, his 'Michael Jackson voice'. 'We're having a challenge here, getting out of falsetto voice, because every other contemporary popular music singer uses falsetto constantly, and if you listen to it enough you just start doing it, especially the fellas. If Wayne is going to go beyond singing the pop ballad stuff, he needs to know his limits and which of them are self-imposed. So we're just trying to get his upper notes into the baritone range of the male voice, not the Michael Jackson shrill voice. Right?' Whenever, throughout the lesson, Helen refers to Wayne's 'Michael Jackson voice', he gives a soft laugh halfway between sheepish and celebratory, and looks at me with a kind of complicit delight.

The vocal exercises begin . . .

To describe a singing lesson is difficult, if not impossible. For much of the time it can be a monotonous stop-start cycle of scales and exercises, a series of feints and short deft manoeuvres with the breath, punctuated by peremptory commands. Frequently there is a great deal of discussion about breathing and the ribs and diaphragm. Sometimes it's pedestrian; sometimes poetic – 'visualise the note floating up into a golden dome in your head'. Above all, it's intensely physical, with a hands-on quality about it. The teacher adjusts the back, corrects the angle of the jaw – 'don't push the voice out, let the voice fall out of your face' – places her hands on the solar plexus, feels for the position of the ribs and the diaphragm, squares the hips, puts her palm on the crown of the student's head – 'think big, volume is mental' – and checks for the position of the feet. 'The bulk of the weight needs to be in the middle of the foot. When you get it right, you'll know. You'll feel safe.' There's a lot of face-pulling – 'give me the subtle sneer' – and strange noises, mostly in the warm-up. There is little that is sweet or elegant or delicate. It's a work-out.

After his lesson, Wayne and I walk to a crowded coffee shop nearby. There, amid the clatter of cutlery and din of conversation he talks into my tape recorder. I note how relaxed he is in this hectic environment, how easily he puts up an invisible screen to shut out whatever distraction hovers around him. Wayne seems to have a quality of deep concentration, of quiet inward focus, and I wonder if it derives from his experience as an athlete, of having to play, year after year, in front of thousands of screaming fans. Or could it be something else?

Why, I ask, does he want to sing?

'Because I always thought I had a voice and now I want to see if I can get it out.'

But why start lessons so relatively late in life? Was there no early encouragement from his family?

Well, he says, he has several brothers, some of them 'into crime and drugs'. He, the youngest, was the most influenced by his mother and his mother was interested in 'all things to do with the voice'.

What does that mean?

'Just anything to do with the voice. Singing, public speaking, broadcasting. And she used to write her own songs. See, I really believe that in my life I'm meant to fulfil the areas in my mother's life that she wasn't able to fulfil. And that gives me meaning for singing.' From time to time, he says, he makes tapes of his latest vocal work and sends them home to his mother in Oakland. He also sends them to his children who live in Adelaide, tapes of spirituals that they can listen to at night in bed.

I tell him that I have recently interviewed an opera singer of note who told me that in his view being a serious singer was in many ways comparable to being a serious athlete. You needed a similar mind-set in order to perform well.

He nods. 'In some ways, being a singer *is* like being an athlete, both are external expressions of who you are. Both are a way to say, here I am, this is me, I've arrived. But there are differences.'

What differences?

Well, he says, basketball is a team game and it's a great relief at last to be a solo performer. 'I was always very aloof and very . . . not self-centred, although coaches always say that, just aloof. And I was independent and I didn't always want to be with the team all the time.

'My first coach didn't like that so he worked out on me. He damaged my self-esteem, I had to rebuild it. The other guys looked up to him. See, I looked up to him, but I didn't idolise him. I respected him, but he was just another person, he was just another coach. I often think I would have been better off as a boxer or someone in an individual sport, because that's where my focus was. As an individual.'

'Like in singing?'

'Exactly.'

I tell Wayne that one of the things that interests me about men singing is that it seems a way for them to express their softer side and he responds to this enthusiastically. 'That's right. See, the singing energy for me, looked at in relation to, like athletic energy, the singing energy is more complete, it's more of a merger between masculine and feminine, whereas when I was playing it was so masculine, that by the time I was able to nurture those feminine parts of my game, I was too old. I was getting to that stage where I was thirty-three, thirty-four, and I was developing more subtleties in my game but by that time I only had a couple of years left in me. So, like, singing is the next progression, it's the follow-on from that.

'Now there's, like, two stages I see as being my next areas of growth. One is I have to get the theoretical side down, which is just repetition for me. And the next is getting comfortable with me as a performer, with expressing not just my voice but everything about me – my manners, my idiosyncrasies, movement, body, being comfortable with all that. Rather like being on the basketball court, understand, when I could go on to the court and think, when I was at my top of my game, *I own the game*. That's how I looked at the game, as though the game were mine, that's how I looked at the court. And that's how I need to look at singing.'

10

'I own the game.' Here I am, look at me, acknowledge me, and not just because I'm here, in the spotlight, but because I'm good.

Wayne has a quality that I've observed in many performers, a quality I think of as *sacré égoïsme;* literally, a sacred egoism. It's a certain kind of inward concentration on self, and it sounds intensely self-ish, but in the sense in which I use it here it refers to something other than blind self-regard. Think of it more as a poetic strategy for survival.

The term, *sacré égoïsme*, was first deployed as part of the language of international diplomacy to describe the belief of men that the welfare of some larger whole justified whatever selfish and duplicitous means were necessary to achieve it. Writ small in the daily life of the individual it becomes a radical form of will bent on self-expression, at whatever cost. Is it always latent, I wonder, or do we acquire it? In suggesting singing lessons to her daughter, did Caroline's mother effect the means of releasing or tapping into something that was already there, or of providing something that before was lacking?

Wherever it comes from, in those who have it the presence of *sacré égoïsme* is almost palpable; they seem to exude it from some hidden reserve in their chest – in a way that can both attract and repel. One can observe traces of it in all kinds of performers but I'm beginning to think that it has some special relationship to the voice, to the mysterious potency of song where it becomes transformed, in an almost alchemical way, into something less egoistic and more sacred.

I get a sense of this when eventually I hear Wayne McDaniel sing in public for the first time. We are at an intimate cabaret space known as the Backspace where some of Helen Todd's students are giving a recital. Immediately Wayne begins to sing it is apparent that he is a very good singer indeed. In the middle of the performance space he stands, quite still, barely moving throughout the two spirituals he is there to sing. There is no 'projection' or self-conscious charisma, no flashing white smiles, no playing to the crowd, no swagger, no charm; it is cool, detached, everything is subordinate to the music, to the song. In the intensity of Wayne's focus I sense the egoism which confidently announced itself in his interview ('I *own* that game') but already in his singing another quality has begun to come into play – a kind of ineffable grace – that draws the spectator into its magic circle so that what is nominally self-centred becomes spellbindingly inclusive. He cannot of course *own* the song. What he can do is place his whole self at the centre of it and, for a time, merge with it. *Sacré égoïsme* gets you to the point where you can get up on your feet in front of a large crowd and make them pay attention. Beyond that, something else, something infinitely more subtle, takes over. But what is it, and why is it so affecting?

11

What happens, I ask Helen, when ordinary, non-professional singers sing in public?

'I think they open up a part of themselves that they've pretty well kept closed off for many, many years. Somehow, through singing, they are rediscovering those parts of themselves that gave them great joy when they were a child, and letting them go again, but letting them go in the company of others. In order to let it go at all they have to go very calmly and very deeply inside themselves and that takes a lot of time. And I suspect the nerves are something to do with: *Will it come out?* I mean, that's the normal question for a singer. Is it going to come out? Is it going to come out in the way I would like it to come out?

'And the nerves are also there because you get tempted to interfere all the time. There's this sense of trusting yourself and keeping out of your own way. No matter how good you become, you can still get in your own way.

'And then there's the question of not only will it come out, but how much of it do I want to let out – though in a way they're the same question. I suspect what all my students are going through is finding their own personal depths and how much of this they are prepared to let out. How damaged might they be if they do? It's a very deep well that you have to get down to. It takes a lot of time to get there, a lot of practice. It's like you throw away that sheer nonsense of being a kid, that undisciplined sunny side. We're actually taking ourselves very seriously when we get up in front of an audience, apart from deciding that we're going to open up a piece of ourselves or, as in Wayne's case, a lot of ourselves. Some young singers get a bit of a shock when they realise how bare they've made themselves. Then there's the singer who just gets up and says: "I'm bare, look at me!"

'Are you nervous for your students when they perform?'

'No.'

'They're on their own at that point?'

'Yes, definitely. They're on their own.'

12

For some reason this reminds me of a story that Beatrice told me.

We are driving home one night and I ask her about the singing group, what it was like before I joined it, and she tells me the story of Julie and how she had haemorrhaged in the middle of a song. They had been standing in the customary circle after a particularly long and intense warm-up. 'Everyone was in tune that night, right from the beginning. It's like everyone came in and, bang, they were straight into it. The warm-up, the sound column, was particularly intense. Things were going really well and for once it all seemed effortless. Then at some point Julie gave a kind of gasp, and I was standing right opposite her and I looked across and there was this red puddle of blood on the floor between her legs. And I'm watching it, sort of mesmerised, and there's this sudden gush, and a stream of it runs from between her legs into the puddle which is just sitting there. And then there's another gush, then another, and two big black clots sop onto the floor. And as I'm looking at her she calmly pulls her T-shirt up over her head – it was a black one – and stuffs it between her legs. And a couple of people crowd around, trying to avoid the clots on the floor. They get her a chair and she sits down and as she sits the T-shirt slips and falls on the floor and the blood begins to seep through the seat of the chair – it was one of those woven rattan seats – and the blood is just seeping through the weave – it was awful – and I look at Julie and she's looking back at me with terror in her eyes. I'll never forget it.'

She pauses at a red light. At this time of night the streets are all but empty. 'Have you ever haemorrhaged?' she asks. As it happens, I have, and I remember that terror, the black sense of being swept away on a tidal . swoon of powerlessness, some kind of fecund dying. But I don't want to talk about it now.

'What did you do?' I ask.

'Maria and Kerry drove her to hospital,' she says, matter-of-factly, 'with the T-shirt stuffed between her legs and a spare one from someone else. After she'd gone we looked in the cupboards for cleaning gear and couldn't find a thing. Sarah came back from the old loo with the dirty old towel they hang there and started to mop up the blood. But it had seeped into the cracks and splinters in the old floorboards and wouldn't come out without a scrubbing brush. There were still some brown streaks in the floorboards the next week.'

'What about Julie?'

'She came back eventually.'

'Abortion?'

'Apparently. And for four months after, she said, she couldn't sing a note. But finally she got back into the circle and it was alright.'

I ask a perhaps trivial question, although it's the kind of detail I always want to know. 'Can you remember what you were singing at the time?'

Beatrice yawns. 'George Gershwin,' she says.

13 *The professional*

There's a phrase from Helen Todd's cool assessment that keeps coming back to me, the one about 'keeping out of your own way'. What does this mean? That you are the conduit for the voice but at the same time, you are its obstacle? It's a paradox that David Brennan, a resident baritone with Opera Australia, elaborates on when I visit him in Sydney later in the month. David is a handsome man in his forties; an eloquent, at times passionate, talker and an acute critic of his own art. I want particularly to ask him this: What is it like for the professional? Does it ever get any easier?

'I still have coaching. Most singers do.'

And what is this thing about getting in your own way?

'Ah,' he says, 'this is the nub of it. Because singing is a great paradox. On the one hand it's very technical, you spend years working on your control and most performers are control freaks, they have to be. On the other hand there's a point where you have to just let go of all that and surrender to the music. The performer has to search for the essential truth of the moment, which is, you know, often terribly subtle. And you have to express this without being either over-controlled or self-indulgently "carried away". You have to achieve a kind of detachment, and that's the hard part. The same detachment which is reading a shooting script to you. You know: you move over here now, you make sure you're ready to hear a knock on the door now, you don't move too far or you'll be out of the light. You're watching the beat very carefully here because you got out last time. And when you run out of other inspirations, the dependence on technique, on what you've repeated, what you've done technically to get you through that kind of dry moment – that will often be the most triumphant, most successful moment. Because you say: I'm exhausted, my throat's dry, my throat's sore, I don't know if I've got another of those notes in my throat, I was distracted for the last ten minutes and this is the bit where Butterfly hears that Pinkerton isn't coming back again. I can't rewind the reel, so I've just got to go on, I remember what I've got to do, I know what I've got to do . . . and often those kinds of emotionally desiccated moments are the moments that are richest.

'Why? Because you're allowing the music, your body, to speak, without a kind of interpretation, without a . . . I'm groping for the exact word . . . *without being your own intermediary.*'

'You make it sound like there are two of you on stage.'

'Not exactly. But there are two voices that are always there in your head. One of the voices is saying, This is beautiful music and I'd really love to do this and I think I can, and the other voice is saying, That note wasn't quite right, and are you sure you're not leaning over too much, and what's that person saying, and was that a sigh I heard, and while you're thinking about what I'm saying you weren't concentrating on what the music was saying a second ago. And the effect of this is? That you're not in the present moment. *You are not in the present moment.* And being in the present moment is what music is. There is no other purpose to music. It is completely evanescent. It's the ultimate Zen experience. It has no purpose other than to be in the moment, and disappear.'

There's another question I want to ask David Brennan, especially since he's a baritone. What's all this fuss about The Three Tenors? Why the mass response?

'Ah, well,' he says, tilting his head back and sighing with a mixture of exasperation and scorn. 'Partly it's an exercise in clever commercial marketing, an essay in the gullibility of the crowd. Some of it is the visceral excitement of responding to a singer at the peak of his powers but the rest of it is a whole lot of bullshit dross, like the three of them singing '*Nessun Dorma*' together.' He groans. 'Wake me up when it's over. I abhor it.'

Is that all? Surely, I remonstrate, there's more. Can tenors be said to have some mystique that baritones lack?

'The tenor voice is the voice of youth,' he replies, after some deliberation. 'Rock singers contrive, no matter what their age, to sound like adolescents. A tenor, even a tenor in his sixties

like Pavarotti, sounds like a young man in his
prime, a prodigiously talented young man at the
peak of his strength.'

'Yes,' I reply, 'but a certain kind of young man.
A man who expresses that strength with an enormous amount of refinement, who opens up his
heart and gives lyrical voice to the most tender of
sentiments.'

'Yes, certainly.'

'Well, it seems to me significant that this spectacle was first launched at a very machismo sporting occasion, the World Cup in soccer. Isn't there
something going on here that is not altogether
about singing but about, say, the social construc-
tion of masculinity? Isn't the sight of Jose Car-
reras, the most lyrical of tenors singing at a
kickfest of headbutters at the very least a striking
contrast in masculine styles?' I tell him about
Wayne McDaniel and his allusion to his "feminine" side.'

'Well, this is an interesting question, a very
interesting question. I mean I do meditate on
what it is to be a male at this time in history, in the
light of a society which has been heavily influenced by feminism. I watch my son, who is now
twenty, growing up, and attempting to find his
own masculinity, and I don't know what to say to
him. I am incredibly lucky. I have my own voice, I
am allowed to sing with and exercise my own

voice, my own unchallengeably masculine voice, and this is a way of finding, or at least, acting, playing my masculinity. I read somewhere that there's a Japanese verb, *to play*, which is, in the mouths of the samurai, to do. Instead of *doing* something, you *play* something.'

'You play the part?'

'No, no. The verb *play* is used in the sense of *to do*. It's an extremely interesting thing, because what I do is play and do, and I can be the impermissable male, in a sense. And so can they.'

'They?'

'So can those Three Tenors. But equally, I would ask: what is happening when we listen to a powerful soprano voice? Isn't there a similarly androgynous appeal at play? Perhaps even more so with the mezzo-soprano who sings trouser roles – Octavian in *Der Rosenkavalier* and so on. There is an extraordinary number of those. A good half of the mezzo-soprano roles are written for women who have to impersonate men. But let's carry this further. Let's look at an operatic soprano, or an operatic female singer. Doesn't *she* take on much of the masculine? The strength, the capacity to fill the hall with her voice, the capacity to take charge of her own destiny and express it? Isn't she every bit as androgynous as the tenor?'

'Yes,' I say, 'but, traditionally women are expected to sing, as part of their ornamental and recreational function – the courtesan, the geisha, and so on. It's not such a break from traditional roles to listen to a woman lament her fate as it is to hear a burly male pouring his heart out in the upper register.'

'I don't know about that. Which traditions are we speaking of? In many cultures it was the role, indeed the privilege of the men *only* to express the moral and political leadership of their society or tribe by singing on all ritual occasions.'

This, I have to concede, is true.

PART 2
MACHIAVELLI'S RIVER

1

Not long after the Port Arthur shootings, when a mood of intense gloom hung over the city of Hobart, I stood in the historic Salamanca Market area by the waterfront and listened to the Sisongke Choir sing a number of slow and affecting African laments. It was a sunny Saturday morning and the market was congested with people and the usual display of colourful stalls. Dressed informally in black T-shirts, forty or so members of the choir stood on the grass verge and sang hauntingly in African words that none of us at that time understood, although this did not make it any the less affecting.

> *thina sizwe*
> *thina sizwe sintsundu*
>
> *sikelela*
> *sikelela izwe lethu*

'*Thina sizwe*' is a song about dispossession; a demand that what has been taken away from us be restored. After only a few minutes I found it unbearable and moved away, but the voices of the choir carried on the sea breeze and seemed to waft behind me. My husband stayed by the verge, listening.

The second time I hear Sisongke sing is in the ornate Town Hall, a minor Georgian masterpiece of pastel blue and gold with Grecian urns on pedestals set in arched wall recesses, a parquet floor, scarlet seats, a huge gilt mirror in baroque gold leaf and exquisite chandeliers. On either side of the stage, above the bronze pipes of the organ and painted on the wall in gold are two of the Muses, one with her books, the other with her artist's palette. Neither is carrying a lyre.

The Sisongke Choir is here for a special concert with visiting singer Valanga Khoza. A former member of SASO, Steve Biko's South African Student Organisation, Valanga fled from South Africa at the age of sixteen and moved to Swaziland as a political refugee. Eventually he completed his formal education in the US and now lives in Melbourne where he makes his living travelling Australia as a performer, and running choral workshops for schools and community groups. This is not the first time Valanga has worked with Sisongke and he is a great favourite with his long dreadlocks pulled back in a bunch, his tiny Zulu 'piano', the *kalimba* that he holds in one hand and uses to tune the choir, and a great line in ironic charm. In the finale, he joins the choir in a stirring performance of '*Nkosi Sikelele*' ('God Bless Africa'), until recently the anthem of 'terrorists', now the official anthem of the new Republic of South Africa. The wall behind Valanga is dominated by three lifesize portraits from the nineteenth century, chief among them, Robert, 4th Earl of Buckinghamshire and Lord Hobart, Secretary of State for the Colonies. The colonial tide is still turning.

But why so much African music? Since Africans are not a large ethnic group in Hobart, each time I heard Sisongke sing, I became more and more curious. Why African? How did this come about?

2

In 1994 black activist Siphiwo Lubambo was living in exile in Sydney. A former choir master in South

Africa and now cultural ambassador at large for the African National Congress, Siphiwo was invited to Hobart for three weeks in February to give a series of singing workshops for the public. This was an initiative of John McQueenie, Arts Officer for the Tasmanian Trades and Labor Council.

John McQueenie gives me a vivid account of Siphiwo's first workshop, a one-off at Risdon Prison. For some weeks Siphiwo had run a programme at Brisbane's Boggo Road Gaol but time at Risdon was limited. For an hour and a half he attempted to persuade a group of Risdon inmates to sing but they were unmoved, refusing to utter a note. As he spoke, they began to make jokes and nudge one another. Singing was for poofs, they said. Well, said Siphiwo, in his culture singing was a mark of manhood and men were proud of their singing prowess. No response. Siphiwo kept talking. He told them about the work of the ANC in Africa and how he had been a weapons instructor there. At that point the mutinous undertow of murmuring began to subside. He was asked: Had he ever killed a man? Sensing that his credibility had suddenly been enhanced and sensing also a change in the mood of the gathering, Siphiwo declined to answer the question. Instead, he began to turn the discussion around and back to the subject of singing. With only ten minutes of the session left he at last managed to persuade the men to make a few sounds; a few vocal exercises, a simple warm-up. But by the time they were ready to sing, time had run out.

Siphiwo had better luck in his principal forum for the summer, a series of workshops for the labour movement. It was John McQueenie's hope that these would result in the formation of a community choir and with this in mind the workshops were offered intensively over the summer break, with over one hundred and forty people turning up for three to six sessions a week. Much of the instant success of the project can be attributed to Siphiwo's flamboyant and energising style and what seems to have been an almost immediate political rapport with the majority of the attendees. Says Victoria Rigney, now performance manager of Sisongke: 'We were always profoundly aware of the situation in South Africa at that time. Siphiwo taught us several songs in three South African languages and every now and then he would stop and tell us a story about his days as an activist.' Unsurprisingly, some connected to the politics of the scene more than others. 'I was deeply affected by Siphiwo's stories,' said one choir member, 'but yet there were always some people in the room who weren't listening. You know, they'd be humming a little tune . . .'

At the end of the three weeks Siphiwo had

pulled the group together for a sell-out concert at Hobart's elegant old Theatre Royal. This proved to be an occasion of some intensity. It was the year leading up to the elections in South Africa, public interest was high and the choir performed '*Nkosi Sikelele*', still an underground anthem. At the end of the concert the singers and audience were linked up by telephone to the ANC office in Soweto and John McQueenie spoke on stage to representatives there. I heard many accounts of that evening, summed up by Victoria as 'incredible. It was very moving.'

When Siphiwo returned to Sydney the local singers voted to continue in some form. They decided they wanted to become a choir and named it Sisongke, a Xhosa word meaning 'side by side'. Victoria: 'None of us knew anything about music, or choral direction. We just knew that we wanted to keep doing what we'd been doing.' A few of the group took on the work of organising a choir and finding a musical director. They approached Micheál McCarthy at the Tasmanian Conservatorium of Music, an Irishman with a wealth of choral experience which included training in Hungary in the Kodaly method. McCarthy agreed to take them on. The next step was to find a venue and eventually they settled on the Quaker Meeting House at the Friends School which seemed more than appropriate. Officially, the choir came into being in June 1994 with joint sponsorship from Community Aid Abroad and the TTLC, which had applied for and been given Australia Council funding for community cultural development.

To say that there were teething problems is an understatement. From the beginning, many in the choir were at odds with the TTLC. 'Things,' to quote Victoria Rigney, 'were a bit scratchy' and the differences came to a head the following February. Victoria again: 'It was one of those summer concerts in the park, a scorching hot day. One of the choir members introduced a song we had learned about East Timor and she said the Australian government was exacerbating the position there at present. Then I introduced a song called "Keep on Walking Forward" and dedicated it to Bob Brown who had just been arrested in the Tarkine Valley and was in gaol that weekend. The audience cheered, and so did the choir, but that was the beginning of the end with the TTLC. We had the most immense fallout the following week. People in the audience had gone straight to them and accused us of being anti-government, pro-Green, environmental terrorists, you name it.

'Perhaps, looking back, we were a bit naive. There was a strong rift in Tasmania between the Greens and the Labor Party, and we had somehow played right into it. We learned the hard way. We wanted our songs to be political but with a small *p*, and not to be aligned with any party. We also agreed then that we wanted our songs to speak for themselves, and that we should avoid provocative introductions.'

At this point the choir embarked on a new phase. They were no longer under the auspices of the TTLC and Community Aid Abroad: they were independent and on their own and they had to decide on some kind of rationale. Why were they singing? What did they want to achieve? What should their repertoire be? Were they serious musicians or were they a glee club? Victoria: 'There was this ongoing debate between those who want to have fun and those who want to progress musically, and how you just keep it in the middle there somehow. In the early days, we got frustrated. Micheál would stop a lovely song and just want to go over and over and over again and again and even his most dedicated followers would think, Oh, come on! Just let us sing, we just want to sing it! He had to modify that a bit, and he did. We also came to see that the Siphiwo concert had largely succeeded because of its emotional appeal, and now we had to improve musically if we were to continue. Once when Valanga came to do a workshop with us, Micheál was sitting in the back row, writing. Someone asked why he wasn't joining in, and I told them to go and watch what he was doing. He was writing out the songs in four parts, as Valanga sang them, so we could keep them in the repertoire after the workshop. A lot of people in the choir can't read music, and to work with someone with those skills is a real experience. So those people who at first resisted the different leadership style came to see how fortunate we were to have this talent in our midst.'

Micheál McCarthy: 'If Sisongke just went to sing for fun, all the time, they wouldn't still be interested in it after two years. Fun is important, but fun is serious work. A sense of play has to be part of the rehearsal process, but it is not for fun's sake, it is for the sake of the music. I prefer it if the sense of fun comes from the achievement. The paradox is that to maintain the sense of fun you have to continue to develop. If you aim *only* to have fun, you may well lose interest. Part of my role is to be aware of this. There can be a certain tension if members of the choir want only to give performances. How can they give performances unless they work hard?'

One of the most fraught of the early issues was repertoire. As Micheál McCarthy says, 'Community choirs are made up of people with particular expectations.' He makes the point that many professional musicians will 'play whatever is put in front of them when it is their job to do that. Amateurs are different.' Victoria: 'We would bring

along songs we loved, perhaps ballads with a
human rights bent, and Micheál could see that
they wouldn't work musically for the big choir. He
would bring along music suitable for a choir, but
it mightn't be what we wanted from the political
or emotional angles. I remember Micheál
brought along a song, beautifully arranged. It
wasn't quite a hymn but was a kind of "spring has
come" celebration and it mentioned God at least
once, maybe twice and there were people there
who just said, "No, we won't sing that, we are not
going to sing about God." And that was the only
time I thought he was going to walk out the back
door and leave us. With a look of complete exasperation on his face he walked this day to the back
of the rehearsal room and stood there for a
moment. Then he turned around and came back
and said, "Just explain why it is that you will sing
about God in Zulu, in Xhosa – you do know, don't
you what '*Nkosi Sikelele*' means?" And people
thought that "*Nkosi Sikelele*" was beyond critique,
you know . . . and rightly so. It's our favourite
song and we do our best and all of that, but it *is*
about God. And a lot of people said, "Oh, okay,
fine."

'So there was a bit of a gap there about where
he was coming from and where we were coming
from. It was all part of our evolution. After that we
came up with a repertoire committee where we'd

work things out. And that was how we all had to grow together. And some of the more radical people who didn't want that degree of formality or process left. But in fact the repertoire committee has now lapsed, we don't need it any more because now we tend to have a lot more mutual trust and understanding.

'It's all that connectedness stuff. First you work it out in the choir among yourselves and then you kind of branch out into the broader community. We decided to look at what music there is in Hobart and began to develop The Hidden Music of Hobart project. We've just done our first one, which is a Latvian song, "*Put Vejini*". Members of the Latvian community came and taught it to us and they perform it with us now, on stage, in national dress. The project relates to our human rights emphasis and we have got a statement of unity about it that says that this is what we are all about. But we are also about recognising cultural and musical diversity within Hobart, and even within the choir we will continue to search out pieces and learn about the communities from which they come. It's a wonderful idea but a hell of a lot of work. To start with it created a lot of stress; people began to feel it was becoming too much like work and not enough like fun. We had to have a meeting and sort out our priorities. But somehow it always works out. That's the interesting thing about the choir as an entity, the way in which the whole is greater than its parts. It's a bit like Machiavelli's river; you can put obstacles in its course, but it seems to find its way around them all.'

2 The choral singer (1)

MARNIE ROGERS, member of Sisongke Choir, Hobart.
'Why do I want to sing? What a question! The real question is: why *don't* other people sing?

'Okay, okay, why do I sing? Well . . . there's a part of me that feels a bit guilty for not being more out there and in the world. I've always been in the world and I was brought up to think I had to participate in the world. And because I don't have a job or any children around any more, and all that sort of stuff, I'm not in the world. I used to be politically active and now I'm not. I really don't care who's in politics anymore – sort of vaguely, but only a bit. And the choir works on both the personal and the political level. I get all these lovely endorphin hits for myself and at the same time, because we're singing the kind of songs we're singing, about human rights, that's my political action.

'But even if it weren't these political songs I could still justify it by saying I contribute to the harmony of the planet. How? Well, I just assume that anything that has a harmonious factor to it, rather than a disharmonious one, is adding a little to the total harmony of the whole. And I couldn't do it on my own, I couldn't sing on my own – I seem to need to butt up against something. I like to know that I have a role in something bigger than I am. I need to feel part of a whole.

'And we sing everything in four parts and that's a great satisfaction, singing in harmony. I need to see – the world needs to see – something in union, instead of scattered and disparate. And I think that's what happens when you have parts. You have four people supposedly holding something different but they're making a whole at the same time. I also want a few male voices as well as female voices, I don't like all male or all female choirs. They're not whole.

'There's a fascinating exercise I should tell you about that relates to this thing called harmony. It's an exercise that people who run workshops sometimes do called "the vocal wheel". Eight people lie head to head in a group, in a circle, like the spokes of a wheel. In a big room you might have six groups or more. You lie on the floor or stand around – it might take an hour – and you just make any sound you feel like, nonsense noises, shrieks and groans – people carry on and carry on. And it all starts by coming out of the bottom of your stomach, real gut stuff, all the anger and vomit, and then you get into doing primal stuff, it might be crying or gurgling or whatever, baby stuff, and then you come through that, as if you were working through the chakras as sound. And then, after a while, people start listening to each other. Whoever is running the workshop might say: Now, listen to the person next to you, pick up on that. That goes on for a while, then you start listening across the room, and after about, say, forty-five minutes or so, people have come out of that and they're actually into some exquisite symphonic sound. It sounds like a composed symphony and everyone has a part in it, like they're an instrument. No words, just sound. In the end it all just comes into an extraordinary harmony. It's fabulous.

'And the interesting question is, will cacophony always end up in harmony if you let it go long enough? I don't know, I've only had three experiences, but I suspect that if you set up an occasion for people to sing they will attune themselves to one another if you give them long enough.'

3 *Choral fixation*

I like the Sisongke story. I like what it says about the politics of culture in general and of art in particular. Getting together to sing is not a straightforward matter; all kinds of value-laden issues come into play. It made me curious about the histories of other large choirs, like the Sydney Gay and Lesbian Choir, and curious about the very institution itself. What is the originary moment of the massed community choir? How did it get to be one of the most resilient of our cultural forms, one that can always be relied upon to reflect the character of its times? Among the many accounts, I am drawn to the one proffered by the music historian, Henry Raynor in his book, *Music and Society Since 1815* (1976). Raynor tells the story of the Berlin court musician, Carl Friedrich Fasch who, in 1787, suddenly realised that his salary had been seriously devalued by the Seven Years War. Seeking to augment it by a few extra-curricular activities, Fasch begins by conducting a singing class for wealthy bourgeois wives, one of whom, the wife of an official in the Prussian War Ministry, offers her garden for rehearsals. Thus is born the Berlin *Singakademie*. Four years later it accepts men into its membership (I would like to have heard the debate on this) and soon after gives its first public performance.

Over the next forty years, similar choirs spring up throughout Germany and Switzerland and later in France, Austria and England, more often than not with agendas that are other than musical. In Switzerland, Hans Georg Nageli, a disciple of the educationalist and social reformer Pestalozzi, believes that singing in groups will produce a sense of social unity and purpose. In 1805 he forms the Zurich *Singinstitut* and from this and his subsequent work there develop a number of festivals, not only in large cities but in small towns and even villages. Nageli's work, like the whole of the Pestalozzi movement, coincides with and is said to express the spirit of the new political organisations of Switzerland which give the nation its modern structure as a democratic state.

Throughout Europe, both the choirs and the proliferating festivals become self-propagating. A combination of local patriotism and a competitive spirit allied to an appetite for the new ensures their spread. Many composers, including Mendelssohn, become enthusiastic supporters of their activities. 'The appeal of choral music in German-speaking Europe,' writes Raynor, 'is that it allows each individual member, man or woman, to become involved in the thoroughly democratic processes that are denied to him or her in political life.' In the choral societies all decisions, democratically arrived at, are the results of general votes of all the members and this gives the choral societies political implications unwelcome to the authorities. The fact that large and efficient organisations can function successfully by democratic methods suggests a criticism of the authoritarianism by which central European states are controlled. Such choral organisations provide a valuable lesson in practical democracy; as such, they become hemmed in by police regulations. They are, of course, almost entirely middle class – apart from activities like the work of the German musician Joseph Mainzer, who institutes large-scale singing classes for the poor in Paris.

This might sound like a simple-minded Whig view of history in which music and democracy march arm in arm along the path of golden Progress but Raynor is alert to the murkier outcomes of the industrial revolution. To begin with, it wreaks havoc on rural families, with devastating effects on traditional folk-singing. People who had once worked at home where they had sung freely now move to the factories in the towns where the deafening noise of the new machines drowns them out. A musicologist's survey of factory workers in Lancashire in the 1850s shows that parents are passing on a rapidly dwindling repertoire of songs to their children.

At this historical moment, John Wesley and the Methodist Revival bring group singing into the realm of the common worker. Wesley wants hymns which the simplest and most illiterate people can remember and sing. As in Lutheranism, the whole congregation is to sing and not, as in the Church of England at that time, sit silently while others sing to it. Singing together, Wesley knew, individual men and women become a community, a congregation. Methodism converted widely in the new industrial town, among a depressed and degraded working-class. And it is at least arguable, writes Raynor, that 'music attracted people to Methodism as much as Methodism attracted people to music'.

Many factory owners encourage the development of work-site choirs, seeing in these an encouragement to a sober and pious (and with luck, docile) workforce. Some of the more enlightened (or the more shrewd) pay for a weekly singing class in work time and contribute to expenses: sheet music, travel to eisteddfods and so on. Dickens' father-in-law and music critic for the *Daily News*, George Hogarth, writes of the proliferation of choral societies among workers: 'their wages are not squandered in intemperance, and they become happier as well as better'. Thus begins a tradition that sees every Lancashire factory, every Welsh colliery have its own choir (and band), and community singing practices become entrenched in ways that live on in the massed singing of the terraces at English football games.

Factors other than religion, however, begin to play a part in the growth of community choirs. During the last half of the nineteenth century, the increasing prosperity of the middle class combined with technological changes means that middle-class women have less work to do at home, yet wives and daughters are not allowed by the conventions of the times to work outside the home or to participate in public and political activities. They take to joining choral groups until, with the beginning of the women's emancipation movement, and its eventual acceptance, these musical organisations begin to decline. Today, however, in the 1990s, they are in revival. Why?

4 *The pied piper*

In February 1995 Julie Clarke wrote an article for *HQ* magazine which looked at the new fad for singing in a cappella groups. Five years ago there were two such groups in Sydney, now there are over sixty, and these are just the ones we know about (and they don't include three or four people who've decided just to get together in their living rooms and sing once a week). Called 'Praise the Lord and Pass the Lipstick', Clarke's article focused on the best known of the Sydney groups, Cafe at the Gate of Salvation, and the work of its founder and musical director, Tony Backhouse.

If there is one person who could be said to be emblematic of the singing revival, it's Backhouse, truly a man with a mission. Regarded by many as Australia's finest gospel singer, since the early nineties he has run voice workshops all over Australia in the belief that singing is 'fundamental to being human' and everyone should do it. 'Everyone can sing,' he asserts. 'It's only fear and cultural conditioning that stops us. It's the first way we express ourselves as babies. It makes work go better, helps breathing and changes brain chemistry resulting in feelings of joy.' All music has the power to change things, he says, but especially singing: 'You can't sing without being changed.' Backhouse is passionate in his espousal of DIY. 'In our culture singing is left to the experts, singers with a capital *S*. It hasn't always been like that. In the good old days everyone sang around the piano, chortling over moonbeams and kisses, dreams and wedding bells. These days we're encouraged not to sing in the rain, on the plane, or anywhere that others can complain. That's a pity because singing is a primal form of self-expression. You don't need to sit down at a piano. It's the most fundamental form of musical expression there is. It opens up the heart.'

The singing that Backhouse is pledged to is black gospel singing because, as he says, 'It's not about the voice, it's about the soul, the spirit.' Not surprisingly his views are reflected in the members of the Cafe. When interviewed by Clarke a significant number of them cited spiritual reasons for joining the choir. 'Every so often I feel spiritually starved, as if there is a special kind of food that I need to be fully alive' (Tamra Hall, 31). Another: 'Singing with the choir is a blessing that provides regular experiences of absorption and transcendence' (David Hall, 38).

According to Judy Backhouse: 'Some conventional Christians are confused by us. They ask, "What church are you from?"'

The Cafe is not from any church; it represents a kind of New Age eclecticism. Anything goes. Not the least interesting thing about the choir is it's betokening of the emergence of a new sensibility, grounded in Baby Boomers and Generation Xers alike. Clarke tentatively defines it as a kind of post-modern spirituality; irreverent, eclectic, hip, tolerant – qualities encapsulated in Backhouse's own manifesto. 'Jesus,' he says, 'is our culture's prevailing metaphor for spiritual excellence, and while the religion built around this metaphor has an unstable and unsound history, Jesus' contribution (non-violent, non-sexist, non-racist, to say the least) is a wonderful thing. I feel comfortable working with the Christian metaphor. Others in the group re-translate the words we sing into political terms or more general spiritual terms. There has to be a place for non-specific spirituality.'

There has to be a place for non-specific spirituality. I am struck by this sentence, each time I read it. What is 'a non-specific spirituality' and is the singing group one of its natural sites? Here is Stephanie Dowrick, a former student of Tony Backhouse's, who accompanied him on a gospel singing tour of the American south.

5 *Gospel*

> Through many dangers, toils and snares,
> I have already come:
> 'Tis grace has brought me safe thus far
> And grace will lead me home.

STEPHANIE DOWRICK, *at home, Monday December 9, 1996.* 'If I had a life to choose I would prefer to be a musician than to be a writer. Why? Because words are always limiting, inevitably limiting, aren't they? And because the contact with the audience is just so *immediate,* and because through music you're reaching to people's hearts in a *very* direct way. You transcend the self through the music, and you transcend the limitations between self and other through the music. There is not another art form that does it so powerfully.

'The liberation of group singing for me is that it's an art form where I don't have to be the best, where my ego is not involved, where I don't have to be ever hoping for a solo, or to shine; where all I need to do is experience the music – experience the music rather than experience my ego through the music. That's the most amazing liberation.

'Why gospel? Well, several reasons. It's a music of worship. That is really important to me. I like the uninhibited worship of it. I like the fact that it's music that comes out of suffering, and transforms suffering, because it developed from the old negro spirituals. It's extremely forgiving music – I mean it's forgiving of the people who sing it in as much as you can do all kinds of things with it so that even if you haven't got a great voice you can still sing it – and, in its actual intention, it's forgiving. I find that really attractive.

'I sang it in classes for five or six months before I went on a gospel tour of the US with Tony Back-house and a group of other gospel singers. When I started I did feel somewhat embarrassed about being in a group of people I didn't know, doing something that I felt very uncertain about, but I'd just had cancer and I thought, hell, you know, I'm just going to sing, because I might die and, I thought, my inhibitions are of no consequence here whatsoever.

'I had sung when I was young, and I'd loved singing, really loved it. And even after school I'd sing sometimes but in the intervening years I hadn't sung, and I'd really, really missed it. I used to sing around the house sometimes, but then I'd feel inhibited and I'd be short of things to sing.

'I haven't got a very good voice now, I truly haven't. But for me singing is about surrendering yourself, and just accepting what you've got. It exemplifies the parable of the talents which I think is a very, very important parable, teaching us to make use of what we've got. That we're all given sing. I remember one memorable occasion when I couldn't speak, we were sitting in this complete kind of doldrum, and I stood up, and started to sing, and then he started to sing with me, and I moved myself out of the pits.

'I think it's partly to do with your breathing; it's also partly posture; it's partly moving your mind, as you do in meditation, on to something very focused. But singing is more energetic than meditation often is. There's so much energy to it, and I think you can tune into a collective energy which reminds you that you are not alone. Of course, when you are depressed, that's when it's hardest to sing. But I had to – it was a *huge* act of will, a huge act of will to do it at all. It felt to me in some moments like a choice between life and death.'

PART 3
THE HEART'S EAR

1

What is the secret of the human voice and where can we expect to find an answer to that question? Is it purely an organic phenomenon to do with the release of endorphins, or does it connect us to a more spiritual dimension? Who is the oracle here: the physician or the metaphysician?

In *Great Singers on Great Singing* (1982) the former bass baritone with The Metropolitan in New York, Jerome Hines, conducts over thirty interviews with opera singers of international standing. Almost all of these are exclusively devoted to issues relating to the soft palate, the uvula, the sinuses, the diaphragm and even the width of the face. Occasionally, someone like Renata Tibaldi will declare, enigmatically, that 'singing is ninety per cent in the mind' but for the most part one gains the impression that the chief artistic consultant of professional singers is their ear, nose and throat physician.

The most controversial of these, who has advised many singers, is the distinguished French physician, Alfred Tomatis (b. 1920). You might think that any survey of the work of Tomatis would begin here with a treatise on the larynx, or the tongue, but it is Tomatis's contention that the key to the voice is in the ear. If we cannot hear, we cannot speak or sing. Mystics like the Sufi scholar Pir Hazrat Inayat Khan teach that the ear and not the eye is the primary sense organ out of which all the other senses develop. Hearing is the first of the senses to be awakened in the womb, at around five months, and the sound of the mother's voice is the first sense imprint on the new self.

Over the past forty years the research of Albert Tomatis focused on these aural beginnings and attempted to unravel their skein of significance within a medical model. Tomatis – whose father, not coincidentally, was an opera singer – devoted his career to analysing the effect that various components of sound, including singing, have on our bodies. His most radical theory is the concept of cortical charge, that it is the primary function of the ear to provide the cells of the body with electrical stimulation and that the cells of Corti deep in the inner ear transform sound waves into electrical input. The function of the ear is to listen and the function of listening is to charge the brain with electrical potential and hence to charge the nervous system. Sounds, especially the ones we make ourselves as singers and speakers, are a kind of primal energy food. This of course is something that most people know intuitively, which is why the first thing a fatigued worker does on arriving home is to put on a music tape or begin herself to sing around the house. It has been Tomatis's lifework to attempt to demonstrate or explicate this intuition in scientific terms.

One of the best known anecdotes about his work as a consultant physician concerns an order of Benedictine monks in a monastery in the south of France which was in a state of decline. A number of physicians had been called in to diagnose the prevailing malaise. One had suggested that the traditional sleep pattern of the monks of from three to four hours a night was insufficient and suggested an increase to six hours or eight. A second consultant recommended adding more animal protein to their diet which was almost wholly vegetarian but for a little fish. The fact that the monks had maintained their prodigious workloads on such a diet since the twelfth century was not considered significant. Fatigue, lethargy, depression and physical ill-health continued to increase. After a time, Tomatis, who had a villa nearby and who knew the Abbé, was called in on an informal basis. After studying the daily routine of the monks before and after the modernising reforms of Vatican Two, Tomatis came to a single conclusion. He recommended that the monks return to the practice they had abandoned post Vatican Two of meeting together eight and nine times a day to sing Gregorian chant. Singing together, he said, would create a mental and emotional focus that would bring the monastery group field into harmony and resonance as a community, as well as profoundly recharging the energy of individual monks. Within six months, he claims, there was a dramatic improvement in the life of the monastery.

Would any singing have achieved the same effect? Not according to Tomatis. The singing must be of a particularly powerful kind, of which Gregorian chant is exemplary. It is partly the effect of overtones on the nervous system, partly the elongated vowel sounds of Gregorian and the special breathing practices that enable them. The slowest possible breathing as required by the elongated vowels of the chant is a sort of respiratory yoga that leads to a state of tranquillity and balance. Doing this in company with others and at the same rate enhances the effect. Symmetry is achieved. Respiratory and heart rates slow down and come into alignment. It's the same sensation, says Tomatis, when you are listening to a great singer. 'You mimic him because, first of all, he excites all of your higher proprioceptor responses, and then you dilate to breathe strongly with him. You become sure of the note that comes next. It is you who sings the note and not him. He invites you to do it in your own skin.' (Tomatis, 1990.) This is the phenomenon of so-called entrainment, where systems come into alignment, as in Huygens' famous pendulum experiment. When individuals sing or chant together, everyone is in a sense tuning together. They lock in, first on the physical plane and then, if you have a mystical cast, on the spiritual plane, to achieve a kind of union. Singing in church is a form of spiritual entrainment. Singing the national anthem or any patriotic song is a form of political and social entrainment (something the Nazis and all propagandists understand only too well). The musicologist Jill Purce tells of running a summer school for teachers and discussing the problem of school assemblies. Traditionally the school assembly was a time for singing the school song and/or some kind of hymn. In recent times both practices have become problematical, but it is Purce's argument that it doesn't matter what you sing, the important thing is to sing *something* since the real aim of any assembly is to tune pupils and teachers into something higher than themselves so that the activities of the school can be harmonious. This reminded me of the observation by a teacher of my acquaintance that the most harmonious schools with the least discipline problems have, in his experience, been those with the most developed musical culture and, in particular, a great emphasis on mass participation in school choir.

Much of Tomatis's work turns on the distinction between hearing and listening. Listening is the key to everything; it is paying attention; it takes you out of yourself and is the first step in making a connection with others. The desire to listen is the human's most ontological desire, says Tomatis, since it is the basis of his desire to communicate. The foetus's first communication is with the world outside, with the sound of his mother's voice. In the womb 'listening to the mother's voice remains the most fundamental perception'. The autistic child, for example, is able to hear but unable to listen. Stuttering is a listening disorder, dyslexia is a listening disorder. The anxious or neurotic subject is blocked in his or her listening. Hearing refers only to the physical capabilities of the ear; listening, including self-listening, is the first step in understanding the self and communication with others. In the broadest sense and on the highest level, it is the auditory function of the psyche. And learning to sing is pre-eminently learning to listen, to hear the notes in your own voice, to hear them in others and then to bring them into the relationship – for example, harmony – that you desire.

In all of this the role of high frequencies is crucial. The thing first heard by the foetus is the voice of the mother, a faint and slightly strident solo in the symphony of bodily sounds. It is a sound which comes to us filtered naturally by bone conduction in some of the high frequencies. These are replicated in certain music and instruments like bagpipes and trumpets, which is why these instruments are used to excite and energise in, say, military charges. It is the bones that sing. The voice essentially excites bone conduction, giving the impression that sound originates from outside or beyond the body. Here is a purely organic explanation for the sensation one sometimes has when singing of the ethereal – of being taken out of oneself.

I find myself greatly intrigued by the character of Tomatis who was a driven man with something of a messianic sense of mission. In this he is at times reminiscent of that mad genius Wilhelm Reich, although, unlike Reich, he has been greatly honoured in his own scientific community despite being controversial. He regarded himself as no mere technician and was a devout Catholic, making a considerable leap beyond the purely technical aspects of his work to the realms of the metaphysical. 'When you are singing, it is God singing with your body like an instrument,' he writes. 'It is the universe that speaks, and we are the machines to translate the universe,' and so on. The leap he makes is a purely personal one since he in no way demonstrates it. It is true, nevertheless, that in all ages and in all cultures there has been a profound connection between singing and religious or ritual practice. And, as leading disciples of Tomatis such as the US music therapist Don Campbell are quick to emphasise, the various forms of sacred chant that occur across a range of cultures, occur in high frequencies. In Tomatis's terms, they are a form of high-frequency audition therapy indispensable to the health of the priestly and shamanic caste and an essential part of their spiritual medicine. We see it in the Indian yoga of sound, mantra yoga, in Tibetan horns and cymbals, Zen gongs, Christian church organs and steeple bells, Hindhu bhajan singing and in the extraordinary Tibetan practices of overtone chanting.

2

Music in the ancient world was a mysterious and powerful tool for the attunement of body and psyche. 'The wise,' writes Inayat Khan, 'considered the science of sound to be the most important science in every condition of life.' 'It is,' as Joachim-Ernst Berendt reminds us, 'the Word made Flesh of the Bible; the *nada* or soundless sound of the *Upanishads;* the *nam* or *Gurbani* of the Sikh Adi Granth; the *kalma-i-ilahi* or inner sound of the Koran; and the *saute surmadi* or *hu* of Sufism. It is also synonymous with Plato's Logos, with the Pythagorean music of the spheres. Buddhism knows it as *Fohat* while Chinese mysticism recognises it as the Kwan-Yin-Tien or the Melodious Heaven of Sound.' (*The Third Ear,* 1988.)

In every culture ritual singing and chanting is employed as a means of awakening a higher consciousness. In Hinduism, for example, the greatest of the arts is singing, the shortest route to the spiritual heights because it is the most direct expression of a man's spirit. Nor is this belief confined purely to Eastern mysticism. Martin Luther believed so strongly in the power of singing to arouse the 'sad, sluggish and dull spirit' that he made it the basis of his reformist liturgical practice and uttered the celebrated dictum that he would not have as a teacher or ordained minister anyone who could not sing. Theology, said Luther, begins where music leads to. Singing is a 'divine creation' by which the human being can be brought to faith, a result of the movement of the Holy Spirit, enabling the soul to 'hear, and trust, and follow', and in consequence the

Lutheran Church began by placing tremendous emphasis on the hymn chorale, on the members of the congregation singing together, in their own music and in their own language.

For Aboriginal peoples the power of the law of the Dreamtime can only be evoked by the appropriate songs. These are permanently tied to nature, to particular local waterholes, rocks, animals, plants and so on. Songs are also maps. Chester Schultz describes it thus: 'These sacred songs are said to be primordial and the authors are totemic ancestors, not human beings. The songs are handed down carefully in a system of age-graded musical education, which at all levels is a medium for religious knowledge and attitude, including history and law. In the higher reaches it is revelation, attainable only by first passing the prerequisite lower stages. To be able to sing the appropriate parts of the repertoire is essential if any child is to eventually take his or her place in society. Some of the repertoire is shared by all, but some is the protected secret of a particular group, defined by sex, clan, or stage of maturity. Songs regulate and instruct every stage of a person's life.' (*Our Place, Our Music*, 1989.)

In indigenous cultures singing has long been used as a healing tool. The Australian anthropologist Diane Bell told me about an occasion when her young daughter was taken ill with food poisoning during a prolonged field trip among the

Kaytej people at Warrabri in outback Australia.
Because of the Kaytej women's acceptance of Bell
and her daughter as kin, they spontaneously
began to treat the sick child as they would one
born to them. Placing her in the centre of a circle,
they massaged her abdomen, gave her quantities
of water and then sang to her for between three to
four hours. The songs the Kaytej women sang
were songs of that part of the country and the
people who belonged to it. As Bell says in her
remarkable book, *Daughters of the Dreaming* (1983),
the Kaytej concept of health is a cosmic one which
entails the maintenance of harmonic relations
between people and place. The individual who is
ill has lost his or her sense of connection. The
singing is a restoration, a 'putting-in-touch-with'
process. The songs of your country reconnect you;
they restore you to harmony with what is around
you, and those to whom you belong.

Such instances were once patronisingly
described as a kind of faith-healing but there are
many recorded instances of resolute sceptics
being greatly affected by ritual singing, and in particular, ritually intoned high frequency sounding.
A group of acquaintances from my university days,
card-carrying rationalists and sceptics all, were
invited on one occasion to attend a meeting of an
Indian spiritual group where, during the evening,
chanting of the usual kind was conducted for

almost an hour; nothing exceptional, such as one encounters in every suburban ashram. By the end of it, one of the sceptical party had dissolved into tears. Another, a young law student, visibly affected, declared that they must have put some kind of gas through the air vents – thereby illustrating how easily, in straining to find a rational explanation within a very limited model, one can tip over into the irrational. This was not a mistake made by that most sceptical of philosophers, the English positivist, Herbert Spencer. Music, he wrote, is one of the few things the rational mind cannot explain: it is 'an incomprehensible secret'.

3

Not the least interesting aspect of Tomatis's conclusions is the way in which they connect up with the work of some theorists in the areas of psychology and psychoanalysis. Like the British object relations school of psychoanalysis, Tomatis placed great emphasis on the role of the mother, in his case going back even to the earliest days of the womb and the power of the mother's voice as primary sensation. More than that, he idealises the prenatal environment as a kind of nirvana which critic, Tim Wilson has characterised as 'an auditory paradise, a condition of "super hearing" to which we aspire throughout our lives to return' (Campbell, 1996). For me there is something in this that resonates with the attempts of British art theorist, the late Peter Fuller, to explain, and defend, the function of art.

Like Tomatis, Fuller has something of a messianic tinge to his work. The atheist son of a church pastor, he turned to psychoanalysis for an explanation of why artistic pursuits, like singing, might be deemed essential to the mental well-being of ordinary people. Drawing on the theories of the object relations school of pyschoanalysis, especially the work of Donald Winnicott, Fuller invokes art as the 'potential space' that enables us to escape from 'the insult of the reality principle', that is, the drudgery of earning a living. On Winnicott's model, one of the effects of the human infant's prolonged infancy is that the infant begins life in a blissfully uncomplicated state but at around the time of weaning, the so-called reality principle – that the world is a harsh place that does not exist purely for the infant's own personal benefit – begins to intrude. This transition from a world that is entirely subjective experience to one that is objectively perceived as outside the self is a painful one. The infant loses his or her sense of oneness with the world having already lost a sense of oneness with the mother in the womb. To compensate and console, the infant establishes an intermediate area of experience between objective and subjective reality, a so-called 'potential space' of play. In this one area, says Fuller, we are free from the insult of the reality principle. How satisfyingly we can be free of it, and for how long, depends on how nurturing our environment is and the valuation it gives to creative play in adult life.

In pre-industrial times, argues Fuller, 'the aesthetic dimension has been hopelessly marginalised and the potential space, at least as the location of adult cultural experience, has been effectively sealed over' (*Aesthetics after Modernism*, 1982). With industrialisation, 'the potential space began to shrink. The insult of the reality principle impinged deeper and deeper into the lives of ordinary people. There was no room for an intermediate area on production lines, at the pit-head or in steel furnaces.' Art was no longer an element in man's lived relation to the world, as it had been in indigenous cultures and even in pre-industrial rural and cottage industry. The artist, says Fuller, became separate and 'special'.

On this model, singing is simply one of the many forms of artistic activity that offer us a break from the established reality principle. And indeed this is strongly echoed in something that Stephen Schafer, the Musical Director of the Sydney Gay and Lesbian Choir, said in an interview he gave to Sydney writer Teresa Savage in 1996. When asked what members got out of singing in the choir, Schafer cited 'the psychology of setting time aside when you can stop worrying about the problems of day-to-day life, of living in a sad household or having a difficult job – it's time out, it's another place, it's art rather than reality. It might relate to reality very strongly, but it is after all not reality as such, it's not the whole thing. It's reflective, or contemplative, interior time. Ironically, when you're all together singing, the last thing you worry about are the day-to-day stresses of being gay and lesbian.'

Micheál McCarthy, Musical Director of Sisongke, makes a similar point. 'You have to look at where singing sits in relation to the rest of our lives. For some people it's very different from what they do during the week. Some have said that it's a real high for them because their normal routine involves sitting in front of computers punching numbers, typing or drafting reports, dealing with benchmarks, competencies, daily measurement targets and the many levels of rationalisation that inhere in certain work. It's a completely different mind-set.'

Undoubtedly it is true that singers in a choir seek to immerse themselves in a subjective, a feeling moment as a way of escaping from stress, but it is also true that they wish to escape into something much more than just a space of 'discharge and release'. This they can do through jogging, or working-out in the gym. But they also seek to escape not just for its own sake, but in order to enter into a space that is powerfully charged with an experience of union. Stephen Schafer captures the inherent paradox of this when he says that singing 'sort of amplifies your self and you lose yourself in it at the same time. That's teamwork at its best. You're part of a greater whole. That sort of stuff is exhilarating, it's thrilling. It's the moment of performance itself, when you're out of time, when the song is it, when you and the choir are making something fantastic, and there's silence and you. That's the universe, that's a great moment, a moment of transcendence if you like.'

What is it that David Brennan says? 'Being in the present moment is what music is. There is no other purpose to music! It is completely evanescent. It is the ultimate Zen experience. It has no other purpose than to be in the moment, and disappear.'

Psychoanalysis might interpret this as a desire to regress to the nirvana of the womb. Social anthropologists might argue for it as an attempt to achieve a sense of community, with the choir, say, as one of many possible communities. In *Aesthetics after Modernism* Peter Fuller quotes Edmund Leach, the English social anthropologist. 'Each of us is constantly engaged, almost from birth, in a struggle to distinguish I from other, while at the same time trying to ensure that I does not become wholly isolated from other.' And this, says Leach (and Fuller), is where art comes in: 'It is the bridge we need to save ourselves from schizophrenia.' If one model of this connection that Leach refers to is the community choir, then this may go some way towards explaining why the choir continues to be one of the most resilient of our social institutions.

The German philosopher, Ernst Bloch, believed that it was the function of music to create a utopian space where inner and outer world, subject and object, mind and nature might be reconciled beyond their present divided condition. Bloch writes of the powerful yearning for a perfected self (shades of *sacré égoïsme*) which behind all superficial egotism is part and parcel of a drive toward a world itself transfigured. In other words, in every narcissistic project of the so-called Me Generation is the seed of a wider Utopian field.

Bloch is just one of a long line of German philosophers (Nietzsche, Schopenhauer, Hegel) to grapple in philosophical terms with the power of music. All agree, though with greatly varying emphases, that in some fashion music enables people to enter into another dimension. One of the most influential of the modern German musicologists, Victor Zuckerkandl, is adamant on this point. Wittgenstein was wrong, he argues, to write that 'what we cannot speak of we must consign to silence'. 'Not at all,' says Zuckerkandl, 'what we cannot speak of we can sing about.' (*Man the Musician*, 1976.) He goes on to postulate the reality of an additional dimension, neither inner nor outer but both at once. The singer experiences inner life as something he shares with the world, not as something that sets him apart from it. Music is a form of self-abandon, 'and this is not a turning away from the self, not a negation, but an enlargement, an enhancement of the self, a breaking down of the barriers separating self from things . . .' (Stephen Schafer: ' . . . [singing] sort of amplifies your self and you lose yourself in it at the same time.')

This is an argument that runs strongly counter to the behaviourist and utilitarian view that music's function is simply the discharge of tension, like quenching your thirst. From the opposite point of view, the most important thing about music is not that it eliminates something from the world but that it adds something to it. The more radical of the musicologists, thinkers of the school of *Musica Speculativa* such as Marius Schneider and Rudolf Haase go even further. Schneider is a distinguished ethnomusicologist with a strong spiritual bent, coiner of the term 'acoustic spirituality' which refers to the belief that the essence of the soul is not air but vibration, sound. The first postulate of speculative music is that sound (or tone, or music) is ontologically prior to material existence. In active participation in music, i.e. singing or playing, man taps into the primordial acoustic energy of creation. This is why, says Schneider, all public ritual is accompanied by music and song, a hearkening back to archaic practices. A student of the Vedas, he quotes from the *Shatapatha Brahmana*: 'Whatever the gods do, they do by song.' Singing calls creation into being and then sustains it: in the *Rigveda* the terms food and hymn are used practically as synonyms.

All songs, says Schneider, are intrinsically songs of praise in that they are about the hunger for and affirmation of life. In the Hindu scriptures, since God resides in the innermost part of every person, to sing the praise of God is to bring about the merger of the human and the divine – one brings one's own innermost nature into harmony with the word of creation from which all creatures have sprung.

In other words we move from separation into union; we are saved from schizophrenia; we embrace the singing cure.

4 *work-in-progress*

It's Tuesday night in the Trinity Hall and it's now the middle of winter and the heating has failed and I am so cold I can barely get my voice out. One of the group is organising a night at the Bruce Beresford film *Paradise Road*, about a group of women in a Japanese prisoner-of-war camp who sing in a choir all through their incarceration. 'At least they were warm,' says Beatrice, *sotto voce*, and rolling her eyes in my direction. She is giving out the sheet music – lost on me since I can't read it, though my newest resolution is that I will have to learn.

When I joined this group, all I brought with me was a vague notion that there was something in my life that I needed to do that I had hitherto left undone. And, lurking in my unconscious, an apparently mundane research finding, courtesy of Aaron, that had once prompted me to a new curiosity about that part of the self that wants to sing. That 'I', clearly, has a fierce desire to draw attention to itself out there in the spotlight, all eyes on me . . . ME . . . Look, look (Look, Mum, look) . . . the narcissistic self, one minute flaunting its wounds, dressing them up in the finest clothes available – 'I will now sing the aria, "*Un aura amorosa*" from Mozart's *Così Fan Tutti* – disguising, titivating, camouflaging the loneliness of the long-distance ego.

Singing alone.

And then, in the group, the ensemble, that other self blooms, the one that wants to forget all that, wants to lose that very thing it thought, or at times thinks, is so precious, that ego in the spotlight; wants to become not one – a supremely refined or developed single consciousness – but One; wants to be part of something larger, some whole; wants not to shine alone but to connect, to be immersed in an oceanic consciousness. *Ecstasis*: to be taken out of.

Singing with others.

Standing here tonight, among these 'others', I don't think there is any one answer to the question of why people sing, any more than there is one answer to the question of why people read books, or garden, or why they want to have children. Winnicott's potential space is much larger and more mysterious than Fuller imagined, something Winnicott himself recognised when he declared, with a humility rare in analysts, that 'the self naturally knows more than we do'. In his last work he went beyond even this to a final paradox which is an acknowledgement of some essential mystery. The self, he wrote, has an urgent need to communicate with others, but a still more urgent need, in its depths, to remain unfound. The self is elusive, the player of hide and seek. It wants to be both separate and connected, to shine alone *and* lose itself in the group.

This had crystallised for me one night here, in the singing group, when we were asked to break into small groups and do a vocal improvisation on our own names. Some groups took to it with relish; mine winced at the idea and made a silent protest by delivering its improvisation in mime. We were agreed on this: we didn't want to draw attention to our own attempts at wit or invention, we didn't want to have to bother with wit and invention at all; we wanted to lose ourselves in someone else's

music. There were others there who put on spec-
tacular and elaborate displays; they were gifted
and urgent soloists, there to be noticed, and that
was fine with me. But there were those of us who
came to sing in order to be lost to sight, to be in it
and at the same time out of it. Not passively and
silently, but actively, and in full voice, unfound.

Meanwhile, I have been invited this evening to
join the basses and try myself out there. For com-
fort. I am still having trouble with 'the mask'. There
is all this empty space in the head – truly – all these
resonating chambers, and I have yet to learn how to
free-float in them, how to 'float the sound'. I know
that once I position myself among the basses with
their earthy, anchored sound, I'll begin to feel restless, and my ear will become attuned to Bridie and
the sopranos, and I will go on singing, as I've
begun, in a state of uncertainty. But that's okay.
One day I'll manage to get out of my own way.

the choral singer (2)
'Wherever I go, I sing. It's like: Have score, will
travel. When I lived in Newcastle for a while, I
joined a choir there. When I was in New York last
year I went and sang in the public *Messiah*. It was
the twelfth of December. No rehearsal, you just
went. You pay a ticket to go in, it's four dollars or
something. You go there to have a hit. There are

three thousand voices in the auditorium at the Lincoln Centre and whole office parties go – that's their end-of-year function, the whole office goes and sings *The Messiah*. You've got to be able to hold your part because you don't know who's around you; you've got a guy on one side singing the bass and a guy on the other singing the tenor part. Is it chaotic? Well, it's fabulously good fun, because you've got to enjoy and trust your voice. You think: I'm not going to be a mouse, I came here to sing this thing. And off you go. And you just have a great time.

'When I was working in England, I sang there as well. I was living in a village called Brightwell. I'd just had a day showing my stuff for the European market and I'd had big rows with our producer over there, and he was mean and nasty . . . and I got back to the village feeling: What on earth am I doing here? Why do I stay here? I still had another three or four months to go of my contract. And it was a miserable grey day and I just fell apart, just weeping for hours, what'll I do? what'll I do? And then I remembered, exactly opposite our house, Brightwell Manor, just over the road, was a little old village church with lots of gravestones and big trees, and the last time I'd gone for a walk there, I'd seen a notice just pinned on a tree saying the choir was about to start. And I didn't know whether it was that week or the last week or the next week, but I was so miserable – and I knew that if you sing you feel better. I was thinking about how when black prisoners of conscience were taken into places of detention like Robben Island in South Africa, the other prisoners would come and take them and say: You must sing, it's the only way to stay up, you must sing. You have to sing, otherwise you'll lose your spirit. I don't know where I read this, but I remembered it. So I went over the road and the notice was still there. And it was actually that very night that the choir was starting. So I took down the phone number and I ran back to the house and I rang up the guy who lived in a village nearby and I just said to him, "Look, I'm an Australian, I'm only here for a few months, I won't be here for when the Christmas concert season is on but I really would like to sing and come to the choir tonight" – which was only a hundred yards up the road in The Free Church. And he said: "Well, of course." He said: "Everybody sings." And it is a tradition in England that everybody sings. Every village has a choir and it's not just a glee club, it's a proper choir with a proper choir director and you sing real pieces. And that evening we were doing *The Messiah* and a Mozart piece – it was real stuff. He was a very nice choir master. And I just felt so much better when I got home and I thought: It's true, you just have to sing and you get your spirit back again.'

ACKNOWLEDGEMENTS

I am especially grateful to Helen Todd for her forbearance and wise counsel during the research of this essay, though she can in no way be held accountable for its limitations.

I am also indebted to the generosity of the following people: Mati-Jo Beams, Diane Bell, David Brennan, Stephanie Dowrick, Beatrice Kelly, Jody Heald, Valanga Khoza, Andrew Lohrey, Brigid Lohrey, Cleo Lohrey, Stacey Loukis, Judith Lukin-Amundsen, Micheál McCarthy, Wayne McDaniel, Victoria Rigney, Marnie Rogers, Teresa Savage, Stephen Schafer, Lyn Tranter, Jasmine Trethewey, Sarah Walker and all the members of the Tuesday night singing group.

ROBERT DESSAIX

'At last the secret'

PROLOGUE

If there are two kinds of chatter polite society affects to disdain, they are metaphysics and gossip. Yet what other kind of conversation is even half as satisfying? What else can hold the attention as gossip and metaphysics can?

In a way they amount to versions of the same thing: we feel a need to know much more about what's going on than we're being told – and we suspect the worst. So both gossip and metaphysics thrive on a lack of hard facts, which no doubt accounts for the bad name they've both acquired.

What delights us about gossip, of course, is its effrontery, its snook-cocking disrespect for someone else's public self, as well as all the little rituals of power that go with it. How gratifying it is, then, to tamper with the conventional boundaries between what is private and what is public (at least in someone else's case), turning their carefully concealed inner stories into eye-opening outer stories. When the music of gossip stops, in other words, everyone is sitting on a different chair and someone has usually been thrillingly dethroned.

More or less everyone gossips – indeed, our sanity as social beings depends on it. If we didn't gossip, then, like parlour atheists, we'd be stuck in complicity with the world of appearances. Gossip serves a comedic purpose in the drama of our lives: it's an impudent, disruptive game with appearances, a potion against concealment and (other people's) secrets.

Metaphysics, some might say, is much the same thing but in a different genre – loftier, although not always tragedy. In fact, the sets are usually Romantic: more the deserted beach than the aromatic café, more the garden in the late afternoon than the kitchen table, although it's not an absolute rule. Still, on the whole, cafés and kitchen tables invite talking *about* things (including metaphysics), which is congenial to gossip, whereas deserted landscapes and solitary gardening encourage *experiencing* things, an altered consciousness.

Yet the suburban metaphysician is hardly different from the gossip in anything that matters: he

usually directs his (sometimes misplaced) inso-
lence at various mock-ups of materialism currently
strutting the stage, although in the end, like the
servants in classic comedies (including 'The
Nanny'), he probably knows his place. He, too,
seeks to turn inner stories into outer ones, to
reveal powerful secrets, to throw light on hidden
patterns and unriddle the world – indeed, sometimes the universe. (And all this while squirting
the aphids with pyrethrum on a sunny Sunday
afternoon.) In other words, the metaphysician
gossips about God, quite often with as little foundation to his conjectures as there is to his calumny
on the neighbours.

The metaphysician gossips about why there is
something rather than nothing and what that
something might be, spreading his rumours on
the basis of very little evidence. His antics cause
the pious and erudite offence and evoke derision
at court where power lies. But he won't stop. He
believes he's onto something, he thinks he knows
something, he's convinced he *saw* something pre-
viously hidden from him as he stepped around a
mound of seaweed where the tide had ebbed. In
fact, the whole exercise is enjoyably oceanic.

(I've said *he* here, not because I imagine a
metaphysical bent is a particularly male character-
istic, but because, to be frank, I'm half talking
about myself.)

In the three short pieces that follow it is this more sublime kind of secret that has been my concern. More precisely, it was less the secrets themselves that engaged my interest than how people very different from ourselves have sought to approach them and make them known. However, I would like to make it clear that, in writing about Egypt during the Eighteenth Dynasty, about the Eleusinian Mysteries centuries before our era and the unimaginably ancient rock art of Cape York in northern Australia, I have written not as a scholar (I am no Egyptologist, no archeologist or anthropologist) but as a curious traveller, armed, to be sure, with intelligent guidebooks, but just a traveller nonetheless. In fact, the rock gallery I describe in 'The Upside-Down Blue Man' is an amalgam of memories of several such galleries I visited rather than a particular site. Wherever I went what interested me above all was what it must have felt like to be in those places when the mysteries, the hidden things about the workings of the universe, were thought to be knowable to certain people at certain precise points on the globe at certain exact times.

In the world we now inhabit we are torn in two directions: on the one hand everything seems about to be known, with an announcement to follow shortly in *New Scientist* or the *New England Journal of Medicine*, and on the other hand it seems possible that nothing will ever truly be knowable at all, that we're deaf, dumb and blind in an epistemological vacuum. Consequently, the only truly important secret left to us, as the 'Seinfeld' series made plain, is our PIN number. At other times in other places, as we know, people saw things differently – and still do, of course – and it's this difference, together with the pattern to it, that caught my dilettante's attention.

Strictly speaking, of course, the task I set myself proved beyond me, as I should perhaps have foreseen. It has been impossible to think myself back into seeing the way the people who once lived on Cape York, on the Nile and in ancient Athens once saw. All I have really been able to do is catch certain echoes, perhaps not even half-understood, before climbing into a bus or jeep to drive back to a world where what I experienced is easily dismissed as vain, unscholarly imaginings. For all that, the echoes were strong, at least when I managed to listen to them alone and focus intently on where they came from. And unscholarly imaginings, in my experience, can on occasion magically make the thickest veils instantly transparent, while the scholar's eye is still examining the intricate warp and weft of the veil itself. In any case, imaginings are all most of us have when we travel, if we want to bring what we're looking at to life.

Now for the gossip about the gods.

THE QUEEN WITH THE GOLDEN BEARD

Djeser Djeseru

Late in the afternoon, when the crowds have thinned and the crags behind the temple are glowing a coppery red, you can suddenly picture how it must have been: Hatshepsut, every inch a king in kilt and elegant head-cloth with gold coil, shaded by a brilliant yellow parasol, sits gazing westwards in silence at the terraces of white carved limestone creeping towards her from the base of the escarpment. This was to be the most beautiful building in all the world.

A clink or two as a mason chips at a stone, the ring of a dropped tool, a shout – strangely disembodied in this vast, dry place – perhaps an egret's cry in the distance. But no mason or egret can break this kind of silence: it gathers here, where the queen attired like a king is sitting, and opens its arms westwards to smother the whole world.

Sitting here like this is what she sometimes did.

Beyond those bluffs to the west, where the sun-god, her father, is swallowed up each night, is the land of death. Death begins right there, a cry away, where the cliff-top, high in the sky above the temple, juts up into the blue. To the east, behind her, not far away but invisible, is life: groves of feathery papyrus along the river, loud with water-fowl at this hour in the afternoon, wharves swarming with fishermen and travellers, feluccas careening across the brown waters, their sails like thick brushstrokes of white paint, and the teeming city, where, even as she sits here, people are cooking, hammering, arguing, writing . . .

Here, though, where Hatshepsut is sitting, squinting slightly under her parasol because even this late in the day the white of the limestone ter-races of Djeser Djeseru is blindingly stark, here in this jackal-ridden valley between the river and the ridge, neither death nor life holds final sway. This is a threshold, there's an exquisite tension in the air recalling that uncatchable instant before a pendulum starts swinging back the other way. Here death calls to life and life prepares its answer. And these terraces, of a colonnaded beauty never before seen in Egypt and not yet dreamt of by the Greeks, are Hatshepsut's answer. After all, this is her mortuary temple, inching towards her out of the cliffs, and these tiers of columns, like row upon row of gigantic alabaster flutes, hiding sanctuaries inside sanctuaries inside sanctuaries, are the façade of her house of death.

Hatshepsut's answer, in other words, is mathematics mixed with magic. She has commanded the burning chaos of rocks on the western escarpment to give birth to mathematical beauty in limestone, alabaster, granite, Sudanese slate and gold from Nubia. Djeser Djeseru ('the Holiest of the Holy') has crawled out of the rocks like a perfectly proportioned, glistening scarab-beetle from its pile of dung.

Not everyone at the time, it must be said, was pleased, more especially her nephew (and also stepson, this being Egypt), Thutmose. Quite clearly a temple of this magnitude and magnificence was calculated to convince Egypt that Hatshepsut, his stepmother-aunt, was the lawful pharaoh, beloved of the gods, when everyone knew in their heart of hearts that a female king was an offence to the right order of things. Later in life, when he was finally crowned pharaoh, Thutmose got his own back by erasing every image he could find of Hatshepsut. Then he marched into Asia and slaughtered with abandon.

Yet even young Thutmose must have sensed a rightness in these symmetries emerging from chaos. His tutors in the harem-school must have taught him how, according to ancient wisdom, being had first appeared out of non-being through mathematics – because mathematics operated timelessly. It was like an early rumble of the approaching Big Bang theory. Perceiving mathematical law and enunciating it, the One became many because it was possible. Through division and multiplication (to put it another way) Wholeness (translated into the sun-god) conquered formlessness, timelessness, darkness and hiddenness. So even Thutmose, strolling by in high dudgeon, must have felt how right these squares and oblongs were against the disordered rockfalls of the cliff.

The Land of Punt

In those days, as she cast her eyes (almond-shaped, of course) around, taking in the scaffolding, the piles of stone from the quarries and the conscripted workmen swarming like wasps in the distance, Hatshepsut must have taken particular pleasure in the myrrh trees clustered around the grand causeway on the first terrace. Needless to say, there's not a single myrrh tree to be seen here these days, just rock, stone and sky – and clutches

of tourists like myself – but we know that Hatshepsut ordered her gardeners to make her temple rise out of a grove of myrrh trees, dotted with
brilliant garden-beds and papyrus ponds. Now,
myrrh had been a half-mystery to her ancestors for
centuries, not unlike moon-rock or the fragment
of a meteorite today.

Burnt, myrrh wafted through their sanctuaries,
as a liniment it was smeared on royal bodies, it was
needed here in this temple to anoint the god, it
was used to fumigate Egyptian houses, it was
chewed in tiny balls to sweeten sour breath. But
where exactly did it come from? It was said to leak
from trees in the Land of Punt, but where precisely *was* that?

For a thousand years or so before Hatshepsut's
day expeditions had been sent to the land where
the myrrh tree grew to barter for resin and pyg-
mies. Or so the hieroglyphs tell us. Yet exactly
where this legendary realm lay remained a secret
known only to the gods and their earthly progeny,
the pharaohs, and was in that sense a mystery to
ordinary mortals. At the time of the Eighteenth
Dynasty, in other words, when the pharaoh owned
everything, although you might try to work your
way backwards from the fragrant lump of resin in
your hand, you could not get past the word *Pwenet*,
Land of Punt, and what *Pwenet* might mean no
one could or would tell you. Was it in the same

order of things as the Land of the Dead, for
instance – hidden and unknowable? Or was it in
the same order of things as the Land of the Hit-
tites – hidden from view but not at all unknowable? In either case it was a mystery, although in
each case a mystery of a quite distinct kind. Hatshepsut, the world's first great queen, sent out a
fleet into the world which made Punt real and
brought the myrrh tree to Egypt.

As we know from the astoundingly realistic
painted scenes on the middle portico, her sailors
found Punt and the myrrh tree came to Egypt.
Ironically, three and a half thousand years later,
we're again no longer quite sure where the Land
of Punt was. Possibly in Somaliland. For us it's
veiled once more in mystery. This is deeply satisfying. It quickens the pulse.

Peering at the lifelike vignettes some years ago,
the guide's voice buzzing in my ear, I tried to
imagine how it must have felt all those millennia
ago to handle myrrh, to perfume the body and
soothe the skin with it, inhale its strong, refined
fragrance, embalm with it, hallow with it the very
Beginning of All Existence (as the god was
known), all the while not knowing where it came
from – or, more exactly, accepting that it came
from somewhere not known to ordinary mortals,
beyond their limits of the known. When Hatshepsut farewelled her expedition to Punt (with great

pomp, I like to think, as befits the desecration of a mystery), she must surely have felt an excitement almost beyond our power to imagine at the idea that what was a mystery – known only in some sense to the gods – was about to become known to everyone. A secret, perhaps, for a year or two, but then just common knowledge. The Land of Punt would no longer float somewhere beyond knowing but would be given coordinates, would lie, say, to the south of Yemen or to the east of the Sudanese goldmines. It would appear on a map.

Despoiling a sacred domain is always an exhilarating experience. It's also a risk. Once myrrh lost most of its mystery, for instance, once it was seen to be just a resinous goo bled from scraggly trees you could glimpse from your upstairs window, might it not lose its power along with its mystery? But Amun-Re the scented sun-god was adamant in the ninth year of Hatshepsut's reign that the time had come to wrest Punt from unknowability and make it real: *I will give you Punt, King Maatkare* (he said to Hatshepsut, using a name which meant 'Truthful Order is the Essence of the Sun-god', which must have pleased her), *the whole of it, on its mysterious shores by harbours of incense, the sacred realm, the divine land, my abode of pleasure . . . And your warriors will load their ships to their hearts' content with trees of green incense and all the good things of that land.* Do it, Hatshepsut, he was saying, encompass

Punt in your realm of the known, let it surrender its power to you. On the night Amun-Re had impregnated Hatshepsut's mother, we might remember, the palace had been mysteriously but pointedly flooded with perfume from Punt – the record is quite specific. So the god had clearly had plans for Puntite myrrh in mind right from the beginning.

There's something about Hatshepsut's expedition to the Land of Punt that sets up deep reverberations in my mind. It's not just the blurred picture that forms of brown and white sailing ships, of hot winds, cobalt skies and dangerous, arid shores, nor even the imagined moment of recognition: *this* is the Land of Punt where the myrrh trees grow, it is connected to Thebes in time and space, so many days' sailing down the Red Sea coast, it can be known absolutely, pinpointed at least crudely on a map.

This is spine-tingling stuff, this moment of making something just told as a tale into something real, but there's more to it than that. I wish I knew the precise taste of it all those years ago – if only there were something to trigger it off inside me. Looking in silence at the depictions of the expedition to Punt on the middle portico helps – certainly there's something utterly demystifying about them: it is spring (we can see the nesting birds), the exotic beehive-shaped reed houses are set on stilts in a forest of ebony, palms and myrrh trees, and the Puntites themselves are by no means just sketched in – they're shown to be a diverse lot, Negroid, Semitic, black, brown and pale. They have dogs and cattle and an obese queen, her flabby flesh and double chins an affront to Egyptian ideas of queenly beauty. And the Egyptians couldn't be more condescending: in exchange for the sacred myrrh-tree, gold, ebony, an ape, a pygmy or two and some boomerangs (truly), they leave behind a few weapons and some beads. The natives are depicted as overjoyed. Punt is now *known*.

One little hair-trigger I might press to spark memories of such moments of desecration is attached to my own version of the Land of Punt. (Admittedly, my Land of Punt can never appear on a recognized map.) There's a surprisingly common disorder whose main symptom is that a significant slice of your waking hours – not, as a rule, your hours of dreaming, oddly enough – is taken up with fantasizing about a land which doesn't exist. You happily acknowledge that it doesn't exist – in fact, that is precisely its value to you. Yet you people it with citizens with personal histories and character traits, you crisscross its mountains and plains with roads and railways of a specific length, you name the streets of its cities, list the plays in its theatres' repertoires, know the temperatures in June and December, the wording of the Social Security Act, the airline timetables, the teachings of famous monks in labyrinthine monasteries whose every cell and corridor you've pictured many times . . . and so it goes on like a kind of madness, spreading in your brain like mushrooms after rain: the plants in the Botanical Gardens, the slump in the silver market, the first salvos fired in the civil war, the name of the governor in Roman times (that is, before the Great Migration), trade with the Vikings, Celtic loan words . . . yet the knowledge I have of my land, whose name begins with K, is dilettantish, I assure you, compared to the truly encyclopaedic knowledge some of my fellow fantasts have of theirs. Details of bank accounts, ingenious solutions to engineering problems, meals enjoyed in non-existent restaurants a decade ago, the exact shade of turquoise of a crater lake in late autumn . . . no Irishman could know Ireland better, no archivist could have more facts and figures, maps and graphs at his fingertips.

I'd love to draw you the map of my land right here and now. It's like an unbearable itch, this desire to draw the map. It's the feeling we all get when we're about to share a secret but then don't. There'd be an almost voluptuous pleasure in taking a sheet of paper and several pens – thick-nibbed, fine-nibbed, black, blue and red – and revealing to you the bays and inlets and rivers and plateaux of my island, with all the towns and connecting roads and railway lines marked in very neatly just like one of those perfect *National Geographic* maps so many of us collected as schoolchildren. As a child I used to draw such maps, carefully annotated in my secret language, but not a single human being knew of their existence or ever heard me utter a word of the elaborate language I taught myself to make my islands' inhabitants more real. To me it was a shameful obsession, so no hint of its existence must ever escape.

In varying degrees what happens in imagined terrains such as mine intersects with historical reality. It has to – this is not Hobbit territory. Some of my fellow fantasts apparently confront the problem of how to make private fantasies merge with public reality by re-creating real lands – a certain Greek island, perhaps, or even a Himalayan kingdom once fleetingly visited – repeopling them, rewriting their recent history, taking control of them and moulding them to conform to private desires. My own solution to the problem of how to make the two worlds converge convincingly is to make everything as plausible as possible – no magic carpets, for example, no pretence that the Vikings once reached China, a near neighbour of my imagined land – invisible but plausible, a blind spot in history only I can fill in. There is no bad faith.

Having once written in the sketchiest terms about the existence of this fantasy (bringing other fantasts helter-skelter out of the woodwork), and having even gone so far, against all my better judgment, as to disclose one small item of my secret vocabulary, I think on reflection I've actually turned something secret into something private – that is, less concealed, strictly speaking, than kept unobserved, more like a garden with a very high wall than a secret garden. There's a difference, although the one doubtless shades into the other. Both strike me as vital to our sanity, to our sense of who we are. And so, although my Land of K is no longer a secret, it is and must remain private. The reason is simple: it is a private map of me. To open it up to observation would be to surrender my sense of control over who I have become. It is the only territory left to me where there is no conflict between what I know and what I believe or perceive to be the case. In other words, I can truly say that I *know* there's a bougainvillaea in flower on the wall of a certain house on a certain street in the city of P. Nowadays, given all the argument about knowledge and perception, that's something I can scarcely say about the bougainvillaea growing in my own back garden. If I say it exists in the city of

P., crimson and three metres high and beautiful, then it does. Once I share this story, I am at sea again, bobbing about, unsure of what I can know and what only seems to be the case – unsure, in fact, if I am there at all, except as a series of borrowed babblings, scattered bits of learnt monologue, signifying little apart from some memory of what I've learnt.

I was crossing a street in Brisbane late one afternoon when someone I scarcely knew came up to me and, out of the blue, asked me the name of the land I'd mapped out for myself. It was an exquisite moment, a sort of neon flash – the whole street lit up in brilliant colours. He'd read the brief account I'd written of this land and a few of its features, and had noted that its name began with the letter K. (An intriguing letter, this K, by the way, so much more mysterious and foreign than a dull, domesticated C, which is usually made to do much the same work. A K has definite echoes of the East – khanates, Karakoram, Kyushu, Krishna, Kathmandu – whereas a C always looks so Roman, so Western, so known – Canterbury, Calabria, Cologne, even Canberra. Why not Kanberra, I wonder, in the manner of Kakadu?) We reached the other side of the street and stood for a moment, neither of us saying anything, while I fought with myself over how to reply.

What could it matter if the door to my walled garden were left ajar for a second or two and a couple of blooms were glimpsed and named aloud? Wasn't it all just a childish game anyway, something it was time to grow out of? Yet, when I opened my mouth to reply, I heard myself say: 'I can't tell you, I'm sorry, I just don't want to tell you.' I now half wish I had, but only half. If my land had been a secret, rather than a matter of privacy, I'd probably have given in and said the word. Secrets beg to be shared, secrets thrive on the tension between silence and furtive intimacy. Think of your own and how your body quickens as you edge towards widening the circle of trust while shrinking the core of things known only to you. There are so few opportunities for true intimacy in the course of the average life that it seems a shame to pass any up.

However, since, as I say, my Land of K is less a matter of secrecy than of privacy, a few gates are probably worth keeping locked shut. Little by little as I've grown older (as happens to almost everyone), privacy has become more difficult – you are increasingly known, managed, probed, positioned (for your own protection) to allow outside intervention. It's all part of a process: at the very end, most people lie completely naked and powerless, even their most private functions a public event. It's vital, surely, for your sanity's sake to keep at least some part of your self walled against intrusion, some part of your self that is still growing.

Hatshepsut's Land of Punt, I couldn't help reflecting as I lingered by the depiction of the myrrh-tree expedition (our guide was anxious for us to move on), while in one sense not the same thing at all as my own Land of K (being more a public mystery, for reasons of power about to be demystified), had things in common with it. Certainly, the shivery moment of demystification was something I could appreciate. The black and brown men of the Land of Punt must surrender power that Hatshepsut might acquire it – she needed all the power she could get, after all, with her nephew-stepson brooding murderously in the wings. In the case of my kind of fantasy (and I now know I'm not alone in this) it's more a case of how much of yourself to surrender to conscious analysis – your own or other people's. Conscious analysis can arm against certain demons and foes, putting them in their place and cutting them down to size. But it can also dry up the creative springs, the source of the stories you hear yourself telling yourself. You can cease to surprise and embarrass yourself. All your railways may start running on time. Nothing may happen.

Point Zero

If you can give your guide the slip, something remarkable can happen to you at the Temple of Hatshepsut, something starkly illuminating. Standing where the pharaoh herself must once have stood, watching all that divine geometry condensing in stone at the base of the cliff, rebuking chaos, you see a ramp rising in front of you to a second level of columns. Once upon a time there was an avenue of red granite sphinxes here, guiding you, bracing you as you made your way slowly upwards, for the pageantry and mystery still hidden from view deep inside behind the colonnades. Each sphinx (indifferent, unimpeachable) bore the face of the queen-king Hatshepsut, and each jaw was embroidered with a golden beard.

Today everything is light and open, there's even a kind of hot brilliance showing through between the upper row of columns. It's light (so it's said) because the pharaoh was light, it's delicate but strong because she was delicate and strong. (Think of flint.)

Emerging onto the second terrace, if you drift over to the far left-hand corner below the next row of pillars, you can move from light into shadow, from the glare of the columned terrace into the darkness of the sanctuary of the cowheaded goddess, Hathor. Once inside the vaulted sanctuary, you realize there's an even darker, smaller inner sanctuary. You want to go in, you want to go deeper inside. You want to know what they could have thought of to put at the centre of the inner sanctuary inside the shrine inside the temple.

What they thought of, it turns out, is a gold image of Hathor, with her tall, winged hat and staff. She's gone now, of course, so what I found was nothing. I remember feeling elated and unfulfilled, both at the same time. Zero at the centre. Hathor the cow-goddess is said to have loved silence.

Back outside on the terrace there's yet another ramp leading even higher and closer in towards the cliff. Another line of columns at the top, concealing yet another smaller courtyard, leading through a gap in the pillars right up to a pink granite doorway in the rock itself. That black rectangle, the very iris of Hatshepsut's stone eye, seems to be staring at me out of the blankness beyond in the Land of Death which stretches westward from this very point, from this selfsame rockface I am looking at now.

To penetrate that blackness into the final sanctuary beyond must have been terrifying. One summer evening every year the queen with the golden beard had to make the journey: in her pleated kilt and angular black wig she moved slowly westwards up the processional way, up the causeway and across the first terrace, up the ramp and across the second, smaller terrace, up the next ramp and steadily on across the last, even smaller terrace, hemmed in by double and triple rows of columns like petrified ghosts, then up the last ramp to this single, black eye, to vanish into the Sanctuary of Amun-Re, hewn with precision out of the red rock. You can imagine the gold disc between the cow's horns on her crown flashing in the torch-light one last time as she stepped across the threshold and was swallowed up.

Inside the first chamber within this last sanctuary stood the barque the god had crossed the river on from Thebes. By now the acrobats, the dancers and the incense-bearers would have melted away. The only sound would have been the unearthly jangling of bronze rattles. On the high walls surrounding the barque the rituals the myrrh-loving queen was to perform were portrayed in vivid ochre and turquoise. Once they'd come alive she'd have stepped even farther towards the threshold of the afterlife inside the cliff, into the last torchlit chamber where the living statue of Amun-Re stood gleaming in a niche carved out of the final wall. This, we must remember, was no house of worship, no mere cathedral. This was the room the god lived in. Hatshepsut was now in the presence of the god she would become one with when she finally rested from life. Here, before the statue, she performed her holiest and most deeply hidden sacraments. They were so natural and real they took almost no time at all.

Now came the moment to face eastwards again, to go back out under the night sky (her star-sprinkled mother Nut, bending over the sleeping world) back down into life, down the causeways towards the canal where her glistening barge was moored, towards the river and the city on the far bank. It's a journey I made myself when the sun dipped down behind the cliff-top, but with far less style.

Walking back to the hotel from the wharf along the Corniche, with donkeys clopping by and grinning touts and pedlars milling everywhere, I found it hard to hold onto what I'd experienced at Djeser Djeseru less than an hour before. The Corniche in modern Luxor is scarcely the ideal place to contemplate such things, especially at dusk: coaches, cars, donkey-carts, buses, all swerving and honking, darting and crawling, tourists looking faintly clownish in their outlandish colours, walking wrongly, hawkers harassing you, kebab grills smoking, shouts from the river, and everywhere that slightly acrid, slightly foetid early evening smell. It's the hour when you suddenly feel more than peckish but don't have the energy to find somewhere to eat. In the end, I remember, I found a quiet spot right at the southern end of the Corniche above the river, across the road from the Old Winter Palace Hotel. A couple of caleche drivers tried half-heartedly to interest me in a jog around town, but after a few minutes I was left more or less on my own. I stared westwards across the river towards where I had been.

Oddly enough, I found my thoughts that evening drifting back to the wilderness inland from Cooktown on Cape York, to what is called Kwinkin country, a name so alive with bewitching meanings it was all I could do even then not to fall into a trance. It was some time since I'd been there, and I hadn't stayed there very long, but the memory of what I'd experienced there was indelible. Although the people in that far-off landscape, like Hatshepsut, had confronted death with stories of an afterlife (also in the west), had communed with the sources of creation and reverenced certain caves, gullies, trees and rocks as spiritually charged, something there had been very different, of a different order. And it wasn't just a matter of the buildings or the land – it was something less obvious, something to do with how the two places invited you to experience them.

In the bush on Cape York I'd had a real sense of *everything* being enchanted – every tree-stump, every rock and birdcall, every breath of wind, the pebbles in the creek-bed, the sky itself – of enchantment being ordinary, just the way things were. In that landscape belief and knowledge had been virtually interchangeable. In other words, there had been a continuity there in the perception of how it all worked – an easy merging of I-you-they, of being and having. There had been a real awareness of some kind of intentionality embodied in creation.

Here on the Nile, by Hatshepsut's time, that perception seems to have been absent, or at best just a misty memory. The enchanted realm, the realm of the gods, was certainly connected to the everyday world of the Egyptians, making its presence felt in a thousand ways, yet it was not one with it. Knowledge and belief had begun to diverge. To keep the mysteries alive vast monuments were needed, bureaucracies, a priesthood, elaborate ceremonies and a recorded rhetoric. The spirits had retreated, or been pushed, into man-made objects in niches in man-made temples. (Not quite – the sky was still alive with gods and dead pharaohs – but it's not a gross exaggeration.) Today in Luxor over three thousand years later they have disappeared altogether. In fact, even thinking about them seemed an overly dainty, ineffectual thing to be doing that evening, especially with Beatles music floating over from the Old Winter Palace behind me.

Eventually I stirred myself and headed across the road to see what might be on the menu in its echoing restaurant. One of the caleche drivers promised me a very special price for a late-night tour of Karnak after dinner.

From time to time, half a world away from Luxor in my suburban house or garden, I still like to bring to mind that terraced progression of the pharaoh at Djeser Djeseru, that measured penetration ever higher and further inside towards the point of absolute zero, because it strikes me as an acting-out of an experience many of us have and find both troubling and exciting. It has to do with the point inside almost everyone where secrets and mysteries intersect.

It happens to me mainly at night. I picture myself back at Djeser Djeseru – or perhaps it's a blurring of Hatshepsut's temple with other shrines and sanctuaries I've visited over the years. I embark on the long walk upwards and inwards, across the wide outer courtyard, the smaller higher courtyard and then through the forest of columns into the smallest, most enclosed courtyard of all. Then I take a deep breath and climb the final ramp towards the last sanctuary. I pass from the light into the boxed gloom inside the rock. It's a tremulous moment because, as my eyes become accustomed to the sweet-smelling darkness, I have to confront the fact that there's only one further step to take to reach the heart of the shrine – the seat of the secret, the point where the mystery resides and is enacted. My fear is that this heart will be dead.

At the centre of the square room I've just entered is one last square vault. In the pure white wall facing me as I stand in the doorway is a square opening. But I cannot see into this last shrine to the vortex of the mystery because, in the Balinese fashion, another white wall just inside the opening blocks my view. To step inside I must go either to the left or to the right around it.

I know, because time has collapsed, that if I pass to the left, what I'll find is an empty room. Nothing. At the core of all this intricate geometry will be a void. If, on the other hand, I pass to the right, I'll find in this selfsame room . . . what? *What will I find?*

Not a barque of gold, nor a god with smoking taper, not a magical hieroglyph, not a diamond struck by a shaft of sunlight at the summer solstice, not a holy scroll on a white shawl, not . . . not . . . I know what I shall *not* find, but I struggle to make myself acknowledge what I *shall* find. It's overwhelmingly tempting to pass neither to the left nor to the right, but to turn around and go back out into the light, back down to the sunlit river, where boats will be careening across the water, sails unfurled, the *souks* and muddy alleyways will be swarming, and you might well just stroll about and enjoy being alive. Yet, if I'm patient with myself, as you can be very late at night in the dark with your eyes closed, I know that if I pass to the right what I'll see at the precise centre of this last chamber at the mathematical point where the unknown meets the known is a flame and a small round mirror. Needless to say, in the morning over breakfast this revelation makes little sense.

Still, even over breakfast, I have an inkling about why it's a flame and a mirror I see in my mind's eye: it's a stab at evoking some sense of presence. (But whose? you might ask.) It's a bid to be seen as what you are. It's astonishingly rare to feel you've come into a presence at the centre of any sanctuary. There might be an altar there with brass symbols, perhaps, or a stone effigy smeared with oil and bruised petals, or even a veiled taboo space – but no presence. As often as not it's disenchantment you feel seeping into your pores when you finally reach the heart of the maze, the conviction that *no, this is not it.* In the end, no one seems to know what to put in the empty room. There's never any ghost at the core of the machine. None is expected, of course, not in this day and age, but expectation is not the same as hope.

Mysteries and secrets overlap, and this half-waking dream of penetrating the holy of holies along a narrowing path focuses light on the cloudy area where this happens. Both secrets and mysteries involve concealing knowledge, after all. In fact, there are languages where one word covers both concepts, a word meaning 'hidden things', 'whatever is unknown' – hidden from whom and by whom being a matter of lesser importance. (I'm thinking, for example, of the Russian word *taina*, which can refer to everything from the activities of the secret police or an adulterous liaison to the liturgy.) Both secrets and mysteries are things which cannot be or must not be discerned.

Every life brims over with secrets, when you think about it, both shameful and innocent: a Christmas present hidden at the top of a cupboard, for example, a working-class boy's passion for ballet, a facelift, money stolen from your mother's purse, your daughter's true father, a vicar's disbelief in God, an embarrassing fetish, your toupee . . . it's hardly possible to go out the front door in the morning without first checking that all the cracks have been smoothed over. Secrets of this kind are legitimate currency, surely, in negotiating who you are as opposed to who others want you to be. In fact, you could be said scarcely to exist as an individual without them.

Mysteries, on the other hand, at least until recently, were things hidden from us by the gods, not just the neighbours: everything from where the sun goes at night to why my nose is shaped like my mother's, from who the Etruscans were to what consciousness is. (And, as if there weren't enough mysteries already, human beings energetically dreamt up new ones – the Trinity, for example, Elvis Presley sightings and the so-called Problem of Evil, none of which is a mystery unless you first accept the premiss.) The workings of the cosmos in these instances, being impenetrable to ordinary human intelligence, were thought to be known only to the supreme intelligence – they were mysteries known only to the gods.

Nowadays, of course, being sceptical about any kind of supreme intelligence keeping knowledge from us, we tend to speak of mysteries only as a joke. 'What she sees in him is a mystery', we say, or 'How they get away with charging those prices is a complete mystery' – that sort of thing. Nothing nowadays is *hidden* – just undiscovered. As Turgenev once wrote about the 'motionless, empty' eyes of the sphinx (in French, naturally): 'they're all the more terrible for not seeking to make you afraid. It's cruel not to know the word [to unlock] the enigma. It's even crueller, perhaps, to tell yourself that there is none because there's no longer any enigma.' He wrote those words in the

summer of 1864, at a time when he himself was
suffering from soul-weariness and the sense of the
futility of each lived life, especially his own, and
when the physical sciences indeed seemed poised
to explain *everything*, to offer us an interpretation
of the universe which took account of *everything*,
leaving nothing hidden at all.

Yet, whatever 'they' might have uncovered,
however assured 'they' might be that mysteries are
an anachronism and that the light of knowledge
will soon illuminate every corner of the cosmos,
most of us, with all our limitations, probably have
a lingering sense that some things are past knowing. Even the kind of template science views the
universe through may be concealing part of the
larger picture.

So, in those night-time hours (especially),
when symbolism and metaphor take on a power of
their own, and you're alone with yourself in a way
you never are in the daylight hours, images of
slowly penetrating a concealed place where the
riddle, like a hieroglyph, is patterned to express
the answer to itself, are still seductive. The narrowing path, the passage into darkness, the piercing of that darkness by some numinous light, the
emptiness which is mysteriously filled, nothingness and being locking horns, fear and awe
becoming one again . . . Hatshepsut's temple is
irresistible. And every time I take that path I am

reminded that, as I stand at the blocked threshold of that final sanctum, what I really yearn for is to be illuminated, not to learn, although learning is almost all I know. It's a desire for initiation into a secret.

And initiation is yearned for, surely, because, at the moment it occurs, belief becomes knowledge. You long for it against all reason. When it comes, you are without words.

THE BURNING BRAHMAN

Speaking of initiation, there was once an Indian
I'd like to know more about called Zarmaros (in
Greek). He was a Hindu Brahman, apparently,
who came all the way from the banks of the
Ganges to a small village called Eleusis just west of
Athens to experience a mystery.

This was in 20 BC or thereabouts when the journey would have been arduous, to say the least. He
may have taken the northern route, making his
way overland on foot, on the back of a donkey and
occasionally, where the roads were in better condition or even paved, in a wagon of some kind,
pulled by oxen or onagers. In that case he must
have spent nearly a year on the road and was

fortunate to arrive in one piece. On the other hand, he may have taken the sea route, riding the monsoon from the southern coast of India to Arabia and then up the Red Sea to Egypt – also extremely hazardous, but quicker and cheaper. If he'd read his Herodotus, he'd have been half expecting to encounter flying snakes guarding the incense trees along the way, not to mention weird bat-like animals whistling through the air above the Arabian marshes. (Still, having also read of gold-mining Indian ants bigger than foxes, he may have taken the flying serpents and giant bats with a grain of salt.)

Whichever route he took to Greece, Zarmaros, not being a merchant, must have been unusually excited by the stories he'd heard of Eleusis to bother going at all. What could he have heard? Quite frankly, not much more than I had when I went there two millennia later, because the Eleusinian Mysteries were and remain a secret. He'd only have heard what could be said: that every year as spring approached thousands of initiates gathered near Athens to purify themselves to experience the Mystery; that in the autumn of the following year they gathered again to perform certain rites and walk along the Sacred Way to Eleusis where, in a great temple built just for this purpose, on a certain night, after the singing of songs and the lighting of a great fire, *something happened that was never spoken aloud.* And the fear of death evaporated.

He went to Greece on faith.

Now, as luck would have it, on the particular Sacred Night when amongst the tens of thousands of other initiates Zarmaros reached the temple at Eleusis and was trembling on the very edge of experiencing the ineffable Mystery, Caesar Augustus was also in the crowd, which is no doubt the only reason what Zarmaros did next has been passed down to us at all. Augustus must have recounted this one small detail of the Sacred Night at dinner tables across his empire, divine ban or no divine ban. But to explain the real enormity of what Zarmaros did that night, there's a need to fill out the picture a little – several pictures, in fact.

At the very time Hatshepsut was building her temple, or perhaps not at the same time but somehow in a *different* time, across the sea from Egypt beside the Bay of Salamis a wrinkled, haggard goddess sat by a well. It was round, of course, and the blue-grey stones enclosing it were terraced in widening circles set in a sunken square. It was not simply deep, this well, but beyond depth or shallowness: it was an entrance to the Underworld. It is still there. You can buy a ticket on a bus, as I did (no. 853 from Eleftherias Square), and go and look at it for yourself. It's just sitting there, a few paces south of the ticket booth near the entrance to the ruins at Eleusis. The day I was there some-one had left a Fanta bottle on the rim. It was once called the Well of Beautiful Dances. There used to be a sign.

To dream yourself out of modern Eleusis into that other time is now almost impossible. On an October morning not so long ago, standing above this well, I looked out across the uneven marble slabs of the temple forecourt (a brilliant yellow-white blur in the autumn sunshine) at the ram-shackle hideousness of the town beyond the gates. I'd crossed the empty, almost lunar hills west of Athens just an hour or so before, my mind filled with ancient stories so vivid I'd hardly taken in the hoardings and rocky fields strewn with plastic bags beyond the windows. As we'd swooped down out of the hills towards the Bay of Salamis my heart had sunk. There under a clay-coloured sky the sacred city lay before me, alive with giant chim-neys belching flame and smoke, its dingy build-ings clustered around refineries and scrap-metal dumps. It had all the magic of a clogged drain. Yet this squalid, stinking town on the E8 to Corinth was once the sacred centre of a Mystery holding half the world in its thrall.

Still, once inside the gates of the sanctuary, I did at least appear to be alone. Nothing stirred amongst the broken pillars and piles of hewn rock. No tourists had yet trekked up onto the small acropolis the temple complex was built around. There was a faint whiff of coffee from the shop across the road on the corner of Dimitros Street and an evocative smell of hot, dry grass. And so, when I came to the sunken well, I sat down on the warm stones just above it and cast my mind back to what I'd read and heard.

The haggard goddess who sat here in that other time was none other than the corn-goddess Demeter, grieving in an earthly way for her ghostly daughter, Persephone. While nonchalantly gathering flowers in a meadow one morning, Persephone had been astounded to see a chariot careering at breakneck speed up out of a cleft in the earth towards her. (Since, to be pedantic, chariots didn't appear here until about 1600 BC, this may be an historical clue or it may be a Shakespeare-in-jeans sort of detail – creative retelling to heighten the impact.) Lashing at the horses, his blood up and roaring with laughter, was a wild-haired god who sprang from his chariot onto the warm spring grass and ravished the divine maiden with what he thought was insistent tenderness. (The word that was later whispered abroad was 'rape'.) Was there a whiff of fermented grapes? Rumour suggested there was. Then he bore her away on a whirlwind journey across the land, pointing out mountain ranges and important rivers, as husbands and lovers still do to this day in the excited flush of a loving conquest, before disappearing with her back into the Underworld very suddenly through another cleft in the earth beside a wild fig-tree near Eleusis. (As the Greeks knew well, spring stank of death much more than autumn or winter. Spring was, and still is, one big *memento mori*, like the young.)

It all happened very quickly – with such speed, in fact, that there was disagreement over precisely which god had done the ravishing. Hades was the name on everyone's lips, but gods were protean beings in those days, so, although the evidence began to point more and more unequivocally in the direction of Dionysus, Hades was never completely absolved of blame because he had the tricky habit of sometimes sliding into being Dionysus. As a matter of fact, even the god of wealth Pluto's name cropped up from time to time, given the connection between wealth and grain, but there was so much now-you-see-me-now-you-don't going on up on Mt Olympus at the time, so much blatant transmogrification, role-swapping (and wife-swapping) and straight-out dissimulation, that any part Pluto may have played in the abduction was soon overlooked and forgotten.

Tearing her diadem from her head, Persephone's mother Demeter wrapped herself in dull mourning-robes and wandered the earth for nine days with two torches, neither eating nor bathing, searching in anguish for her ravished daughter. On the tenth day the sun-god Helios could bear the corn-goddess's grief no longer and told her what she already half-suspected: the culprit was Dionysus. The earth had swallowed up her daughter forever. The corn-goddess had been suddenly made barren. The trail of meaning, so to speak, had been brought to an abrupt end.

Demeter was seized with anger. She'd been spiralling in her torch-lit moon-wanderings closer and closer to stony Eleusis, searching for the maws of hell. Now she sat on the circular step enclosing the Well of Beautiful Dances, rocking with grief and fury, hardening her heart against oblivion and endings. In her agitation she wandered on to a nearby palace, where she was treated to an evening of cheerful dancing, witty recitation and obscene songs. Although she smiled from time to time, as we have all done in a similar situation, the ache of meaninglessness and loss was only dulled, not assuaged. Since they could hardly in all conscience offer the bereaved goddess wine, her hosts hastily concocted a new beverage: barley-water and pennyroyal, a minty drink which both agreeably refreshed the drinker and snubbed Dionysus at the same time.

Tiring of the well-meaning attempts to soothe her pain through conviviality, and at this point possibly a little unhinged by the depths of her bereavement, Demeter began to behave very strangely indeed, at least from the point of view of the worldly revellers and their *comme il faut* hosts. In a display of what must have looked like demented surliness, instead of cooing over the royal baby Demophoön rocking by the fire, she seized him, basted him in ambrosia and threw him into the flames amongst the roaring logs. A goddess may be a goddess, but even today this abrupt incineration of an innocent must strike us as bizarre. After all, she'd curried favour in the first place with the king and queen by promising to nurse their son. In the frantic uproar that followed, Demeter said, in that tone of voice typical of the divine, that she would remove the burning baby from the fire and make him whole again, but the price would be the child's mortality. In what must have been a hideously messy procedure, Demeter whisked him out of the fire and then threw him back in again night after night until the king and queen made up their minds. Understandably enough, they chose mortality. Whether or not they ever took time to ask themselves what Demeter's real point was in this gruesome bargaining is not recorded. The king smoothed over any wrinkles in his conscience, by the way – so pragmatic, so male, so of this world – by arranging for the peasants to be instructed in sound agricultural practices in honour of the corn-goddess.

By this time the cosmic ramifications of a corn-goddess without issue were making themselves felt at higher levels. In fact, Zeus himself was becoming involved in the unfolding drama. Needless to say, it wasn't the odd ravished maiden that troubled Zeus – after all, he wasn't above snatching at a tasty morsel himself, when tempted beyond endurance, as Ganymede could testify. Indeed, it was generally held that his own coupling with Demeter had been little short of rape. No, it was more the *semantics* of the affair which were beginning to trouble Zeus, the growing sense that a corn-goddess without issue was impossibly meaningless. So, pulling rank, Zeus sent a messenger to reason forcefully with Hades, who took his point and sent Persephone back to the surface of things in his chariot on condition she return to the Underworld each summer. He also made her eat one blood-red pomegranate seed, which was a sign of so many things it almost meant nothing at all. Demeter's joy was unbounded. An accommodation had been reached with death and a meaning of sorts restored to living.

Now, none of this is secret knowledge – this story, more or less as I have retold it, was known in ancient times in one form or another from the Iberian peninsula across Asia Minor down through India to (some have claimed) remote islands in what is now Indonesia. It's doubtful

whether there was even anything particularly mysterious about the story: it seems to have emerged
from a common fund of wisdom about the need
to confront death and meaninglessness by considering regeneration in nature. Yet, in itself, of
course, at this storytelling level of wisdom, the
myth of Demeter and her daughter (who are, by
the way, often intriguingly portrayed as aspects of
a single being) is scarcely satisfying. Yes, we understand that 'life goes on', yes, I am part of a chain
of being, yes, my dust feeds the grass which feeds
the cow which feeds the child who . . . and so on,
down the ages, across an infinity of blades of grass
and cows and children, but am I consoled? Is my
anxiety allayed? No, hardly at all. Deep down, who
cares about future cows and the children grown
fat on their meat and milk? At some point in a life
(I have the growing feeling), not to mention in a
good story, a baby must be thrown on the fire.

Now, Demeter, mother goddess, life in the
grain, knew this. In throwing an actual baby onto
an actual fire, she stated the problem (so to
speak) in all its starkness: that is, as a rule we
choose between meaning in a single lived life in
the mortal sphere and unending meaning in
unending life. But are there only two choices? On
restoring Demophoön to perfect mortality, Demeter also announced the birth of a Mystery. Revealing to her hosts that she was the corn-goddess, she

ordered the yearly celebration of the mystery of
lived unending life, which initiates would experience in the month of Boedromion every autumn
in return for keeping their experience *secret.*

Why, one might wonder, was secrecy the price?
Some secrets must not be communicated because
knowledge would obviously jeopardize the balance of power. The Sufis put it more poetically, if
a trifle over-dramatically: the master archer
should keep the secret of his skills concealed from
even his most faithful pupils – otherwise they will
use those skills to slay him. And no doubt there
were considerations such as these in the silence
forced on the Eleusinian initiates – the Mysteries
became, after all, a cult replete with hierarchies of
power, political, economic and religious. However, until quite recently, muteness and mystery
were connected for other reasons as well.

Some things, a true *mystes* (as an initiate was
called) might aver, simply cannot be put into
words. They can only be experienced or, as earlier
thinkers might have put it, seen. Not, of course,
that this belief has ever stopped mystics talking –
in fact, they rattle on interminably about the futility of seeking to express the inexpressible, and
have always done so. From Paris to Peking, the
world is littered with their treatises and books of
wisdom, their poetry, their guides and wordy flyers
for their seminars on the ineffable. Yet, in a sense,

once it is expressed in words, the mystery is no longer itself – that is, experience. The Sufis (as usual) put it even more colourfully, likening Sufic wisdom to the disease *biram*: when he first falls ill the sufferer raves like a madman, but once the disease takes hold of him in earnest, he is struck dumb. Another Islamic philosopher, Rumi, used the tricky metaphor of mirrors and vision:

> *I am a mirror, I am a mirror, I am not a man of speech,*
> *My state becomes visible when your ear becomes an eye.*

Demeter, it seems to me, had muteness of this kind in mind when she named her price for experiencing the Mysteries.

Interestingly enough, some thousands of years before the Eleusinian Mysteries took hold of the Greek imagination, and before there were Greek-speakers, Latin-speakers, Hindi-speakers and Germanic tribes, linguists assure us that somewhere to the north-east of Eleusis on the plains around the Caspian Sea or possibly in the mountains of Asia Minor the word *mu* was occasionally to be heard. What it meant to those ancient Indo-Europeans was something akin to *muteness, sealed or inarticulate lips*. Indeed, its echo is probably still faintly heard in our English word *mute*, in the Greek word *muein* meaning *to close the mouth* – and, in fact, by coincidence (and although it seems trivial to mention it, meaningless coincidences do tickle the post-modern sensibility) in that one word-root from my private language I chose to reveal in an earlier book. But the echo becomes an insistent reverberation in the word at the core of all these reflections on hidden things: the word *mystery* itself. The *my-* in *mystery* is a transformed *mu*, reminding us of the unspeakable nature of certain hidden things. So the first initiates into the Mysteries at Eleusis were called *mystai* – those who close their mouths, close up like night flowers, just being themselves.

A post-structuralist at the end of the twentieth century might be inclined to point out that even if ears were to become eyes, there would still be no escape from language in a broader sense – both self and the world, they might say, can only be perceived or known through the prism of language, never directly, in themselves. You cannot, in other words, just open your eyes and *see*. You see what you have learnt, or in some cases been taught, to see. (Why this must *always* be so is not clear, although it seems to be a workable description of how human beings, if not other species, interact with the world much of the time.) Perhaps, though, it's time for a few post-post-structuralists to canvas the idea that a mystery is a problem a given language cannot solve, a phenomenon our language does not equip us to interpret, leaving it to individuals to decide for themselves whether or not they can know without language. For two thousand years or so at Eleusis hundreds of thousands of *mystai* clearly thought they could. Their silence seems not simply to have been enjoined, but to have resulted from what they experienced.

For whatever reason, for some two thousand years the system of secrecy appears to have worked perfectly – so perfectly it's almost a mystery in itself. Hundreds of thousands of initiates came every year for two millennia from all over the known world, even, as we've seen, from India, and on the Sacred Night in the temple at Eleusis experienced the Mystery. Yet what they experienced we still don't know. The secret was kept. Virtually no one over two thousand years, having lived through that Sacred Night, felt moved to ridicule it, ignore the secrecy and demystify it. (Those few who did were killed, and, even so, what they said has had no echo.) Can you imagine, for example, the majority of Irishmen today being the holders of a secret about something they had all experienced at least once in their lives on a certain night every year since Julius Caesar in the company of hundreds of thousands of other Irishmen, *and no account of what it was they experienced ever once leaking out*? It strains credulity, it goes against human nature, yet the evidence is there – or, rather, the lack of it. What on earth took place during the

Sacred Night at Eleusis? What sealed all those lips?
As with any secret, the impulse to nibble away at it
is irresistible. Indeed, resistance, as I sat beside the
well, was the furthest thing from my mind.

Yellow-skied Eleusis, as I've said, with its cement
factories, traffic jams and scrappy cypresses seems
scarcely the place to contemplate numinous experiences. The desolation is complete. Better to
lower the eyelids just a fraction and try to imagine
a chilly February morning near Athens – let's say
in 340 BC: Plato is not long dead, peace has been
made with Philip of Macedon and the sanctuary at
Eleusis is as monumentally developed a site as it
ever will be, at least until the Romans add a few
final grandiose touches. Under the bare branches
of the plane trees on the banks of a small river just
outside the city walls thousands of men and
women have gathered to begin the rites of initiation into the Mysteries, the Mysteries that hold the
world together. There are no criminals amongst
them and no barbarians – foreigners, yes, from
every corner of the world, but no one who speaks
no Greek. In this outer circle of the Mysteries, this
forecourt of mystery, so to speak, we are still very
much in the world, language-ridden, children of
the earthly, earthy Demeter.

There is little that is secret here on the banks

of the stream at Agrai. There is exhilaration, trepi-
dation, the first quakings of awe, but this is still the
world of *signs*, not *experience*. In droves the initiates
are herded half-naked into the freezing stream in
a ritual of purification, fires are lit, pigs are
washed in the sea and then slaughtered on the
spot to be roasted on huge spits and feasted on,
torches flame, mythic stories are intoned, songs
are sung, strange, ritual dances are performed in
the flickering half-shadows ... a threshold has
been crossed. Or perhaps not even crossed, but
stepped up to. And in the dead of night – let's
imagine a half-moon – the *mystai* drift off through
the frosty air amongst the plane trees like ghosts,
back into the city to wait in perfect readiness, but
still in the forecourt, for the sign to step inside the
next circle. It's a long wait, as a rule: through two
springs, two summers, an autumn and another
winter, over a year and a half, and throughout all
those weeks and months the *mystes* must in spirit
stand ready to cross into the next circle of secrecy.
(Occasionally at about this time, if a word was spoken in the right ear, special arrangements could
be made to shorten the waiting period – Caesar
Augustus didn't wait a year and a half, for
instance.)

It's now September or thereabouts in the following year. There's a mellowness lying across the
fields and hillsides outside Athens, a contented

hopefulness that comes with sowing, an overripe air wafting into the streets of the city. The moment has come.

This time the *mystai* make their way down to the sea and bathe themselves again to reaffirm their purity, their receptivity to the Mysteries. And over the next nine days there are sacrificial ceremonies, there are feasts and there is strict fasting (in memory of Demeter's abstinence), there are sacraments and liturgies in the Eleusinian temple just above the *agora*, and sacred objects, brought the night before across the hills from Eleusis, are displayed to the initiates. Excitement, a slightly crazy feverishness, ripples across the city. Yet this is all still far from being the Secret. It is 'unspeakable' (*aporrheton*), but not 'inexpressible' (*arrheton*). This is more just sacred theatre – seduction, performance, catharsis, ritual. (These days, it would seem, the seer, whether in Baghdad or Bucharest, has little need of ritual or seduction, infuriating the priestly caste of whatever shade. Priests sell secrets, after all, that is what they traffic in, requiring ignorance as doctors require illness in order to live. They're cursed and run to in equal measure.)

All the same, while not the Secret, not the *magnum mysterium*, these rites and ceremonies performed in the temple above the *agora* in Athens are already under the law of silence – *aporrheton*, not to be told. People have told, naturally enough, and even painted the unspeakable on vases and urns, which is why I can picture them now. Law, signs, rites – this is all too human, this is Demeter grieving, sitting by her well, wandering with torches. On the sixth day of the rites, however, it is time to enter the next, tighter circle of secrecy. The pitch of excitement is raised a notch, lips are more firmly closed and eyes more alertly open.

The sun is just up and the air is still sharp. As it moves off through the potters' quarter towards the Sacred Gate, the crowd of initiates is a little light-headed – its spirits overheated, but weak in a febrile sort of way from fasting. Most of the *mystai* have myrtle twigs in their hair. They are officially in mourning for Persephone, still at one with the grieving Demeter, but once they reach the bridge over the River Rhetoi just outside the city, they can begin to rejoice. Now, as the day warms up and the rawness goes out of the air, they can start to dance their way along the Sacred Way to Eleusis, to sing bawdy songs in memory of Demeter's night in the palace where she burnt the baby and to watch comic actors performing their antics, refreshing themselves with barley-water flavoured with penny-royal (of course). In some cases the barley may have started to ferment, just slightly, we can't help suspecting, which might explain in part the

remarkably high spirits, the air of boisterous frol-
icking, but it would be ungenerous to discount
other, less crudely chemical sources of their joy.
These men and women from all over Greece, from
Crete, Syria and Sicily, from settlements as far away
as the Gates of Hercules and the Caspian Sea, from
beyond the Indus and beyond the third cataract of
the Nile . . . this vast, rejoicing throng is genuinely
(by all accounts) in a state verging on rapture as it
makes its noisy, multicoloured way westwards
along the narrowing path towards Eleusis.

Yes, westwards again. And that westerliness is
not the only Egyptian echo to be heard, if faintly,
at Eleusis. Indeed, some scholars (largely discred-
ited, I'm sure) have advanced the theory that
Eleusis was mainly a transplant from Egyptian soil,
while Demeter was simply Isis in Greek clothing
(even Herodotus thought as much). Certainly,
late in the afternoon as we approach the small
white town of Eleusis perched above the Bay of
Salamis, we can't help noting, if we're amongst
those hordes of Greek tourists who have gone
sightseeing up the Nile recently (leaving their
coins, their broken sandals and graffiti behind
them), that, just like Hatshepsut's Holiest of the
Holy, the sacred complex here at Eleusis, where
the Underworld opens up to swallow life, also
pushes eastwards out of a cliff to the west in a
series of geometrical statements refuting chaos.

And like Hatshepsut's Holiest of the Holy, the most sacred hall of all here at Eleusis, the Telesterion, containing within itself a small room called the Anaktoron where the ineffable is not only about to be seen but *to take place*, grows outwards in geometric configurations from within the raw rock itself.

Scholars can no doubt trace the web of influences governing the shape such sanctuaries have taken, untangling the Cretan and the Mycenaean strands from the Egyptian and even more exotic. Yet what strikes me now about both Thebes and Eleusis, given my night dreams, is the way in both places the initiate confronted death by moving westwards out of the city, crossing a river and then taking a narrowing path towards a rocky outcrop out of which a temple designed with mathematical precision, low and spreading, emerged in steps towards him. He then moved slowly upwards through ever narrower gates, ever smaller forecourts towards a sacred chamber (large, in the case of the Telesterion, an amphitheatre hewn out of the rock) and once inside the sacred chamber he found an even smaller chamber, the heart of everything, apparently empty but in fact the place where the Secret would be not just declared or acted out but would *happen*.

It's so still on this particular October night (if we can transport ourselves back again briefly to the road glowing white in the gathering dark amongst the fields outside Eleusis) that the cries of *Iakchos! Iakchos!* from the ghostly, seething crowd begin reaching the sanctuary from quite some distance, long before the leader's torch can be seen dancing mysteriously in the blackness to the east. Now (and we know this actually happened) a tremendous light flashes out from the roof of the sanctuary. What produces it no one knows – that is not only a mystery, but a secret. It comes from a point in the Telesterion at the centre of all the diminishing circles and forecourts of secrecy. What is happening is incommunicable, *arrheton.* (Yet, paradoxically, its luminescence is for everyone: it dazzles watchers far across the Bay of Salamis, for example; shepherds on the hilltops and fishermen in their boats on the bay are awestruck by the uncanny incandescence.)

At a signal from the bare-chested, godlike youth holding his torch aloft at the head of the crowd, there's an explosion of tambourines and cymbals, the pipes and cross-flutes start to swirl, and the *mystai* surge forward dancing. They dance their way upwards towards the sanctuary, in through the gates and across the first courtyard, ablaze with holy fires. 'And the starry ether of Zeus himself takes up the dance,' Euripides has already written about another such night, 'the moon goddess dances, and with her the fifty daughters of the Sea-god dance in the sea and the eddies of the ever-flowing streams, honouring the Daughter with the golden crown and her holy Mother . . .' As the initiates snake in an almost endless, undulating line inside the massive walls of the sanctuary, they're swallowed up by the mystic geometry of the place where death will be looked in the eye. Here, now. They're passing into the very antechamber of the Mystery.

Those left outside the walls cannot know what will be seen. It will be beyond words, beyond conveying. It must be unbearable to be so hermetically excluded. Everything human in you wants to know – half a syllable would do, the merest glimmering of a blurred reflection of what takes place inside. So I'll tell you what I've heard.

To be candid right from the outset, I should say that we have hardly even an inkling, so it's scarcely worth repeating. Whispers, rumours and hints of rumours – that's all we have to go on. And I can't help feeling there's something futile, even shameful, about trying to put into words an event whose whole point was that it passed beyond language. But the temptation to gossip very briefly – just a word or two muttered over my shoulder as I move on – is too great.

What will happen next is probably, or at least possibly, this: crowding into the brilliantly lit inner courtyard, leaving historical time and measurable space behind, the vast crowd of *mystai* will be addressed, perhaps in verse – at least in language refined and enriched by poetic density – by a priest standing above them on the platform jutting out from the Telesterion. There will almost certainly be a re-enactment of the abduction of Persephone. This is still to some extent theatre, this is still a rite of purification, this is mood-setting (let's be frank). Through the leaping shadows and smoky air the *mystai* will be able to glimpse frescoes and carvings at the edge of the crowd, depicting scenes from the story of Demeter and Persephone. There is a lifting now, there is a ripening in the air, but the initiates are still anchored to the earth, still wandering with that earthiest of Mothers, Demeter.

What will then happen, it would seem, although literally no one can utterly confirm it, is that the crowd will begin to leap and whirl through a narrow doorway into the columned Telesterion itself. And somehow it will cohere inside the rectangle of the great temple into a semicircle of attention on the sloping fan of stone seats. And there will be a shattering gong, 'like thunder', electrifying not just those hurtling, motionless, towards the divine instant there in the cavernous Temple of Purpose (of *telos*, 'goal'), but also the men drifting in boats in the darkness way out across the bay, waiting, the farmers and their wives and children waiting in doorways, lost in the blackness far away across the fields . . . indeed, it will be heard in Hell itself, not accidentally. Hell is very close here, we must remember, hardly a blink away in a fast chariot. And then it will all begin to happen.

The Hierophantes (no mere priest, by the way, but 'he who makes the mystery manifest') will now astonish the crowd by appearing on his throne – *now not there, now there,* as if he had never not been – and then 'a great light will burst forth' from the core chamber, the holiest of all holies, the Anaktoron, close by the throne. Some volatile, tightly packed core of essential being (perhaps) has been ignited. The seeing is beginning, the *epopteia,* the state of 'having seen'. This is no longer theatre. This now has nothing to do with theatre. This is now beginning to be *it.*

There will be a shout from the throne: 'The Mistress has given birth to a holy child!' In the blinding furnace of the Anaktoron Demeter has given birth to life. Some say a child will be glimpsed, a perfect child will take form before the initiates' eyes . . . some also say that a miraculous ear of corn will grow in the radiance of the holy fire. All eyes are focused on a presence.

We're wheeling around towards an infinite zero now at such a speed that something strange begins to happen: our flight is turning into light itself, the velocity at which everything just *is*. And the indescribable is lived through, Persephone is there, at one with the effulgence, like an instant stretched at the speed of light to infinity, hovering, detached from the earth, neither high nor low, at the exact centre of all things, which ripple away in an infinitude of circles, like a rose as endless as the universe itself. And the vision is here, and hope swells beyond all bounds, and fear is burnt right away, evaporating too quickly to see, and there is rapture and blessedness and a flaring up, a lambency, that will never in all eternity die down.

But it's only hearsay, I can't absolutely vouch for it. Still, what isn't only hearsay is that these thousands, perhaps tens of thousands of initiates will go back to Athens at first light, and on to the northern steppes or Spain or Africa, wherever they must go, and never tell the Secret. They will live on as if they have seen and experienced an event that was real yet beyond language, an event which has banished the terror of death, made the afterlife in some way contiguous with what they each are now. This is simply recorded fact.

It's that ancient Greek concept of *theos* – without any article, note, no *a* or *the*, just *theos* – that is making itself felt here, surely. *Theos* – god more as event than as entity. This is what was made manifest to the *mystai* and it's an angle on the divine which has been long eclipsed in the West. (Indeed, it is an angle on the divine energetically crushed by Byzantine Christianity with its personification of the godhead.)

And intention: I can't help believing – it's more a scent in the air than a structured belief – that the Mystery made plain something connected with Intention, the intentionality characterizing all existence, despite the impossibility of such a thing. Intention lurks between desire and action. Still a disembodied mystery, it hints uncomfortably at the notion that consciousness may be the something that is there instead of nothing. Somewhere in there, between desire and action (between Demeter, perhaps, and the wilful Hades) Persephone is floating and won't come down to earth.

This is why, from my point of view, two thousand years later and in possession of virtually no reliable information whatsoever, I am convinced that Zarmaros the Brahman got it all quite wrong. What happened to Zarmaros is this: at the moment of Persephone's appearance at the flashpoint where two universes collide, Zarmaros, wanting to go one better than the common herd, rushed over to the Anaktoron and flung himself, 'his naked body gleaming with oil', into the inferno. He was utterly consumed. As theatre it was undoubtedly dramatic, but as an epiphany it was quite wrong-headed. In trying to leap physically into the afterlife, it seems to me that Zarmaros had missed the point of the whole Mysteries business. The point, surely, was to be acted *upon*, not to act – or perhaps, more exactly, to be the act: the elision of death through seeing life differently. Still, at this distance, it's impossible to say. Even conjecturing, I realize now, is rather absurd.

In 391 the Christian emperor of Byzantium, Theodosius, pious mass-murderer and scourge of pagans, put an end to it all. No more folksy corn-goddesses on imperial territory, no more floating Persephones, no more epiphanies in the Telesterion at Eleusis. No more secrets, in other words, not owned by Theodosius. Just for good measure, Theodosius' barbarian allies, the mead-swilling Visigoths, sacked the sanctuary at Eleusis four years later. Since the experience of the Mysteries was unwisely tied to one place, the Telesterion west of Athens, the destruction was utter. And so the mysteries of the afterlife passed into other, far more powerful hands. Henceforth they would be revealed on a more rational, calculating basis. And at one remove: the new sacraments were to be performed 'in remembrance' of Christ, as Luke put it, or as the *visibile verbum* ('the visible word'), as St Augustine put it, as if faithful memory and understanding were the heart of the matter. To the Eleusinians that had all been a 'forecourt' matter – the word, the respectful memories, the re-enactments, the rituals, the theatrical loosening up of consciousness. What Eleusis had offered *everyone* once a year on the Sacred Night (even women and slaves) was not doctrine, but the thing itself.

From where I was sitting beside the well (in point of fact, the booklet from the Greek Ministry of Culture I was thumbing through now told me, a 6th century BC reconstruction of an earlier Mycenaean well several hundred metres to the south) I could see a crude reminder of the victory of Theodosius perched on the edge of the acropolis above me: a small Byzantine church, half-abandoned now, just an undistinguished rectangle of stone with a reddish tiled roof. Almost insultingly nugatory, contemptuously nondescript. But undeniably still there.

Right beneath its curved back wall, as I discovered after a stroll along the remains of the Sacred Way, the eight tiers of seats hewn from the raw hillside still faced east, the very seats, without their marble dressing, on which the *mystai* had once (at least in my imagination) seen what could not be said in words. The hypostyle roof had gone, the walls and porch had gone, the Anaktoron had disappeared as if it had never been – not so much as a sooty smudge to be seen, although I looked. (All the same, somewhere there, on one of those slabs towards the centre of the floor, if only I had the vision to see it, there is presumably to this day a microscopic trace or two, an infinitesimally small smear, of the body fat of Zarmaros.) To all intents and purposes the Telesterion has vanished. As I watched, a solitary tourist, slung about with cameras, a bum-bag and a backpack, clambered slowly from row to broken row up the tiered back wall towards the church. I hoped she knew what she was doing.

Are there any ghosts left at Eleusis? If you stare long enough at the spot the Anaktoron once stood on or the Well of Beautiful Dances or the paving stones of the Sacred Way, can anything be rekindled? Almost nothing. And the reason, it struck me then, is that for our minds to open up to mystery we need one of two things: geometry or nature. Ritual, dancing, aromas, music, chanting, storytelling, sacrifice, fire, libations, dread – they may all play a part in the cathartic theatre of mystery, may all predispose us to desire to see, but are not the mystery and do not open the eyes. As Hatshepsut knew, and as Demeter knew when she ordered the first temple to be built here, nothing happens without geometry – without patterns forming out of chaos. Or without its opposite, nature, the gods' untended garden. Theodosius and the Goths removed the geometry from Eleusis nearly two millennia ago. And nature, I can't help thinking, squinting into the yellowish glare enveloping this blighted city, is something no less rigorously banished from Eleusis than the Mysteries themselves. Demeter and her daughter are quite dead.

THE UPSIDE-DOWN BLUE MAN

You have to go alone. You have to zigzag up the scree amongst the sandstone blocks, dodging the vicious little clusters of green ants on the vines, all alone. Otherwise it doesn't happen.

Above me on this particular morning, like a school of dying whales, loomed the pink and grey bluffs on the edge of the escarpment. In the shimmering air you could almost see them breathing, slowly heaving. I stood for a moment, I remember, halfway up the jagged slope, just where a string of lolly-pink rock-orchids cascaded over the edge of a slab of warm sandstone above my head, and looked back down the scree towards the creek below. Somewhere down there in the moist gully

amongst the saplings and spear-grass the rest of
the group was dozing by the tea-coloured water.
One or two of them might be paddling across to
the sandbar, sharp-eyed, no doubt, despite the
heavy blanket of heat – there were eel-tailed catfish and mottled eels about, and not far away, just
past the bend in the creek, a young freshwater
crocodile. Someone had sighted it the day before.
Shy, we were told, but we stayed on the lookout for
slowly floating logs with yellow eyes just the same.

Out here amongst the gorges and creeks a
day's journey west of Cooktown it was supposed to
feel ancient. Everyone had said it would feel inde-
scribably old. Civilized people had lived here
amongst these rocks and rivers for tens of thousands of years – their paintings were hidden just a
few yards away under the overhang at the top of
the scree. In fact, someone (although no one
seemed to know exactly who) seems to have been
roaming around here hunting and methodically
burning off well over a hundred thousand years
ago. And even those first people had arrived here
a mere blink of an eye ago – the vast, lush paradise of Australia had been waiting just over the
horizon for a good fifteen or twenty million years
before that. And had been drifting north like a
stupendous, swarming, surreal zoo, adrift in the
southern oceans, for some thirty million years
before that. There were mountains here they said

were over a billion years old, whatever that might mean.

Yet, as I stood there in the midst of it, it didn't feel old at all. If anything, it had a sense of *now* about it I'd scarcely ever felt before. Knowing that the black cockatoos wheeling above my head had been shrieking harshly like that amongst these bloodwoods and acacias for aeons, beyond thought, knowing the scrub turkey had been scrabbling about in these vine trees for longer than I could begin to conceive of, even knowing that men and women like me had trudged up this higgledy-piggledy track to the overhang a million times, eating the tart lady-apples as they went, seeing the ferns and ants I was seeing and hearing the chitter-chitter sounds I was hearing now – none of that made it feel old. Not even a little bit. On the contrary, the powerful feeling I had was that the people living here had just gone out for an hour or two but would be back shortly. As a matter of fact, if you held your breath for a moment and stood tree-still, time fell in a heap. A category mistake. The wrong frame for the picture.

But then, of course, you begin breathing again, and it's an unbearably steamy Friday morning in early April – *kabakabada* was the word actual lips and tongues used on this hillside for thousands of years to describe this 'under-water-time' after the long wet – and the climb up from the fern-choked gully has exhausted you and you don't belong here. You also have the eerie feeling that your presence here has been *noted* – by what? by whom? the rainbow lorikeets? – and that you are being judged. Don't stumble.

In my walled garden in the city, I now realize, nothing much changes with the light. The ferns stay dark and spinachy, the irises a wicked blue and the clouds of eucalyptus leaves against the western wall stay more or less grey-green, whatever the weather, whatever the light. Up here in the far north, though, everything changes from minute to minute. The pink and grey bluffs are turning a rich brown before my eyes. The tunnels of green along the creek below me are turning black. The sky looks enamelled now, the soft, newly washed look has faded. All the reds in the bush around me, so scant they were invisible just moments before, are suddenly alight.

There are moments in the city, I admit, just before a storm in the late afternoon, when a strange kind of orange sunlight washes over everything and all the greens begin to glow and the trunks of the ghost-gums at the bottom of my garden grow luminous. But up here that kind of sudden burst of bright yellow half-light shivers the greens as if a spell has been cast, filling the air with the whoosh of wings and rapid bird-calls. At home it's certainly a moment to close the windows, but

here it has always been felt to be fraught with spiritual danger: this is the time when dogs howl at the
scent of souls' shadows darting amongst the
bushes, the time when trickster spirits, clustering
like bats in their crevices amongst the rocks, begin
to chirrup and flap about, intent on mischief in
the yellow gloom. And when those rascally wind-
gusts start ripping through the foliage – first here,
then there, then suddenly way off on the opposite
hillside – the pot-bellied imps hiding in hollow
trees spew out dozens of little pot-bellied doubles
of themselves to swoop about on the corkscrewing
air and spy out occasions for evil. Just before the
storm breaks, they suck them back into their bellies and sit and ruminate on causing havoc.

I pick my way upwards. Ants everywhere. If you
brush against a branch they're swarming on
almost invisibly, green on green, in a flash they're
scurrying up your arms, under your shirt, up your
legs, nipping fiercely everywhere. You tear at your
clothes and slap and yelp and forget all about
taipans and wild boars – nothing in the universe
matters except escaping the ants. Yet even as
you're thrashing about there like a demented
clown the dim suspicion grows that something or
someone is watching your antics and thinks it's a
great joke. You're here on sufferance.

There's an alertness, even a sentience about
your surroundings, but no sense of *mystery* as you

near the lips of the overhang – none at all, that's not what's exciting. I'd expected it, even hoped for it, but what I now felt was something else. Killing-sticks, rainmaking rites, messages from totemic animals, prowling shadows of the self, tabooed caves ... I'd heard stories about these things, of course, and here in the country where it all (for all I knew) still happened I'd thought I might catch something in the air at least, some aroma of mystery, of hidden things, little electricities. But, oddly enough, the enchantment here was so *real* it felt as unmysterious as sunlight or sudden rain.

I came on the frescoed overhang abruptly. The track up the hillside towards the bluff had led me in and out of bushes, through clefts in rocks and then smack up against a sheer red wall. I'd veered left around a huge, lopsided boulder embroidered with sculpted roots and found myself at one end of a long, sandy-floored gallery – at one corner of a gigantic open mouth, so to speak, high above the valley. This temple in the rock (if that's what it was) clearly had no need of geometrical entrances, of forecourts and stairs, mathematically designed to induct the seeker into secrets. It, too, like Egyptian and Greek temples, had its inner sanctums, its *geography*, if you like, but of a subtler kind. I had the immediate sense, right there at the corner of those lips, that these people had mathematically ordered their world differently from my people, more intuitively, and that their symmetries, if you will, must have been felt in other kinds of configurations – in the lacework of kinship, perhaps, or the complex choreography of language. But not in stone.

There was a faintly greenish light in the gallery from the crowns of the lady-apple trees growing just below the lip on my left. (And they were only growing here, far higher than they should, I knew, because once upon a time someone had sat up here in the cool, lunching on lady-apples, and had spat the seeds out over the edge. In this kind of temple you could do that.) What I had come to see, though, was on my right. It was astonishingly just there.

Glowing against the pink-grey rock I saw first a flattened, black echidna outlined in white, and then a creamy, fat-legged kangaroo, bounding along, ears pricked. Further on and higher up where the wall curved over like a wave to become the ceiling, a long, red-ochre crocodile, with jutting, stumpy legs. And lumpy yams, an evil-looking catfish, and a smudgy dingo, claws stretched downwards. I felt quiet, but nothing prickled yet. I tried to make the paintings feel ancient, I tried to think of that crocodile hovering there just like that, being stared at, the day Caesar landed in Britain, the day the first *homo sapiens* crossed from

Siberia into the Americas. But they refused. They didn't want to be looked at like that. But how *did* they want to be looked at?

I was just about to squat down and think about what I was seeing – about what was monochrome and *very* old, for example, about what the bands on the kangaroo might mean, and how the echidna's sweet flesh was taboo to anyone except grandfathers – when figures further along the gallery caught my eye. Now the rock began to seem more impregnated with feeling, more literally *impassioned*. These were *imjim* figures, these were the 'bad buggers', little frog-like men and women, four-fingered and four-toed, with knobbly knees and elbows and *no mouth*. At night they didn't flit like ghosts – they bounced about like froggy wallabies in a nightmare, the men on their massive, balled stone penises, their wives on their distended breasts, leaping half a mile or so in a single bound. Imagine huddling here in the middle of a moonless night, listening to them crashing crazily about in the spirit-filled darkness, bent on harm. Imagine feeling the land was so full of intent. Thunder at dusk, midnight storms – smashing his stone axe-elbows against the ground, the *imjim* sent lightning crashing amongst the cliffs, thunder rolling down the gullies. The *imjim* gloated like frogs when the downpour began and slithered back into the cracks in the rocks.

At times like this you don't either believe or disbelieve these ways of experiencing things – or, at least, I didn't. You don't contemplate the choice. You just feel drawn to trying, however faintly, however impossibly, to feel what was felt *then.* Especially about lightning. Once, a thousand miles away in the far north, I stood on a hill and gazed out (as I'd been told to do) at the mouth of a chasm in the pink Arnhem Land escarpment far away to the east across the green floor of the valley. This deep gash in the cliff-face, we were told, was the home of Namarrgon, the Lightning Man. (We'd seen Namarrgon depicted on a nearby rock-face not half an hour before: a white, skeletal, frog-like figure with axe-heads on his elbows and knees and huge, distorted genitals.) When provoked, we were told, Namarrgon would fly into a fury, hurling himself out into the sky above the cliffs to storm across the hills and valleys, roaring with rage and striking at the earth with his axe-heads. We all stared in silence at the chasm, smoky black, across the valley. It was a *sacred* place, we were told in English – forbidden, mortally dangerous to any intruder.

Of course, on reflection, we all had much more reliable information at our disposal about what caused storms to sweep over Kakadu – that is, reasoned explanations which, if forgotten, could eventually be re-established – but not one of us there that day, I'm convinced, would have entertained for a second the thought of ever entering that chasm. Not so much from fear of Namarrgon's retribution, although we were all by then at least half-bewitched, but because we had a powerful sense of not belonging here, of being in a land where different rules applied.

On that occasion I hadn't been alone. When you go somewhere alone, it's much easier to become a transparency, if you allow yourself – *not to reflect*, in other words. In this there's both delight and danger. Wandering further along the gallery on this morning I could feel myself dissolving, as it were . . . But no, that's perhaps not quite right – let me find other words: wandering further along the gallery that morning, with the rocks and greenery falling away into almost blinding brightness on my left, throbbing with interlacing patterns of tiny sounds, and on my right image after image (icons, really) of timeless presences in this very land, I feel what is *made* in me becoming *unmade*. (According to the theorists who are having their day where I come from, needless to say, this is an impossibility, a silly illusion, perception itself being *made*. Perhaps they should reflect less and see what happens.) For example (to continue my reflections), I can definitely feel my skin disappearing, that enclosed sense of self, the one that stops at the skin, beginning to evanesce – or do I mean expanding to absorb or be absorbed by the presence of other things? I don't seem to stop *here*, at the tip of my nose and toes, as I still did down by the creek.

Now shivery, elongated, mouthless spirit figures swim up before my eyes, slim as snakes, arms raised thinly to the sky like a whoo-whooing cry (no mouth is needed, their arms and saucer-eyes are crying out). And then I see him, right at the end of the overhang, just where the sandy path is squeezed into a dark slit between the wall and a massive, brooding boulder: the upside-down blue man. He's splayed across the rock-face, head down, legs and arms awry, a luminous, creamy, moonstruck blue, almost as if he's been spat there, you can sense the hatred. Pecking down into his armpit – the paint has smudged, the loathing was so frenzied – is a long-beaked, vicious little bird. This is *purri purri*, sorcery, strong black magic. This is a curse. This painting was *sung* onto the rock with terrible words. And there are people not too far away from where I'm standing, I've been told, who still know how to sing like that. I crouch down on the sand and stare at the hate-filled blueness. Had the magic worked?

I begin to wonder what it must have been like to be here on the day this image first appeared on this rock-face. How must it have felt to be here on the day the man who painted that painting dipped

his fingers, or perhaps a feather or the chewed
end of a soft stick, into the pale blue clay, tinted
with a special coppery mineral from far away, and
began to sing and paint his abomination onto the
rock? Yet, crouching in the sand, I find I can't
even begin to conceive of *that* day, that day warns
me off, and so I lay my mind open (against all the
odds – what difference does it make?) to a day
one month before that day, for argument's sake.
What was seen and felt here on that day that made
all these things possible?

If I pick a day just when the hot time was beginning, around October, by our calendar – *wungar-
iji*, as the people gathered here on that afternoon
probably called it (or something very like that) –
let's say five thousand years before Hatshepsut
thought of ordering her temple built, just when
the country hereabouts had settled comfortably
into being wet again after nearly twenty thousand
years of drought – what would I have seen? Just
like me today, the dozen or so men and women sitting here trying to keep cool and dry could have
looked out through the branches of the lady-
apples at the stringybarks and vines scattered
across the scree and perhaps have heard their
children shouting things up from the creek, lost
amongst the pandanus palms and nonda-fruit
trees choking the valley. (The walls of the little
fish-farm built where the creek widened out into a

pond had probably been broken down by this time of the year, releasing the fingerlings to fatten and spread out downstream.)

They'd have seen and heard abundant food everywhere, of course, as I can't – hanging from the trees, scuttling, standing frozen, darting, loping – they'd have seen a kind of living richness my eyes simply can't recognize. I remember walking through a coastal rainforest once with an Aboriginal woman who belonged there, feeling almost blind in her presence. 'See that lizard up there on the trunk of that tree?' she'd say, nodding vaguely towards the east where the trunks of at least five hundred trees were visible. A few minutes later, if I was lucky, my eye might chance on the minute silhouette of the lizard she'd noticed without trying, clinging to the bark of a tree way off in the distance a hundred feet above the ground. 'Well, now, what we did with him when we caught him was this . . .' And even as she spoke she'd be fingering the tiny berries on some bush by the track, whose juice, when fish was steeped in it . . . And so it went on – the bush was alive with good eating.

Speaking of food, by this time in the afternoon a few of the women were probably starting to prepare the evening meal, squatting on the soft paperbark-matting floor amongst the nonda-fruit seeds to scrape out a shallow hole.

Flying Fox à l'étouffée

*Line shallow hole with layer of pebbles, layer of
    kindling and second layer of pebbles. (Where
    available a clean termite nest may also be used.)*

*Light kindling and wait until fire is very hot.
    (Firesticks made from matchwood are preferred but
    not essential.)*

*Place flying foxes (one per person) in flames to singe
    off fur and char skin. Remove and place to one
    side.*

Rake pebbles and coals.

*When pebbles and coals have reached a constant high
    heat cover with thick layer of eucalyptus leaves.*

*Smash bones with heavy rock and lay flying foxes on
    bed of leaves.*

Cover with layer of paperbark and thin layer of sand.

Cook for approximately one hour

*Garnish with ground pandanus nuts or other fruits
    in season and serve.*

The dark red, aromatic meat, when it is served, will be delicious.

I suppose they must have talked, as we do, about what had been happening to whom, what goannas had got away, who had been unbearably pompous yesterday about this or that, who had been making eyes at whom, how stiflingly hot it was, who'd had a stomach-ache the night before and so on. The rules about what who could say about whom, naming names, must have been different from those governing conversation around a Carlton kitchen-table, but they must have chatted about these things, surely, here in this gallery, because they happened. Bawdy jokes were almost certainly told at someone or other's expense. Fly-whisks must have been flapped about and dilly-bags rummaged in, even woven perhaps with one of the little weaving-sticks lying by the back wall with the pile of threaded grasses.

It would be nice to think that at some point in the afternoon one of the adolescents spent an hour or two learning how to perfect the art of hand-stencilling – filling the mouth with liquid white clay and spraying it abruptly over a hand pressed up against the rock. But there isn't an infinite number of these stencils to be seen in the caves and galleries in these parts, so it's a little fanciful to expect it to have happened on this particular day. I must remind myself, too, that the clay they spat across their hands was white because red ochre was by this time taboo. The people I was imagining had after all been as astonished as I was now to find these galleries dotted with red hands, as well as paintings of all the other animals and plants, when they first reached them after twenty thousand years of absence during the great drying out. They saw them as part of what was given by the ancestor spirits, as natural as the bluffs, the streams and the wallabies. So red became taboo, at least for stencilling.

When night falls over the country and the October moon comes out, there's a perceptible change of mood. It's now not only sugar-gliders and night-parrots flitting through the darkness, not only dingoes prowling and possums slithering – there are other hunters abroad. This is the time when the Kwinkin spirits slide out of their hollow trees and damp crevices to sit like gigantic stick-insects, brimming over with evil intent, just outside the ring of light around the fire in the shelter. The squatter, froggier Kwinkins crouch behind rocks and, craning their ugly necks, peer out with their huge, round eyes to see what is happening around the fire. Their monstrous penises are rearing, iron-wood hard, ready for rape. All the men can do is set quartz crystals in a ring around the huddling group to catch the firelight in their magic eyes, blinding any spirit who might try to attack.

Actually, there were other things you could do as well, other ways you could contact living presences in the land and assure yourself of their willingness to help you and your people make your way further, in safety, along the track you'd been following. You might find them in a comet or a snake or a spherical stone, or a tortoise or catfish or even a yam. What you could do all depended on knowledge – knowledge of a kind which could not be rediscovered from evidence – and knowledge was not equally shared amongst everyone. It was a secret.

Communion with ancestor spirits, or eternal presences, was granted in return for ritualized pain and service, beginning in adolescence. As boys grew into men and into grandfathers their knowledge of secrets became more refined and access to the most sacred places, where the objects allowing communion were kept, was slowly opened up – wooden maps of the ancestors' meanderings, for example (and they wandered here, so these were maps of here), stones of a significant hue, oblong objects particularly, of stone or wood, as well as oval, round and cylindrical objects, incised pearl-shell, staffs with pointed ends . . . Perhaps even just before the day we're imagining a sacred bullroarer may have been taken from this storehouse to bring on the rains, as usually happened when the wet was building up, and made to roar on a jutting rock nearby but out of sight, curdling the blood of the women and young children with its unearthly booming whine. Intriguingly, the wooden objects from this sacred collection were understood to have been waiting inside the trees they were eventually carved from for the enlightened carver to release them. Never not there, just unrealized.

The store of objects would have been perched

serenely, reminds you of the cycles of loss which
must be endured. That's why, I suppose, you can
feel almost intimate with the moon in a way you
never can with the sun. It's you up there, being
chipped away at every night until you disappear.
The sun is so majestic, so unimpeachable by com-
parison. I have to go back down into Sunland in the
morning – Sunraysia, the *Herald-Sun*, Sun Alliance,
the Sunshine Coast, Sunnybank Apartments, fun in
the sun . . . the *Daily Moon* or Moon Insurance
clearly don't have the same ring, in fact they sound
quite menacing. Still, down there is where I belong,
I'll grow back into my skin quite quickly, probably.

When morning came I was *lulled* awake, first by
the blue-winged kookaburra, with his chortle-
chortle-chortle, and then, as the blueness spread,
by the laughing kookaburra, egging me on into
wakefulness. By the time the rosellas and lorikeets
began squawking and chattering, I was back in my
skin, focusing sharply on the day. (I could see why
the people who had lived on this river had feared
being jolted awake: a sudden awakening means
that the night-time self and the daytime self don't
have time to slide back together again peaceably –
the night-time shadow can get caught still out and
about, off the leash somewhere miles away. I don't
belong on that river and so explain it to myself differently, but the local explanation is surely much
more evocative.)

As I climbed back into the jeep I could feel the dissolving of that strict sense of self as head, torso and limbs, plus I-memories, going sharply into reverse. Of course, as we move from box to box in our boxed-in lives in the city, any other sense of self is almost inconceivable. It was just that here, for a short time, I really had experienced an *I* that meant something else – it included *you* and even *them* (those people and even those things). Perhaps it was just the mugginess and the solitude.

Or perhaps it really was part of an awareness – something new for me – of an enchanted landscape which had turned out to be the opposite of the kind of enchanted realm fairytales had prepared me for. (I thought about this, staring out of the window of the jeep as our luggage was loaded in from the back. A cockatoo was whistling shrilly way up in the sky. It had its eye on us.) In European tales of moonlit, haunted castles, of frogs turning into princes and pumpkins into carriages, there was always something fantastical about the enchantment, something almost unwonted – what the French call *insolite* and *irréel* – not *unreal* exactly, but phantasmagorical, an intrusion from another realm. Here, though, along the banks of these creeks and up amongst these crags, there was only one realm – enchantment was completely ordinary and the ordinary was completely enchanted. It had been both disappointing and enthralling at one and the same time.

Even the westward drift into the afterlife had had a seamlessness about it here which down in the city (at Sunnybank Apartments, for example) was but the faintest of folk memories. You rose up through your funeral post to sit for a while on the spreading roots of an upturned matchwood tree, contemplating what you must do, and then set off westwards where the taproot was pointing until you came to the gates of *woolunda* – perhaps *heaven* in English, lying near the spot where each month the moon waited for three days, presumably – and then once you'd proved your fitness to pass through the gates (shown signs of your status in sacred knowledge) in you went to be reborn in a true and good relationship to all that surrounded you. Nonsense, of course, if you take it at face value, but then taking it at face value would be a foolish thing to do.

And so off we went, jolting along the sandy track amongst the pandanus and wattle, frightening the life out of frill-necked lizards basking in patches of sunlight in our path. Eventually, after many hours, you come to a very strange corner in your journey eastwards down to the coast. At this point you're speeding along a smooth, black road towards a mountain. All around you it's empty, dry and still, everything grey-green and red – a single eagle, perhaps, wheeling slowly high above you, but otherwise nothing moves. You curve around the base of the mountain, come to T-junction with another smooth, black road and turn left. And in the twinkling of an eye – I couldn't believe it – you've woken up in another world. In the distance you could throw a ball it's suddenly lushly green, the hillside is dotted with farms with silly names, there are lychee orchards, riding schools and Bed and Breakfast signs. There's writing everywhere and everything's in squares. There's salt in the damp air. Something has vanished.

We'll hit the coast quite soon now and, as in one of those Escher prints, all the swans we thought we could see will suddenly be obviously rabbits again, even though not a line has moved on the paper.

EPILOGUE

Consider the humble teapot. Not long ago in a Berlin museum I looked at an exhibition of teapots: there were angular art deco teapots, smart little look-at-me Italian teapots, stylish English silver teapots, and also, in the very last display case, chubby modern teapots, exactly the kind of teapot that sits squatly on the kitchen bench at home, leaving little rings on the laminex. What struck me was how artificially designed our ordinary household teapot suddenly looked in this company, the very teapot which for years had looked to me just like a teapot, almost nature's teapot, almost not designed at all. I needed to see it with all its forebears to grasp how carefully contrived it actually was. This teapot effect is worth holding onto.

Something fades after you leave Hatshepsut's inner sanctum, wander away from the Well of Beautiful Dances or clamber back down the scree from the Upside-Down Blue Man – of course it does. The enchantment evaporates – that acute awareness of feelings and ways of seeing so different from your own that you almost feel bewitched. What doesn't quickly fade, however, is the light the experience casts on established ways of seeing – conventional wisdom – in the world we inhabit every day.

It's unsettling, this discrepancy, this divergence in how we have experienced the world. In your disquiet you'll try to hold onto whatever it was you experienced in those far-off places, to give it a name, to define its essence, but the words won't come or else they sound banal. All the same, today's accepted wisdom and today's empty, intentionless universe now look to you as stylized as Hatshepsut's hats.

The Spanish film-maker Buñuel tried to put his finger on the difference. 'I'm lucky to have spent my childhood in the Middle Ages,' he said, referring to the forsaken village in Aragon he grew up in. Quoting Huysmans, he called the medieval epoch 'painful and exquisite . . . painful in terms of its material aspects perhaps, but exquisite in its spiritual life. What a contrast to the world of today!' 'Spiritual life' has overtones I'd rather avoid, but it's undeniably evocative, it points in the right direction. For Buñuel, clearly, after a child-hood spent in Aragon, *the room was never again quite empty*. In 'the world of today' it usually is.

On a Greek island not so very long ago my cousin and I took some big, brass keys and, with much jabbing and clanking, unlocked the doors of the family church just below the rambling, mouldering family house on a hillside looking out on Albania. It was chilly inside. The eye went first to a striking silver candelabra hanging from the ceiling and then, of course, to the gaudy iconosta-sis. Now, I've always wanted to go behind the iconostasis, to step through those golden doors into the secret, sacred place beyond – I've always wanted, as you'll have gathered, to know what it would feel like to stand breathing in such a sanc-tum, what signs there might be of a miraculous presence. We did step through, but all we found, apart from a centuries-old Bible covered with a simple cloth, was the odd coffee-cup, a ceremo-nial bowl or two and a shirt on a hook. Disen-chanting stage-props. We couldn't think of anything to say to each other at all. We peered about for a moment or two, clanked our keys and left. We had just had a modern experience.

Crossing back over the Nile from Djeser Dje-seru, too, or Deir El-Bahri, as it's called today, to

Luxor, traffic-clogged and seething with touts, I think I experienced the contrast Buñuel had in mind between a spiritual exquisiteness and the world of today. I certainly did when I stood on the floor of the Telesterion at Eleusis and contemplated the dingy industrial squalor surrounding the sanctuary on every side. And again when I turned that corner in Far North Queensland and saw the first orchards and Bed and Breakfast signs. Each time the world of today knocked enchantment out of me.

For a brief moment or two in each of those places I'd thought I'd understood what it may have felt like to experience the world as *created* – as the expression of hidden intentions, as embraced by consciousness, rather than the other way around. In each of those places what was hidden had governed what was seen, while power had resided in access to what was hidden. Gradually, as knowledge and secrets became distinct categories, this access had become open to almost everyone: what was known only to certain male elders in Kwinkin country was available to almost everyone in ancient Greece – only the rituals were left in privileged hands.

In the world of today, it would seem, the clear light of knowledge now illumines every last nook and cranny of the universe. Mysteries are no longer thought to be realities hidden from us by the gods, like the nature of Namarrgon's lightning bolts or Hatshepsut's oneness with Amun-Re, but simply problems we can't yet nut out, like the provenance of the Turin Shroud or the popularity of pasta. Indeed, nothing now is said to be *hidden* from us, except, perhaps, by language and other people. So secrets in this world of today have been reduced to the banal level of silent telephone numbers and affairs at the office – snippets of information we withhold from others to keep some small part of our lives to ourselves. And ritual, in some ways, has fared worst of all. No longer a forecourt to experiencing another reality (since none is rumoured to exist), it has turned into nothing more than the repetitive rearrangement of surfaces: New Year's Eve, Santa Claus, the Sunday roast, yoga on Tuesdays, birthday celebrations, even the Eucharist for most people. Consequently, the numinous moment in today's world means little more than an altered sense of who *you* are (rather than what *it* is), available to all and sundry through night courses, instruction manuals, drugs, bushwalking, concerts, poetry . . . in other words, it's not really *numinous* as such at all.

As if this were not dispiriting enough, seekers after the exquisite moment may all be on a wild goose chase, according to another group of thinkers, for other reasons entirely: not because, as Turgenev feared over a century ago, all is about to become known, and the room is about to be found quite empty, but because nothing can ever be known. Seeing face to face, as the Bible would have it, turns out to be actually impossible. Hatshepsut, advancing in her glowing, angular robes up the final ramp, the delirious Athenians, prancing up the road to Eleusis, even suburban dreamers, rehearsing in their image-clotted minds their much more solitary approach to what they might call the Mystery – they are all, according to this view, doomed to dance about in a fun-house of distorted reflections, never able to step beyond perceptions to *know* – to see, undistorted, what is there in truth. 'Knowing' becomes just a word pointing to other words which point in their turn to other words in a futile, self-referential cycle. Everything, it transpires, has just been theatre, re-enactment and rehearsal all along. In Kwinkin country, for example, all those secrets about the afterlife, rainmaking and goblins bent on rape turn out to be little more than transparent devices for keeping women powerless. Disenchantment is common sense.

There's a kind of half-light, though – perhaps Buñuel stood in it all his life – in which a kind of re-enchantment seems within reach. Once on a steamy night in a Darwin carpark lit by powerful amber lights on tall concrete stanchions, I went to stand at the very edge of the cocoon of light, just

beyond the last row of cars, and stare out into the
blackness that began right there, at the end of the
fingertips on my outstretched hand. Behind me in
the glare of the arc-lights was the modern world –
glass and concrete, lines of vehicles, sharp, metal-
lic sounds, the hum of machines, everything new,
functional, rationally planned, explicable. In
front of me was a wall of nothingness which I
could people with whatever presences I chose.
That penumbral moment, between two kinds of
world, is in its way exquisite. It has a keenness, a
kind of piercing, faintly menacing sort of beauty,
which brings memory lustrously to life, *astonishing*
the storyteller into speech. Into gossiping disrup-
tively, really, about the gods.

Still, it's only a halfway position – gossip always
is. It's not the experience itself. 'If the Way is
made clear,' as the Taoists say, in their slightly irri-
tating way, 'it is not the Way.' Well, precisely. Once
you'd actually glimpsed *that*, you'd presumably
fall silent.

ACKNOWLEDGEMENTS

Among the books I turned to for help with historical detail in these essays were *Hatchepsut: the Female Pharaoh* by Joyce Tyldesley (Viking, London, 1996), *Eleusis* by C. Kerényi (Bollingen Foundation, New York, 1967) and *Dream Road: A Journey of Discovery,* Percy Trezise's detailed account of the discovery of the Kwinkin rock art sites in Cape York (Allen & Unwin, Sydney, 1993). I also am particularly indebted to Michael Cooke of Batchelor College in the Northern Territory for sharing with me his insights into an Aboriginal way of seeing the world. Credit for the excellent recipe for roast flying fox, however, is due to Percy Trezise.